兎用心棒
THE
USAGI
YOJIMBO
SAGA

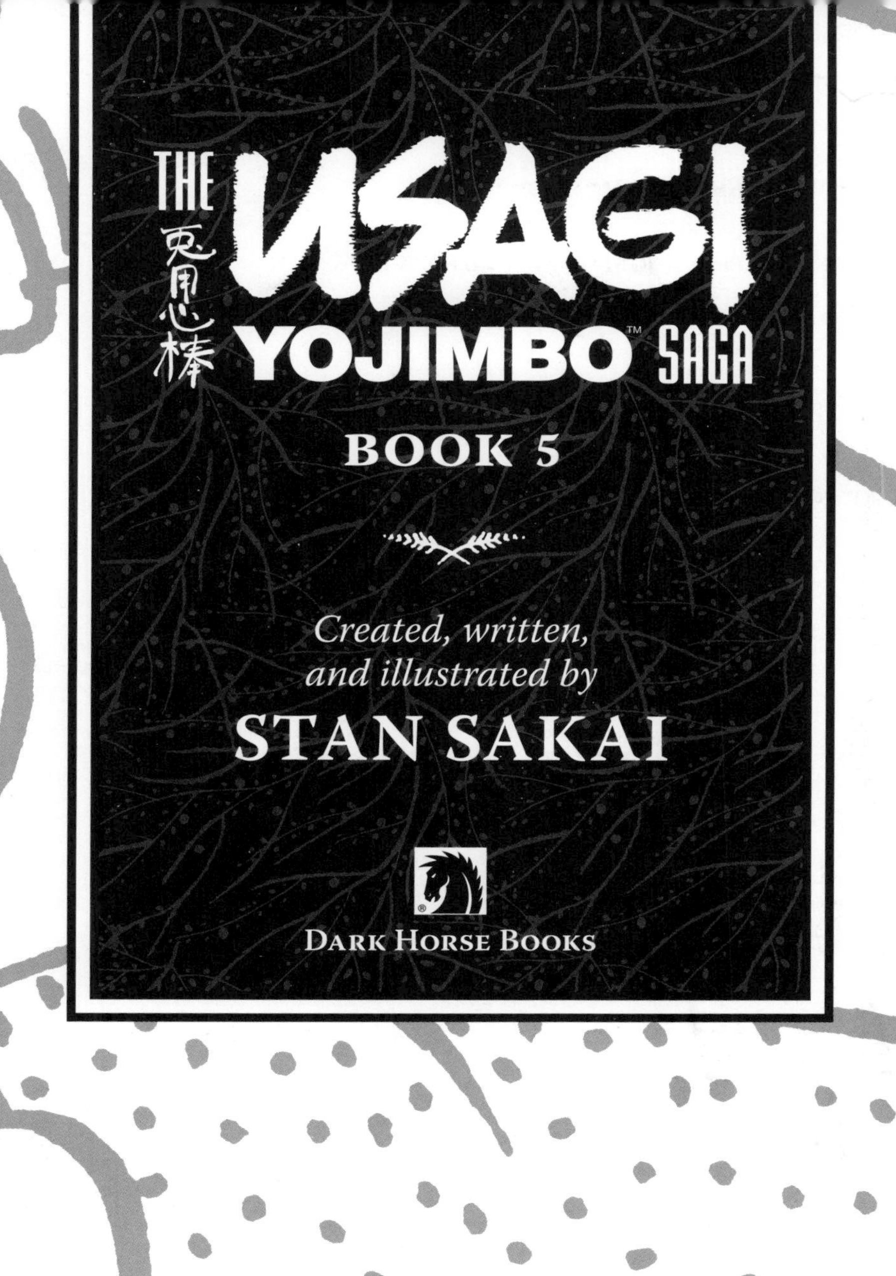

THE USAGI YOJIMBO™ SAGA

兎用心棒

BOOK 5

Created, written, and illustrated by

STAN SAKAI

DARK HORSE BOOKS

Publisher
MIKE RICHARDSON

Collection Editors
JUDY KHUU, PHILIP R. SIMON, *and* **ROSE WEITZ**

Original Series Editor
DIANA SCHUTZ

Designer
CARY GRAZZINI

Digital Art Technicians
CARY GRAZZINI *and* **ADAM PRUETT**

THE USAGI YOJIMBO™ SAGA BOOK 5

This volume collects "Cooking Lesson" from the Central Reproductions Ltd. Anthology *Drawing the Line*, issues #76–#94 of the Dark Horse comic book series *Usagi Yojimbo Volume Three*, and "The Doors" and "Fox Fire" from issues 2 and 3 of the Fantagraphics comic book series *Usagi Yojimbo Color Special*. "Tomoe's Story," first published in issue 1 of Fantagraphics's *Usagi Yojimbo Color Special*, was entirely redrawn for the *Tomoe's Story* collection. The Dark Horse issues were also collected as *Usagi Yojimbo* Book 20: *Glimpses of Death*, *Usagi Yojimbo* Book 21: *The Mother of Mountains*, and *Usagi Yojimbo* Book 22: *Tomoe's Story*.

StanSakai.com
UsagiYojimbo.com
DarkHorse.com

Published by Dark Horse Books
A division of Dark Horse Comics LLC
10956 SE Main Street
Milwaukie, OR 97222

To find a comics shop in your area, visit comicshoplocator.com

Library of Congress Cataloging-in-Publication Data

Names: Sakai, Stan, writer, illustrator.
Title: Usagi Yojimbo saga / writen and illustrated by Stan Sakai.
Description: Second edition. | Milwaukie, OR : Dark Horse Books, 2021- | v. 1: "This volume collects Usagi Yojimbo Volume Two #1-#16 and Volume Three #1-#6" | Audience: Ages 10+ | Audience: Grades 7-9 | Summary: "Celebrate Stan Sakai's beloved rabbit ronin with the Second Edition collections of the comic saga featuring brand new original cover art by Stan Sakai"-- Provided by publisher.
Identifiers: LCCN 2020036007 | ISBN 9781506724904 (v. 1 ; paperback) | ISBN 9781506724911 (v. 1 ; hardcover)
Subjects: LCSH: Graphic novels. | CYAC: Graphic novels. | Samurai--Fiction.
Classification: LCC PZ7.7.S138 Ur 2021 | DDC 741.5/973--dc23
LC record available at https://lccn.loc.gov/2020036007

Second Edition: March 2022
EBook ISBN 978-1-50672-541-3
Trade Paperback ISBN 978-1-50672-495-9

10 9 8 7 6 5 4 3 2 1

PRINTED IN CHINA

Dedicated to
Hank and Nancy Kagawa.

GLIMPSES OF DEATH

THE MOTHER OF MOUNTAINS

TOMOE'S STORY

After the death of Lord Mifune in the battle of Adachi Plain, retainer **MIYAMOTO USAGI** chose the warrior's pilgrimage, becoming a wandering *ronin* in search of peace. Practicing the warrior code of *bushido,* Usagi avoids conflict whenever possible, but when called upon, his bravery and fighting prowess are unsurpassed.

Trained in her father's Falling Rain school of swordsmanship, **TOMOE AME** serves as personal bodyguard and chief adviser to the young Lord Noriyuki of the Geishu clan. Tomoe is perhaps Usagi's equal as a fighter, with their duels to date ending in ties.

A descendant of samurai nobility, **MURAKAMI "GEN" GENNOSUKE** fell into poverty while his family pursued a vendetta and, vowing never to be poor again, turned to bounty hunting. Gen never fails to stick Usagi with the check for a meal or an inn and swears to be concerned only for himself, but his soft side sometimes briefly emerges.

A street performer who believes "a girl has to do what she can to get by," **KITSUNE** makes extra money as a pickpocket, but steals only from those who deserve it. She and Usagi have been friends for many years, since the day she stole his purse and he stole it back.

Using his keen mind to solve mysteries beyond the skills of his fellow detectives, **INSPECTOR ISHIDA** remains committed to justice, even when corrupt officials and other police find it inconvenient, a quality that has earned him enemies in the city government but also a true friend in Usagi.

Inhabiting the body of the swordswoman Inazuma since his apparent death, the demon **JEI** again haunts the countryside with his black blade. Despite claiming to be an emissary of the gods sent to wipe out evil on earth, Jei appears indiscriminate in his killing and has specifically targeted Usagi for death.

GLIMPSES OF DEATH

I WANT TO BE STAN SAKAI

I FIRST GOT TO KNOW STAN in early 1998, when I helped organize a forum in Tokyo for North American and Japanese cartoonists and comic book artists. I acted mainly as a coordinator and interpreter for the forum organizer, Tezuka Productions, but I also got to help select some of the artists from the States. It was easy to propose Stan as a candidate, since I had long admired his work.

The manga industry has become gargantuan and global, so much so that some people in the business in Japan have begun to look down their noses at North American cartoons and comics, or to consider them limited to superhero fare. In selecting artists for the forum, one of our goals was therefore to introduce people to the wide variety of work being done in North America. In retrospect, to many of the forum's Japanese participants, Stan must have seemed original to the point of being mind boggling. Born in Japan of a Japanese-American father and a Japanese mother, but raised in Hawaii and culturally very much an American, he draws American comics heavily influenced by Japanese samurai movies, set in feudal Japan, but populated with furry-animal and occasional dinosaur characters. To merely call Stan's *Usagi Yojimbo* "original" is a terrible understatement.

I was recently reflecting on what it is that I like so much about *Usagi*. I was watching Yoji Yamada's 2004 film *The Hidden Blade*, the follow-up to his immensely popular *The Twilight Samurai*. It harks back to the golden era of samurai movies, à la director Akira Kurosawa and others, and was so good that it made me hunger for more. It also made me want to go back and read *Usagi Yojimbo*, too, for I realized that *Usagi* has the same wonderfully rich, detailed, immersive, and otherworldly quality that I love about early postwar samurai films. And of course *Usagi*'s also got another favorite of mine—furry animals! I know that Stan grew up watching samurai films in Hawaii, and also was probably glued to the box on Saturday morning watching the furry-animal TV cartoon masterpieces of his day. But until Stan came along, I doubt if anyone had ever thought of combining these two worlds, at least in such an entertaining, well-researched, tongue-in-cheek, and only slightly (but deliberately) historically inaccurate way. If all these adjectival phrases sound as though they shouldn't coexist, well, in *Usagi* they get along like dear old friends.

One would think that someone with as much talent as Stan might be a difficult person, occasionally given to smashing hotel rooms and to checking into rehab, but he isn't like that at all. I don't know anyone who is so original, who seems to enjoy his work so much, and who is also so well adjusted. And it shows in his work. To say that I admire Stan and his work is an understatement. I would love to *be* Stan Sakai.

FREDERIK L. SCHODT

COOKING LESSON
BEFORE USAGI SERVED LORD MIFUNE AS A SAMURAI, HE STUDIED THE WAYS OF THE WARRIOR UNDER THE MOUNTAIN HERMIT KATSUICHI-SENSEI.*
HI-YAHH!
YOUR TIMING IS SLOW, USAGI, AND YOUR MOVEMENTS ARE ERRATIC.
YOU ARE SPENDING TOO MUCH TIME THINKING ABOUT YOUR NEXT STROKE.
KLAK!
YOU NEED TO INCREASE YOUR PRACTICE SESSIONS.
* TEACHER

WITH PRACTICE, THOUGHT WILL BECOME INSTINCT. INSTINCT WILL BECOME ACTION.
KLAK!

ACTION WILL BECOME VICTORY.
KLAK!
YOW!
1.

IT'S NO USE, SENSEI. I'LL NEVER LEARN THE WAY OF THE SWORD. IT'S JUST TOO HARD.
ADVERSITY CAN STRENGTHEN ONE'S CHARACTER, USAGI. IT DEPENDS ON HOW ONE DEALS WITH IT.

WHAT DO YOU MEAN?
BOIL THREE POTS OF WATER.
HOW CAN HOT WATER STRENGTHEN MY CHARACTER?

AND SO...

OKAY, THEY'RE BOILING. NOW WHAT?
COOK THIS DAIKON RADISH IN THE FIRST POT.

IN THE SECOND POT, BOIL THIS EGG.

SCATTER THESE DRIED LEAVES IN THE THIRD.

DAIKON, AN EGG, AND DRIED LEAVES?! WHAT KIND OF LESSON IS THIS?
2.

SOON...
THEY'RE DONE, *SENSEI*.
GOOD. TAKE OUT THE *DAIKON* AND THE EGG.

THE BOILING WATER REPRESENTS LIFE'S HARDSHIPS.

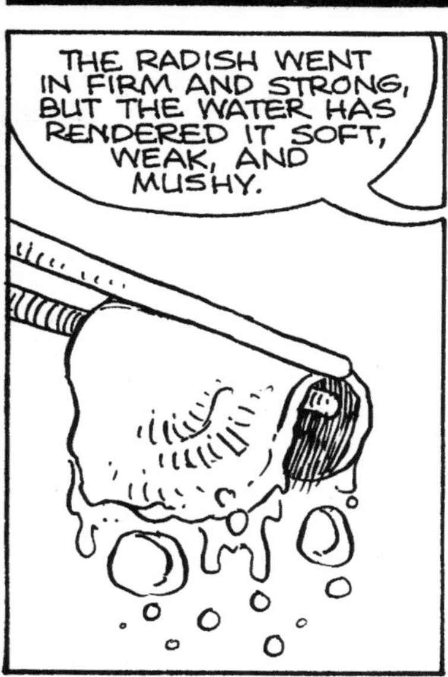
THE RADISH WENT IN FIRM AND STRONG, BUT THE WATER HAS RENDERED IT SOFT, WEAK, AND MUSHY.

THE EGG, ON THE OTHER HAND, WAS ONCE FLUID IN ITS SHELL.

THOUGH OUTWARDLY IT LOOKS THE SAME, THE INTERIOR HAS HARDENED.

ADVERSITY HAS CHANGED BOTH THOSE TWO.

WHAT ABOUT THESE CRUMBLY LEAVES?

THE LEAVES HAVE CHANGED THE BOILING WATER INTO A SAVORY, AROMATIC TEA.
SIP!

IN THE FACE OF ADVERSITY, WHICH OF THESE THREE ARE YOU?
HUH?

ARE YOU THE *DAIKON*, AT FIRST STRONG AND RIGID, BUT SOON BECOMING SOFT AND WEAK?

PERHAPS THE FRAGILE EGG? AFTER LYING IN THE BOILING WATER, ITS HEART BECAME HARDENED AND ITS SPIRIT STIFF.

OR ARE YOU THE LEAVES, WHICH DID NOT SUFFER FOR THE WORSE, BUT INSTEAD CHANGED THE VERY CIRCUMSTANCES THAT WOULD HAVE BROUGHT PAIN? AS THE WATER BECAME HOTTER, THEY RELEASED THEIR FRAGRANCE AND FLAVOR, ALTERING THE SITUATION AROUND THEM.
ANY QUESTIONS, STUDENT?

UH... JUST ONE, SENSEI...

MUSHY *DAIKON*, A HARD-BOILED EGG, AND SOME TEA... IS THAT ALL WE'RE HAVING FOR SUPPER?

THE END

CONTRABAND

I REALLY MISS JOTARO'S COMPANY.
I WONDER WHERE HE IS NOW.

I REGRET NOT TELLING HIM THAT I AM HIS FATHER. HE HAS A RIGHT TO KNOW, DESPITE THE CONSEQUENCES.
I'LL TELL HIM THE TRUTH THE NEXT TIME I SEE HIM...
IF THERE IS A NEXT TIME.
1.

?
UHH...

DRUNK.

HMMM... HE DOESN'T SMELL OF LIQUOR.

OOH...

ARE YOU ALL RIGHT? I'LL TAKE YOU TO AN INN TO SOBER UP.
UH...

!
YOU'RE BLEEDING!
UH...
2.

HELP! I NEED A DOCTOR!
N-NO, SAMURAI. STOP.

WHAT?
YOU MUST GET THIS PACKAGE TO AYANE AT THE RED PEONY INN.
PLEASE.

GO-- GO AND TAKE IT TO AYANE.
BUT YOU'RE HURT.

THIS...IS MUCH MORE... IMPORTANT... THAN...MY LIFE.
T-TAKE IT... PLEASE...

REMEMBER, SAMURAI...
A-AYANE... RED... PEONY...
AHHHHH

MISTER? MISTER?

WHAT IS THIS THAT IT IS WORTH DYING FOR?

AND SO...
TWO BLOCKS DOWN-- ON THE LEFT.
THANKS.

HERE IT IS AT LAST-- A BIT RUN DOWN AND NOT IN THE BEST PART OF TOWN.
IT LOOKS CLOSED.

HEY, OPEN UP!
BAM! BAM! BAM!

HEY! OPEN UP, I SAID!
BAM! BAM! BAM!

WHAT'S ALL THE RACKET?
DON'T YOU KNOW WHAT TIME IT IS?
IDIOT.

OH, UH... SAMURAI. I DIDN'T KNOW IT WAS YOU.
COME IN, COME IN.
WHAT CAN A POOR INN-KEEPER DO FOR YOU?

I'M LOOKING FOR AYANE.
MY SISTER-IN-LAW? WHAT IS YOUR BUSINESS WITH HER?

I AM TO GIVE HER THIS PACKAGE.
PACKAGE, YOU SAY? WHAT IS IN IT? MONEY? I WILL GIVE IT TO HER.
UH... NO. I THINK I'LL GIVE IT TO HER PERSONALLY.

HAVE IT YOUR WAY, *SAMURAI*. *FEH!* STUPID GIRL'S PROBABLY IN TROUBLE AGAIN.
SHE'S IN THE KITCHEN.

AYANE-- THIS *SAMURAI* HAS A PACKAGE FOR YOU.
A PACKAGE FOR ME?

YES, FOR YOU.
AHEH. HEH HEH.
DEAR SISTER-IN-LAW.

YOU CAN LEAVE US NOW.
HUH?
OH.
GRUMBLE! GRUMBLE!
DO I KNOW YOU, SIR?

I AM CALLED MIYAMOTO USAGI. A DYING MAN GAVE THIS TO ME WITH INSTRUCTIONS THAT I PASS IT ON TO YOU.
A DYING...?

TH-THIS IS FROM MY FATHER!

WHERE IS HE? TAKE ME TO HIM!

HURRY!
HEY! WHERE ARE YOU GOING?! WHAT'S IN THE PACKAGE?

HURRY, USAGI-SAN, HURRY!
COME BACK HERE, AYANE!
DISHES DON'T WASH THEMSELVES, YOU KNOW!
6.

IT'S NOT FAR NOW!

STOP! GET OUT OF SIGHT!
WHAT?

STAY BACK!
HE'S BEEN FOUND...AND I DON'T LIKE THE LOOKS OF HIS DISCOVERERS.

I TOLD YOU HE COULDN'T GET FAR--NOT WITH HIS INJURIES.
HE SHOULD NOT HAVE ESCAPED IN THE FIRST PLACE.

NOW, WHERE IS IT?
7.

HE DOESN'T HAVE IT!
THEN SOME PASSING THIEF MUST HAVE FOUND THE BODY AND TAKEN THE PACKAGE.
LET ME SEE, *SAMURAI.*

NO, IT WAS NO THIEF. HIS PURSE IS STILL HERE.

THEN HE'S PASSED IT ON.
YEAH. BUT TO WHOM?

OUR RECORDS SHOW HE HAS A DAUGHTER IN THIS TOWN.
WE'LL FIND HER, WITH VERY LITTLE TROUBLE.

ALL THIS TROUBLE IS ***YOUR FAULT!***
K! CK!
OH--!
8.

WHAT WAS THAT?
WHAT WAS WHAT?
CHH

I THOUGHT I HEARD A NOISE.
STAY BACK.

CLIK!

HEY-- WE'VE WASTED ENOUGH TIME. WE'VE GOT TO FIND HIS DAUGHTER.
I GUESS IT WAS MY IMAGINATION.
LET'S GO.
9.

WAIT-- WAIT UNTIL THEY'RE OUT OF SIGHT.
OKAY, THEY'RE GONE.

FATHER!

THOSE SAMURAI WERE AFTER YOUR FATHER. NOW THEY'RE LOOKING FOR YOU.
WE'D BETTER REPORT THIS TO THE AUTHORITIES.

NO! YOU CAN'T!
WHAT? WHY NOT?

THOSE SAMURAI--
--THEY ARE THE AUTHORITIES!
10.

WHO ARE YOU?
WHAT'S IN THE PACKAGE?

IT CONTAINS NOTHING HARMFUL, USAGI-SAN. ONLY GOOD WILL COME FROM IT.
I SWEAR IT.

NOW WE'VE GOT TO TAKE THE PACKAGE TO HIRATA IN THE NEXT TOWN.
NO. I AM NOT GETTING ANY MORE INVOLVED IN THIS.

YOU HAVE GOT TO HELP ME, SAMURAI. IT IS NO COINCIDENCE THAT IT WAS YOU WHO FOUND MY FATHER.
PLEASE.

NO, I WON'T.

FWEET! FWEET! POLICE! WHAT ARE YOU DOING THERE? STAY WHERE YOU ARE!
LET'S GET OUT OF HERE! IT LOOKS LIKE I'M INVOLVED AFTER ALL-- AT LEAST FOR A WHILE.
11.

MY FATHER HAD STUDIED HERBS AND MEDICINE EVER SINCE HE WAS A CHILD.

LAST SPRING, HE WAS ASSIGNED AS A DOCTOR TO NAGASAKI, THE INTERNATIONAL PORT CITY ON THE ISLAND OF KYUSHU.

AS YOU KNOW, NAGASAKI DEALS WITH FOREIGN TRADE WITH THE BLACK SHIPS FROM THE SOUTH.

HE WAS ONE OF THE FEW PEOPLE IN OUR COUNTRY WHO'D HAD CONTACT WITH FOREIGN TRADERS.

FOR A WHILE, HE EVEN STUDIED UNDER A FOREIGN DOCTOR.
YOUR FATHER MUST HAVE LEARNED MUCH FROM HIM.

TOO MUCH, THE PORT AUTHORITIES THOUGHT.
12.

WHEN IT WAS TIME FOR HIM TO RETURN TO HIS COUNTRY, THE FOREIGN DOCTOR GAVE MY FATHER A GIFT.

I HAVE HAD SOME EXPERIENCE WITH SOME OF THE "GIFTS" THESE FOREIGNERS GIVE--THE COUGHING DEATH, THE EXPLOSIVE BLACK POWDER. NOTHING GOOD EVER COMES FROM THEM.

NO, NO--! IT IS NOT LIKE THAT! THE DOCTOR WAS A GOOD PERSON! HE WANTED ONLY TO DO GOOD!

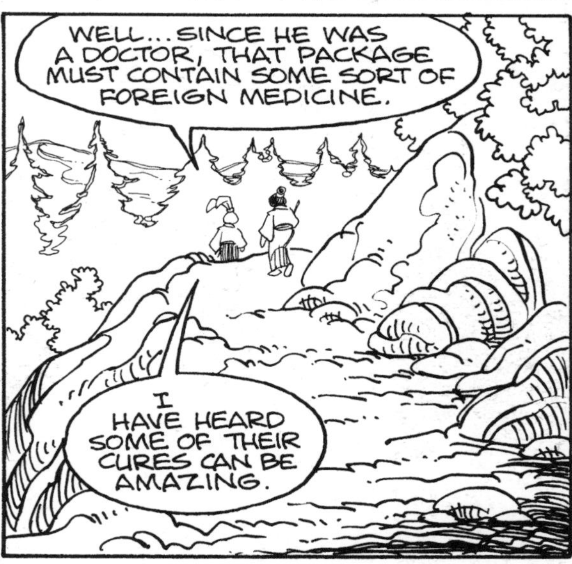
WELL... SINCE HE WAS A DOCTOR, THAT PACKAGE MUST CONTAIN SOME SORT OF FOREIGN MEDICINE.
I HAVE HEARD SOME OF THEIR CURES CAN BE AMAZING.

DID HE WANT TO GIVE IT TO THE PEOPLE RATHER THAN TO LET A FEW MERCHANTS PROFIT FROM IT?
YES...

IT HEALS... AND IT IS FOR **ALL** THE PEOPLE.
13

BUT YOU REALIZE THAT WHAT YOU CARRY IS CONSIDERED CONTRABAND. IF WE ARE CAUGHT WITH IT, THE PUNISHMENT IS DEATH.

THEY KNOW WHO YOU ARE. EVEN TO RETURN TO YOUR HOME WOULD BE FATAL.
YES...

BUT I HAVE NO TIES THERE NOW. MY HUSBAND ONCE OWNED THE RED PEONY.

WHEN HE DIED, HIS BROTHER, TAJO, TOOK OVER THE INN. TAJO IS NOT A PLEASANT PERSON. I AM GLAD TO BE AWAY FROM THERE.

LATER...
WE ARE MAKING GOOD TIME. IT SHOULDN'T TAKE LONG TO REACH HIRATA.

LISTEN.
HOOF-BEATS.
14.

CLOPCLOPCLOPCLOPCLOPCLOPCLOPCLOPCLOPCLOPCLOPCLOPCLOP!

THEY'RE ON OUR TRAIL--FASTER THAN I EXPECTED.
THEY MUST BE DESPERATE TO RETRIEVE THIS PACKAGE OF YOURS.

HURRY--BEHIND THESE BUSHES...AND HOPE THEY HAVEN'T ALREADY SEEN US.

STAY DOWN!

HURRY--SHE COULD NOT HAVE GOTTEN FAR!
15

YAAAHHHH
SHUT UP, YOU FOOL!

TH-THAT WAS TAJO!
WHAT IS HE DOING WITH THOSE SAMURAI?

THEY MUST HAVE PAID HIM TO IDENTIFY YOU TO THEM.
THAT GREEDY SCUM!
WHAT SHOULD WE DO?
WE'VE GOT TO GET THE PACKAGE TO HIRATA AS SOON AS POSSIBLE!

THE ROAD IS BEING PATROLLED!
THEY'VE PROBABLY SEALED THE ENTIRE AREA.
WE CAN'T GO BACK.

AND THE MOUNTAINS ARE TOO STEEP TO CLIMB.
WE CAN ONLY CONTINUE ON AND HOPE SOME OPPORTUNITY SHOWS ITSELF SO WE CAN SLIP PAST THEM.
16.

BUT SOON...
THEY'VE ALREADY SET UP A ROADBLOCK JUST BEFORE THE CROSS-ROADS. THEY'RE CHECKING EVERYBODY.
AND THERE'S TAJO! WE'LL NEVER GET PAST THEM!

WE'LL HAVE TO GO BACK. PERHAPS THERE'S A PATH THAT WILL TAKE US AROUND THE ROADBLOCK.
BUT EVEN IF WE FIND ONE, IT MAY BE GUARDED AS WELL.
YES.

THE LONGER THIS IS OUT IN THE OPEN, THE GREATER THE CHANCE THAT THE PORT AUTHORITIES WILL GET IT.
GET DOWN BEFORE THEY SEE YOU.
SEE ME...? YES...

HERE. TAKE THIS TO HIRATA THE FISH-MONGER. HE IS THE NEXT LINK IN THE CHAIN.
CHAIN? I DON'T UNDER-STAND.

THANK YOU FOR YOUR HELP, USAGI-*SAN*.
WHAT ARE YOU GOING TO DO?
17

STAY IN HIDING, USAGI SAN.
WAIT! COME BACK HERE!

TAJO--YOU MONEY-HUNGRY SCUM!
!

YOU WOULD BETRAY YOUR OWN SISTER-IN-LAW?!
THERE SHE IS! THERE'S AYANE!
GET HER!

PLEASE, USAGI-SAN, I'M DEPENDING ON YOU. DELIVER THE PACKAGE TO HIRATA.
18.

GET HER!
DON'T LET HER ESCAPE!
STOP!

I SAID--

ZWIT!
--STOP!
SLASH!

F-F-FATHER...
STUPID WOMAN!

PLOP!
TURN HER OVER AND SEARCH HER.
FIND THAT PACKAGE!
DO I GET MY REWARD NOW?
19.

SHE--
SHE LURED THEM ALL AWAY.
SHE GAVE HER LIFE TO CREATE A DIVERSION.

I CAN'T LET HER SACRIFICE BE IN VAIN.

MY, HE'S IN SUCH A RUSH.
THOSE SAMURAI ARE ALWAYS IN A HURRY.
THEY'RE CRAZY--EACH AND EVERY ONE OF THEM.

SHE DOESN'T HAVE IT!
WHAT?! SHE COULDN'T HAVE PASSED IT ON SO QUICKLY!
THAT LONG-EARED SAMURAI...

WHAT LONG-EARED SAMURAI?!
HE GAVE AYANE THE PACKAGE IN THE FIRST PLACE! HE ACTED REALLY SUSPICIOUS! HE WOULDN'T TELL ME WHAT WAS IN IT!
THEY LEFT THE RED PEONY TOGETHER.
20.

YOU FOOL! WHY DIDN'T YOU TELL US ABOUT HIM?
YOU JUST ASKED ABOUT AYANE. IS THERE A REWARD FOR HIM? DO I STILL GET MY MONEY FOR AYANE?
THE GATE IS UNGUARDED!
YOU TWO-- DID YOU SEE ANYONE SLIP PAST THE CHECK-POINT?
YES, SIR!

I'VE NEVER SEEN ANYONE RUN SO FAST! THAT SAMURAI MUST BE HALFWAY TO KYOTO BY NOW! HA HA!

WHICH ROAD DID HE TAKE?
HE RAN UP THE NORTH PATH--UP THE MOUNTAIN.
DID HE HAVE LONG EARS?
WHY, YEAH.

YOU TWO-- STAY HERE AND GUARD THE GATE. THE REST OF US WILL CHASE DOWN THAT SAMURAI.
YES, SIR!

HURRY-- UP THE NORTH ROAD!
21.

HURRY--
HE'S ALREADY
HAD A GOOD
HEAD START
OVER
US!
22

HIS SHOP SHOULD BE SOMEWHERE IN THE MARKETPLACE.

I'M LOOKING FOR HIRATA THE FISH-MONGER.
THAT'S ME, SAMURAI. HOW ABOUT SOME FRESH TAI? I JUST GOT IT IN THIS MORNING!

AYANE ASKED ME TO--
AYANE? SHH--! COME INTO THE BACK ROOM, SIR!

I NEVER WOULD HAVE TAKEN YOU TO BE ONE OF US, SAMURAI.
OH? ONE OF WHOM?
UH...

THIS ORIGINALLY CAME FROM THE NAGASAKI DOCTOR.
AH...WE HAVE BEEN EAGERLY AWAITING ITS ARRIVAL!
23

FAREWELL.
WAIT, SAMURAI. OUR GROUP WILL BE MEETING SOON. WON'T YOU STAY?

NO THANKS. I DID WHAT I PROMISED TO DO. I HOPE I NEVER SEE THAT PACKAGE AGAIN. I'M GLAD TO BE RID OF IT.

THAT--WHATEVER IT IS--HAS CAUSED ENOUGH PAIN.

I'M SORRY YOU DIDN'T STAY, SAMURAI.

IT IS NOT PAIN THAT THIS BRINGS, SAMURAI...

...BUT, RATHER, SALVATION.

THE END

"I'M HUNGRY, MA!"
"I KNOW, DEAR."
"AND COLD!"
"WE ALL ARE."

"I WISH PAPA WERE HERE."
"SO DO I."

YOUR FATHER HAS BEEN OUT OF WORK FOR SO LONG, AND WHAT LITTLE HE EARNS IS BARELY ENOUGH TO SUPPORT US.

LET'S HOPE THAT HIS LUCK WILL IMPROVE TONIGHT.

COME...SNUGGLE CLOSER. AT LEAST WE CAN KEEP WARM.

1.

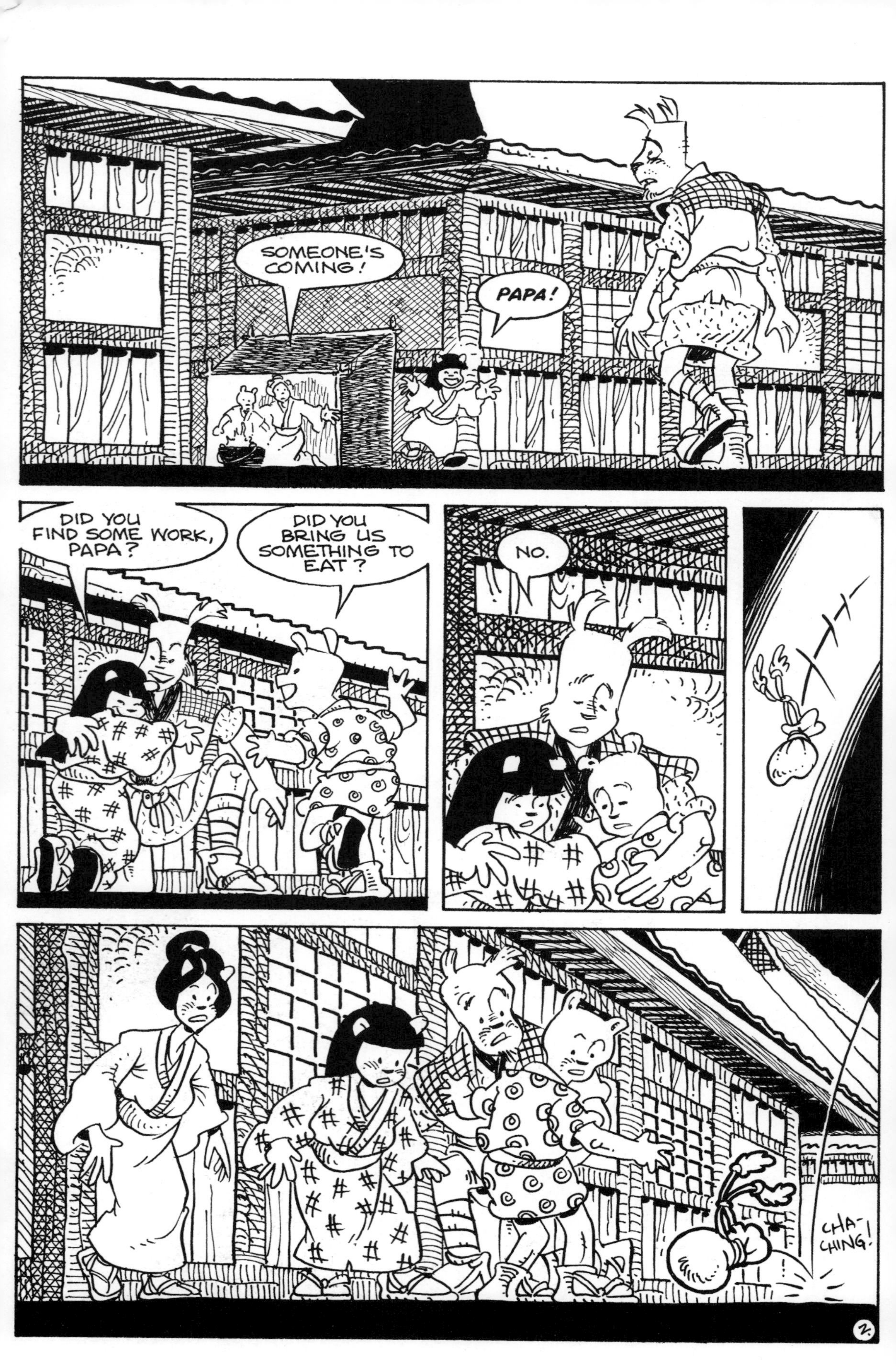
SOMEONE'S COMING!
PAPA!
DID YOU FIND SOME WORK, PAPA?
DID YOU BRING US SOMETHING TO EAT?
NO.
CHA-CHING!
2

I-IT'S FILLED WITH MONEY!
BUT... HOW--? WHO--?
LOOK!

WHAT--?!
UP THERE!

IT'S NEZUMI*!
*"RAT"

THANK YOU, NEZUMI-SAN!

THANK YOU.

AFTER THE RAT

GET MEN ONTO THAT ROOF--
--AND THE NEXT! WE'LL CAPTURE HIM THIS TIME!

BE CAREFUL-- THE FOOTING IS TREACHEROUS!

HA! WE'VE GOT HIM NOW!

WAP!
OW!
WAK!
UH!

STAY STILL, YOU--!

YOW!

AHHH!

YAHHH--!

OW!
THUD!

ONE OF YOU-- SEE TO YOUR FALLEN COMRADE. THE REST OF YOU--AFTER NEZUMI!
UHH--!
6.

SURROUND THE AREA! HE HAS TO COME DOWN SOMETIME!

THERE HE IS-- THIS WAY!

THE POLICE HAVE GOT NEZUMI TRAPPED!
HE'S HELPED SO MANY OF US!
HURRY! HE'S TRAPPED UP THERE!

IT'S OUR TURN TO HELP HIM!
COME ON!

HURRY, BEFORE HE GETS AWAY!
7.

YOU'RE RUNNING OUT OF ROOF, NEZUMI!

WHERE DID HE GO?

DON'T TELL ME I'VE LOST HIM! THE MAGISTRATE WILL HAVE MY HEAD!

MAYBE I'LL SAVE HIM THE TROUBLE AND TAKE YOUR HEAD FOR MYSELF, INSPECTOR ISHIDA.
ULP!
DON'T TURN AROUND.

YOU'RE IN ENOUGH TROUBLE. DON'T ADD MURDER TO YOUR LIST OF CRIMES!

I STEAL ONLY FROM WEALTHY MERCHANTS, AND HELP THOSE WHO NEED IT. WHAT CRIME IS THAT?
YOU CANNOT RATIONALIZE YOUR ACTIONS TO ME!
8.

NEZUMI...?

RATS.

INSPECTOR ISHIDA--ARE YOU ALL RIGHT?
I'LL GET YOU, NEZUMI! I SWEAR IT!

SO... HE'S ESCAPED, HUH?
SLIPPERY DEVIL. HE SHOULD BE CALLED "EEL" INSTEAD OF "RAT"!

THERE WILL BE OTHER OPPORTUNITIES.
SO--YOU WANT TO GO OUT FOR SUSHI?
YEAH. OKAY.

POLICE HEADQUARTERS.
NEXT MORNING.

HE ESCAPED AGAIN?!

THE MERCHANTS ARE IN AN UPROAR!
THEY'VE PETITIONED LORD YAMAHASHI, DEMANDING NEZUMI'S CAPTURE.
SO I HAVE HEARD, CHIEF INSPECTOR ITO.
WOULD YOU LIKE SOME TEA?

YOU HAD HIM CORNERED LAST NIGHT, AND YOU LET HIM GET AWAY!
WELL?
SIP!

THE TOWNSPEOPLE PROTECT HIM BECAUSE HE HELPS THEM.
10.

THE TOWNSFOLK ARE FOOLS! NEZUMI GIVES THEM A FEW COINS--A PITTANCE OF WHAT HE STEALS--AND BUYS THEIR LOYALTY.

MULTIPLY YOUR PATROLS. IF NEZUMI IS NOT CAPTURED SOON, THE MERCHANTS WILL INCREASE THEIR PRESSURE ON ME...

...AND I WILL NEED TO FIND A ***SCAPEGOAT***. DO I MAKE MYSELF CLEAR?
SIP!

YES, MAGISTRATE ITO.

GOOD. I'M GLAD WE UNDERSTAND EACH OTHER.

NOW, ON TO OTHER BUSINESS.

THERE IS A WAVE OF PICKPOCKETING IN TOWN.
OH--?
11.

HAVE THE EXTRA PATROLS BEEN ASSIGNED, INSPECTOR NII?
YES, SIR.

MANY ARE IN CIVILIAN GARB TO BLEND IN WITH THE CROWDS. IF NEZUMI SHOWS HIS FACE, WE'LL GET HIM FOR SURE.

NO ONE CAN COMMIT A CRIME AROUND HERE.
I GUARANTEE IT!

HELP! POLICE!
EH?
12.

I'VE BEEN ROBBED! MY PURSE HAS BEEN STOLEN!
THE PICKPOCKET IS HERE! SEAL OFF THE SQUARE!

WHAT DO YOU INTEND TO DO--SEARCH EVERYONE IN THE AREA?
WELL...

IT WOULD BE FUTILE. THIS IS A CLEVER THIEF WE ARE DEALING WITH. HE IS GONE BY NOW--OR HAS ALREADY DISPOSED OF THE EVIDENCE.
THEN WHAT CAN WE DO, INSPECTOR ISHIDA?

WE CAN ONLY MAINTAIN OUR VIGILANCE.
YES, SIR.

?
...AND NEZUMI JUMPED OVER THE ROOFTOPS AND ESCAPED THE DIMWITTED COPS.
13

HEY! HOW DARE YOU RIDICULE THE POLICE?!
I SHOULD ARREST YOU FOR YOUR DISRESPECT!

NO DISRESPECT INTENDED. I'M JUST A GIRL DOING WHAT I CAN TO GET BY.
PLEASE DON'T ARREST US, SIR.

OH, DON'T WORRY ABOUT IT, MY DEAR. I ENJOYED YOUR STORY.
THANK YOU.

I AM INSPECTOR ISHIDA, AND YOU ARE--?
I AM CALLED KITSUNE, AND MY YOUNG FRIEND IS KIYOKO.

OH MY, YOUR BOWL IS STILL EMPTY. DID YOU JUST SET UP?
YES, SIR.

WE DON'T MEAN TO INTERRUPT YOUR WORK. PLEASE CONTINUE SO WE MAY ENJOY YOUR PERFORMANCE.
WITH YOUR PERMISSION, THEN.
FLICK!
14.

MY, SUCH CLEVER LITTLE FINGERS YOU HAVE.
WHY, THANK YOU. YOU HAVE SUCH A HONEYED TONGUE.

THERE IS A PICKPOCKET IN TOWN WITH FINGERS JUST AS CLEVER AS YOURS.

BE CAREFUL. IT WOULD BE A PITY IF YOU WERE MISTAKEN FOR THAT THIEF.
OH, DON'T WORRY ABOUT IT. WE'RE VERY LAW-ABIDING STREET ENTERTAINERS.

ARE YOU STAYING IN TOWN A WHILE, OR MERELY PASSING THROUGH?
WE WERE THINKING OF STAYING...
...BUT I THINK WE'LL JUST CONTINUE ON OUR WAY.

I SEE. GOOD. GOOD.

HERE IS SOMETHING TO HELP YOU ON YOUR WAY.
THANK YOU, INSPECTOR ISHIDA.
15

WHAT A FUNNY LITTLE MAN.
NOT AS FUNNY AS YOU THINK, LITTLE SISTER. THAT WAS A WARNING.
HE'S SHREWD, THAT ONE. INSPECTOR ISHIDA IS SOMEONE TO BE WARY OF.

BUT--ENOUGH OF HIM. LET'S GET BACK TO WORK.
GATHER 'ROUND! GATHER 'ROUND AND SEE HOW NEZUMI ESCAPED THE DIMWITTED POLICE!

INSPECTOR ISHIDA! INSPECTOR ISHIDA!
EH--? WHAT IS IT?
MURDER!
WHO?

MERCHANT HASAMI OF THE GREEN LOTUS INN--NEZUMI IS THE MURDERER!
NEZUMI? HOW DO THEY KNOW HE IS THE KILLER?

THERE WERE WITNESSES!
MOVE ASIDE! MOVE ASIDE! WE'RE ON OFFICIAL POLICE BUSINESS!
16

STEP ASIDE! STEP ASIDE!

DID YOU HEAR THAT?
YEAH. NEZUMI IS A KILLER! THAT CHANGES A LOT!

OUT OF OUR WAY! LET US IN! IF YOU HAVE NOTHING TO DO WITH THE INVESTIGATION, GO HOME!

WHERE IS THE BODY?
UPSTAIRS, SIR.
THEN I'LL START DOWN HERE.

THIS LOOKS LIKE ANY OTHER KITCHEN.
HMM...

I GUESS THAT IS EVERYTHING WE CAN LEARN HERE.
NOW LET US LOOK AT THE BODY.
17

HAS THE BODY BEEN TOUCHED?
NO, SIR, BUT THE BODY REMOVERS SHOULD ARRIVE SOON.

SO MUCH BLOOD...

HMM... LET'S SEE. STABBED IN THE CHEST...

...A SHALLOW GASH TO HIS SIDE...

...AND A POWERFUL BLOW TO HIS SHOULDER, HACKED TO THE BONE. NO DOUBT THIS IS THE SOURCE OF MOST OF THIS BLOOD.

THE MONEY BOX IS EMPTY, EXCEPT FOR A FEW COPPERS.
THEN CLEARLY ROBBERY WAS THE MOTIVE. IT HAS TO BE NEZUMI'S WORK!

WHO ARE THE WITNESSES?
HASAMI'S SONS. THEY'RE WAITING IN THE NEXT ROOM.
I'LL GO AND SEE THEM NOW.
18

THESE ARE THE MERCHANT'S SONS.
I'M SORRY FOR THE LOSS OF YOUR FATHER.

NOW, TELL ME WHAT YOU SAW.

I'M THE OLDEST, SO I'LL DO THE TALKING.

"WE HAD CLOSED THE INN, AND THE SERVANTS WERE CLEANING UP DOWNSTAIRS. WE THREE CAME UP TO HELP FATHER ADD UP THE DAY'S PROFITS, AS WE USUALLY DO. BUT WHEN WE SLID OPEN THE DOOR...
!
!

"...WE SAW NEZUMI CROUCHED OVER THE BODY OF OUR FATHER, A BLOODY *KATANA* IN HIS HAND."

HE PUSHED PAST US, AND ESCAPED UP THE ATTIC AND ONTO THE ROOF.
I SEE...
19.

HMM... WHY RUN PAST YOU AND UP THE ATTIC? IT WOULD HAVE BEEN MUCH EASIER TO ESCAPE OUT THE WINDOW, AND ONTO THE ROOF THAT WAY.

THE WINDOWS FACE THE STREETS. HE WOULD HAVE BEEN SEEN, AND, WITH ALL OUR MEN IN THE AREA, HE WOULD HAVE BEEN CAPTURED FOR SURE.
OF COURSE.

SO WE ONLY HAVE THE WORD OF YOU THREE THAT NEZUMI WAS HERE.
IT HAPPENED JUST LIKE HE SAID!
YEAH.
WHAT ARE YOU IMPLYING?

I'M NOT IMPLYING ANYTHING. I'M JUST THINKING OUT LOUD.

THIS LEADS UP TO THE ATTIC, DOES IT?

YES, THIS ATTIC WOULD MAKE A VERY GOOD ACCESS TO THE ROOF.
20.

INSPECTOR ISHIDA, THE CHIEF INSPECTOR HAS ARRIVED.
OH, HAS HE? HELP ME DOWN.

AH, ISHIDA! NEZUMI IS NOW A MURDERER! THAT'S A DIFFERENT MATTER THAN ROBBERY! THE PEOPLE WILL TURN AGAINST HIM NOW!

IT'S ONLY A MATTER OF TIME BEFORE WE GET HIM!
PERHAPS NOT.
WHAT DO YOU MEAN?

NEZUMI DID NOT KILL MERCHANT HASAMI.
WHAT?!
THEN WHO DID?

NII, ARREST THOSE THREE.
WHAT?!
WHAT PROOF DO YOU HAVE?
21.

YOU SAID NEZUMI HAD A BLOODY KATANA LONG SWORD. HE CARRIES A TANTO KNIFE. I, UH, HAPPENED TO GET A GOOD LOOK AT IT ONCE.
YOU'RE CRAZY!

THERE WERE THREE DISTINCT WOUNDS, MADE BY THREE DIFFERENT BLADES, ONE OF THEM SURELY A CLEAVER.

I NOTICED THERE WERE THREE KNIVES ABSENT FROM THE KNIFE RACK IN THE KITCHEN.
GULP!

I BELIEVE EACH OF THE THREE BROTHERS DELIVERED A SEPARATE CUT.

THAT WAY, NONE COULD LATER BLACKMAIL THE OTHER, BECAUSE ALL THREE ARE GUILTY.

ANOTHER THING--NEZUMI COULD NOT HAVE ESCAPED THROUGH THE ATTIC. THE COBWEBS UP THERE ARE UNDISTURBED.
B-BUT WHY?

NO DOUBT THEY DID NOT WANT TO WAIT ANY LONGER FOR THEIR INHERITANCE, AND NEZUMI MADE A GOOD SCAPEGOAT.
ARREST THEM, NII!
GOOD NIGHT.
22

IS IT TRUE, INSPECTOR? IS NEZUMI A KILLER?
NEZUMI IS GUILTY OF MANY CRIMES, BUT MURDER IS NOT AMONG THEM.

DID YOU HEAR THAT?
HE'S INNOCENT!
HOORAY!
I KNEW HE COULDN'T HAVE DONE IT!

DUM DE DUM DUM... YOKOHAMA GIRL...

WELL, ARE YOU GOING TO SHOW YOURSELF?
23.

YOU'RE GETTING BETTER, INSPECTOR ISHIDA.
THANK YOU FOR PROVING MY INNOCENCE.
I DID NOT DO IT FOR YOU. I JUST LISTENED TO WHAT THE EVIDENCE TOLD ME.

THEN I'M GLAD I DIDN'T CUT OFF YOUR HEAD, OR YOU WOULDN'T HAVE EARS TO HEAR THE EVIDENCE. I OWE YOU A FAVOR, INSPECTOR.

YOU OWE ME NOTHING, NEZUMI. YOU ARE A CRIMINAL, AND I'LL CAPTURE YOU ONE DAY SOON.

SO, IT'S A GAME, THEN... A GAME OF CAT AND MOUSE.

JUSTICE IS NOT A GAME!

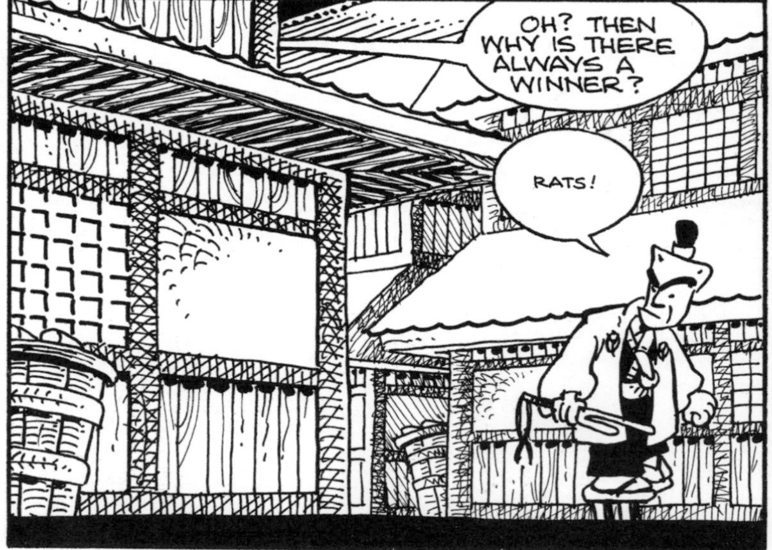
OH? THEN WHY IS THERE ALWAYS A WINNER?
RATS!

THE END

SAMURAI FOR HIRE
1.

G' MORNING.

YOU-- STOP!

WHO? ME?

I AM TRAVELING NORTH. YOU WILL BE MY ESCORT.
NORTH?

BUT I'M TRAVELING EAST, AND...
HARUMPH!

WOULD YOU FORCE AN OLD WOMAN TO TRAVEL THIS DANGEROUS LAND ALONE?
BUT...

WELL...WHEN YOU PUT IT THAT WAY, I GUESS I CAN TAKE YOU TO THE NEXT TOWN.

I AM MIYAMOTO USAGI.
HRMMPH!

YOI-SHO!

WELL?
HUH? "WELL" WHAT?

PICK UP MY BAG. IT'S NOT GOING TO WALK BY ITSELF, YOU KNOW. HARUMPH!
IDIOT.
HUH? OH... SORRY.

HURRY! COME ALONG!
UGH! WHAT DO YOU HAVE IN HERE-- ROCKS?

THAT IS NONE OF YOUR BUSINESS! SUCH IMPERTINENCE!

NOW HURRY ALONG! I DON'T LIKE SLACKERS!
YES, MA'AM.
4.

?

WHAT'S THE MATTER NOW? WHY DID YOU STOP?

YOU ARE A HIRELING.
I AM?

HIRELINGS WALK FIVE PACES BEHIND THEIR BETTERS.
THEY DO?

COME ALONG, COME ALONG. I CAN'T STAND A HIRELING WHO DALLIES.
YOU CAN'T?

NICE WEATHER WE'VE BEEN HAVING, HUH?
I EXPECTED IT TO BE A LOT COLDER BY NOW.
I DON'T ESPECIALLY LIKE THE COLD.
THE COLORS OF THE LEAVES ARE CHANGING, THOUGH.
DON'T YOU LOVE THE LEAVES OF FALL?
THE FALL HAS ALWAYS BEEN MY FAVORITE TIME OF YEAR.
WELL, AFTER SPRING AND SUMMER, THAT IS.
WINTER IS OKAY TOO...
...EXCEPT FOR THE COLD. DID I TELL YOU I DON'T ESPECIALLY LIKE THE COLD?
6.

HOURS LATER...
WE'LL TAKE A MEAL THERE.
GOOD. I'M HUNGRY.
AND MY ARM COULD USE A REST.

HA--A DRINK HERE... A BOWL OF RICE THERE... SERVE...CLEAN UP... YOU'RE ALWAYS IN A RUSH. THE MONEY'S NOT WORTH THE EFFORT.

IT'S WHAT YOU HAVE TO DO WHEN YOU OWN A BUSINESS... EVEN ONE AS UNPROFITABLE AS MINE IS.
THAT'S NOT FOR ME. A GUY WITH MY BRAINS CAN GET BY WITHOUT SUCH HARD WORK.

RATS! I'M OUT OF SAKE'. HOW ABOUT GIVING ME A BOTTLE ON THE HOUSE, HUH? I ONLY HAD ENOUGH CASH FOR ONE BOTTLE.
NO MONEY? THAT'S WHAT NOT WORKING GETS YOU!

FEH! AFTER A DAY'S LABOR, WHAT HAVE YOU GOT TO SHOW FOR IT? YOU CAN'T EVEN BUY ME A LOUSY BOTTLE OF SAKE'. HA! YOU'RE NO BETTER OFF THAN I AM!
7.

AFTER A WHILE, I'LL HAVE ENOUGH SAVED TO OPEN AN INN IN TOWN.
THEN I WON'T HAVE TO SERVE RIFFRAFF LIKE YOU!
I WOULDN'T DRINK AT YOUR INN IF YOU BEGGED ME.

WHO NEEDS PATRONS WHO DON'T HAVE ANY MONEY?
¡YAWN!¡

¡ZNORE!¡
EXCUSE US...
AH! **PAYING** CUSTOMERS! WELCOME!
I'VE GOT A NICE TABLE FOR TWO.
NO.
TWO TABLES FOR ONE. I DO NOT EAT WITH HIRELINGS.

UH, YES... OF COURSE. THIS WAY.

HERE'S A FINE TABLE FOR YOU, MA'AM.
¡*HARUMPH!*¡ IT WILL HAVE TO DO.
8.

AND A TABLE FOR YOU, SIR.
THANK YOU.
ZZZ...
I CAN'T WAIT TO PUT THIS DOWN!
FEH! FILTHY!

WHEW!
BE CAREFUL, YOU IDIOT!
THUD!

THAT HOLDS WHAT IS **PRECIOUS** TO ME! TREAT IT WITH RESPECT, YOU CLUMSY OAF!
"PRECIOUS"?

OH, SORRY.
FEH! YOU CAN'T GET GOOD HIRELINGS NOWADAYS.
THAT BAG LOOKS AWFULLY HEAVY.

I WONDER WHAT PRECIOUS THING COULD BE SO HEAVY... **GOLD,** MAYBE?

IF I COULD LEARN WHO SHE IS, I COULD PROBABLY GUESS WHAT'S IN THAT BAG.

THE INNKEEPER MIGHT KNOW HER.
9.

HEY-- WHO IS THAT ILL-NATURED OLD LADY OUT THERE?
SHE OWNS THE BIG FURNITURE STORE IN TOWN.
EVEN VASSALS OF THE GREAT LORDS PATRONIZE HER SHOP.
I GUESS IF YOU'RE THAT SUCCESSFUL, YOU CAN AFFORD TO BE DIFFICULT.

BUT I'VE NEVER KNOWN HER TO LEAVE TOWN. HER BUSINESS IS HER LIFE, OR SO I'VE HEARD. SHE MUST BE ON A BUYING TRIP OR SOMETHING.
SLOOOP!!

MAYBE IF YOU WORKED AS HARD AS SHE DOES, YOU WOULD BE RICH TOO! HA HA!
RICH, HUH?

A LADY LIKE HER MUST TRAVEL WITH A LOT OF MONEY-- THAT'S PROBABLY WHAT'S IN THAT BAG OF HERS.

THE *RONIN* CAN'T BE MUCH OF A SWORDSMAN IF HE TAKES THE AMOUNT OF ABUSE SHE DISHES OUT.
IDIOT.

10.

LATER...
I HOPE YOUR MEAL WAS SATISFACTORY, MA'AM.
FEH! I'VE NEVER EATEN SUCH UNAPPETIZING FOOD--EVEN THE TEA WAS GREASY!
SIP!

COME ON, CLUMSY--WE'VE GOT TO CONTINUE ON OUR WAY.
B-BUT, MA'AM... THE COST OF THE MEAL...

FEH! DO YOU EXPECT ME TO PAY FOR SUCH A POOR MEAL? MY HIRELING WILL TAKE CARE OF YOU.
ME?!

OF COURSE. DO YOU THINK I WOULD HAVE COMMERCE WITH ONE SUCH AS HE?

AND HURRY ALONG! YOU'RE SO LAZY!
I'LL BE GLAD WHEN WE REACH THE NEXT TOWN!
11.

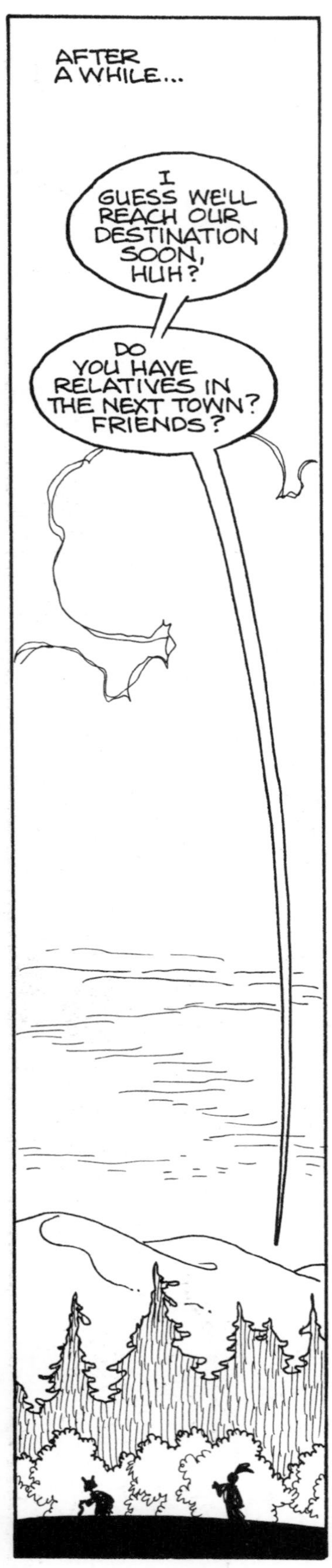
AFTER A WHILE...
I GUESS WE'LL REACH OUR DESTINATION SOON, HUH?
DO YOU HAVE RELATIVES IN THE NEXT TOWN? FRIENDS?

HIRELINGS SHOULD NOT JABBER INCESSANTLY LIKE CROWS! THEY SHOULD KEEP THEIR MOUTHS SHUT AND OBEY.
...
I'VE HAD ENOUGH! I AM NOT YOUR HIRELING! OLD WOMAN OR NOT, YOU CAN CONTINUE ON YOUR OWN!
THUD!
I WON'T TAKE ANY MORE OF YOUR ABUSE! I WASN'T EVEN GOING THIS WAY IN THE FIRST PLACE! I HELPED YOU BECAUSE I FELT SORRY FOR YOU!
YOU WON'T CONVERSE WITH ME--YOU WON'T EVEN TELL ME YOUR NAME! YOU'RE JUST A RUDE, CANTANKEROUS OLD WOMAN!
12.

I'M LEAVING! YOU CAN GO WHEREVER YOU WANT-- ON YOUR OWN!
GO AHEAD-- YELL AT ME! I DON'T CARE!

.....

BWAHH!
!

WAHH! SOB! SOB!
UH...

LOOK... I WAS A BIT HARSH. I'M SORRY. I HAVE SUCH AN UNCONTROLLABLE TEMPER. ARE YOU OKAY?
SOB!

THE NEXT TOWN IS NOT FAR AWAY, AND I'M IN NO PARTICULAR HURRY. I'LL BE GLAD TO ESCORT YOU THERE. YOU DON'T EVEN HAVE TO TALK TO ME. OKAY?
SOB!
13.

I HAVE A CLOTH SOMEWHERE THAT YOU CAN USE TO WIPE YOUR EYES. THEN WE CAN CONTINUE ON OUR WAY. OKAY, LADY?

UH... LADY?

HAYASHI.

WHAT?
I AM CALLED HAYASHI, AND, NO, I DO NOT KNOW ANYONE IN THE NEXT TOWN.

SO, THEN...UH... ARE YOU ON A SHRINE PILGRIMAGE?
NO.

ER... THEN, WHY...?
I--

I'M RUNNING AWAY FROM HOME!
14.

AND SO...
MY HUSBAND AND I BUILT UP A SUCCESSFUL BUSINESS. AFTER HE DIED, OUR SON TOOK OVER THE DAILY OPERATIONS.

BUT I STILL OVERSAW EVERYTHING. AFTER ALL, I WORKED HARD ALL MY LIFE TO ESTABLISH THE SHOP. WHO KNOWS THE BUSINESS BETTER THAN ME?

THIS MORNING, THAT SON OF MINE TOLD ME I WAS NO LONGER NEEDED AT THE SHOP...THAT I WAS TOO OLD, TOO RUDE TO THE CUSTOMERS, THAT I DIDN'T KNOW THE BUSINESS ANYMORE.

WHAT AM I TO DO? I'M NOT A HOMEMAKER. THAT IS WHAT HIS WIFE IS FOR. MY PLACE IS RUNNING THE SHOP.
IT IS THE ONLY THING I KNOW.

UNGRATEFUL-- THAT'S WHAT HE IS! HE WOULDN'T HAVE WHAT HE HAS IF IT WERE NOT FOR ME!
MY HUSBAND WOULD WEEP IN HIS GRAVE IF HE KNEW HOW SHABBILY OUR ONLY SON TREATS ME!

LET'S GO. I WANT TO PUT AS MUCH DISTANCE AS POSSIBLE BETWEEN ME AND THAT INGRATE!
DON'T FORGET THE BAG.
15.

SURELY THERE MUST BE SOME REASON WHY YOUR SON--
BAH!

HE CLAIMS THAT I INTERFERE... THAT I'M RUDE... THAT I SHOULD ENJOY MY GOLDEN YEARS. HAVE YOU HEARD ANYTHING MORE PREPOSTEROUS? WELL, WE'LL SHOW HIM.

WE'LL GO TO THE NEXT TOWN, OPEN UP A NEW SHOP, AND DRIVE THAT UNAPPRECIATIVE SON OF MINE OUT OF BUSINESS!

"WE"?!

MAYBE YOU SHOULD GO HOME AND TALK TO YOUR SON. I BET HE'S SICK WITH WORRY ABOUT YOU.

IN FACT, I BET HE'S OUT LOOKING FOR YOU RIGHT NOW!
BAH!
16.

I WOULDN'T GO BACK TO THAT SON OF MINE IF HE BEGGED ME--THAT UNGRATEFUL INGRATE!

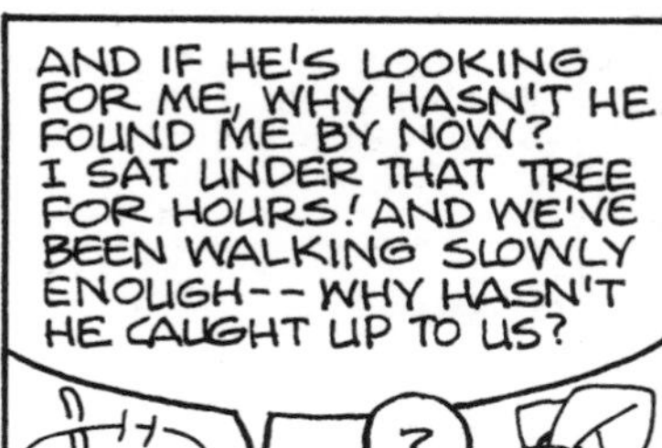
AND IF HE'S LOOKING FOR ME, WHY HASN'T HE FOUND ME BY NOW? I SAT UNDER THAT TREE FOR HOURS! AND WE'VE BEEN WALKING SLOWLY ENOUGH-- WHY HASN'T HE CAUGHT UP TO US?

?

HE'S SO INCOMPETENT, HE'S PROBABLY GOTTEN HIMSELF LOST!
I LIKED HER BETTER WHEN SHE WAS SILENT!

NO, THE BEST THING FOR US TO DO IS START OUR OWN BUSINESS.

AND IT'S NOT A PARTNERSHIP, MIND YOU. YOU'RE JUST A HIRELING!

SO DON'T THINK YOU'LL GET RICH ON MY EFFORTS!
HERE THEY COME!

I DON'T KNOW--THAT SAMURAI LOOKS TOUGH.
HA! HE'S A COWARD. EVEN THAT OLD LADY IS TOUGHER THAN HE IS. LOOK AT THE WEIGHT OF THAT BAG. THERE'S A FORTUNE IN THERE, FOR SURE!
YOU HANDLE THE SAMURAI. I'LL TAKE CARE OF THE OLD LADY.
17.

COME ON, COME ON! QUIT DRAGGING YOUR FEET! WE'VE GOT TO GET THERE BY DARK.

WAIT-- THERE IS DANGER AROUND.
BAH! YOU DON'T KNOW WHAT YOU'RE TALKING ABOUT!
YOU'RE JUST MAKING EXCUSES FOR YOUR SLUGGISH-NESS!
HURRY ALONG!
SLACKER.

HIYAAHHH!!
!
!
HAND OVER THE LOOT!

HEY, WATCH OUT!
HYAH!

HA! GIVE UP, COWARD! YOU HAVE NO CHANCE AGAINST--

ZONK!
--ME-- OW!
18

LET HER GO.
D-DRAW YOUR SWORD AND...AND I'LL KILL HER, SAMURAI!
LET ME GO, YOU RUFFIAN!
IF SHE DIES, YOU'LL DIE.
GULP!

UH...LOOK, ALL WE WANT IS WHAT IS IN THAT BAG.
NO--! DON'T GIVE IT TO THEM! I NEED IT TO OPEN ANOTHER BUSINESS!

"OPEN ANOTHER BUSINESS," HUH? SO THERE IS MONEY IN THERE! OKAY, SAMURAI, TOSS IT OVER.
NO! DON'T!

NOTHING IN HERE IS WORTH A PERSON'S LIFE. HERE, TAKE IT.

YOU'RE SMART, SAMURAI. NOW STAND BACK, AND DON'T EVEN TOUCH YOUR SWORD. TAKE EVEN ONE STEP CLOSER, AND I'LL KILL HER!
NO! DON'T LET HIM TAKE IT! IT'S MY FUTURE!
DON'T HURT HER!
HURRY--CHECK THE BAG.
19.

WHAT THE--?! A HAMMER... A PLANE... A SAW... THESE ARE TOOLS! THERE'S NOTHING IN HERE BUT JUNK!
WHAT'S GOING ON? WHERE'S THE GOLD?!
GOLD?

WHAT GOLD? THOSE ARE MY HUSBAND'S TOOLS! TOGETHER WE BUILT OUR FURNITURE BUSINESS!

WITH THEM, I WILL FOUND A NEW ENTERPRISE! WORKING WITH HIS TOOLS WILL BE AS IF HE WERE WORKING RIGHT ALONGSIDE ME. WE CANNOT FAIL!
HIS HAMMER...HIS PLANE--

SHE'S CRAZY! COME ON--LET'S GET OUT OF HERE!
--THESE THINGS ARE PRECIOUS TO ME.

"SHE'S TRAVELING WITH A FORTUNE AND A USELESS BODYGUARD." BAH! YOU AND YOUR STUPID IDEAS!
SHUT UP!
NEVER BEFORE HAVE I ENCOUNTERED SUCH INCOMPETENT THIEVES.
20

LET ME HELP YOU GATHER THESE UP.
BE CAREFUL WITH THAT, YOU CLUMSY OAF! IT'S FRAGILE! DON'T BREAK IT!
IT'S A HAMMER.

MOTHER! MOTHER!

MOTHER! I'VE BEEN LOOKING ALL OVER FOR YOU!
HA! THAT'S MY SON! I KNEW HE WOULD COME BEGGING FOR ME TO RETURN!
HE CAN'T RUN THE BUSINESS WITHOUT ME!

MOTHER--YOU LEFT WITHOUT TELLING ANYONE WHERE YOU WERE GOING! I SEARCHED ALL OVER TOWN, AND THEN A COUPLE OF WOODCUTTERS TOLD ME THEY SAW YOU ON THE ROAD.

SAY...! WHAT'S GOING ON HERE?
WHO ARE YOU, SAMURAI? WHAT DO YOU WANT? DON'T YOU HURT MY MOTHER!
21.

FORGET THE SAMURAI. HE'S HARMLESS, BARELY COMPETENT. LET US RETURN, AND I WILL OVERSEE THE SHOP ONCE AGAIN.
I KNEW YOU WOULD COME TO YOUR SENSES!

UH... MOTHER, YOU CANNOT WORK IN THE SHOP.
WHAT?!

YOU CAST ME OUT, THEN BEG ME TO RETURN? WHY SHOULD I GO BACK WHEN YOU WILL NOT LET ME WORK IN THE BUSINESS THAT I HELPED CREATE?

BUT YOU'RE RUDE TO ALL OUR CLIENTS!
BAH! I'M AS COURTEOUS AS ANYONE DESERVES.

JUST YESTERDAY YOU INSULTED OUR LARGEST BUYER--A HIGH-RANKING SAMURAI. YOU CALLED HIM A HIRELING! WE HAD TO SEND HIM A VERY EXPENSIVE GIFT TO SOOTHE HIS PRIDE. IT WILL TAKE US MONTHS TO MAKE THAT MONEY BACK!

AND HE'S NOT THE ONLY ONE WHO'S COMPLAINED ABOUT YOUR BEHAVIOR.
THERE IS NOTHING WRONG WITH MY BEHAVIOR! I STARTED THE BUSINESS, AND I KNOW WHAT'S GOOD FOR IT!
22

AND WHAT WOULD I HAVE TO RETURN TO? YOU WON'T LET ME WORK, AND HARUMI HAS NO TROUBLE MANAGING THE HOUSEHOLD. SO IT'S BETTER THAT I LEAVE AND START ANOTHER SHOP!

BUT THERE IS SO MUCH TO DO, ESPECIALLY WITH THE COMING BABY.
BABY? WHAT BABY?

WE TOLD YOU MONTHS AGO, BUT YOU NEVER HEAR US! YOU JUST THINK ABOUT THE BUSINESS.
I THOUGHT HARUMI WAS JUST GETTING FAT. WELL, THIS CHANGES EVERY-THING.

THAT WIFE OF YOURS CANNOT EVEN ORGANIZE A HOUSEHOLD. HOW CAN SHE RAISE MY GRANDCHILD?
I'LL NEED TO TAKE CARE OF EVERYTHING AT HOME.

COME ON!
WHAT? BUT HARUMI MANAGES OUR HOUSEHOLD WONDERFULLY! YOU SAID SO YOURSELF!

WHY ARE YOU STANDING THERE LIKE AN IDIOT? COME ON, AND DON'T FORGET MY BAG.
WHAT ABOUT THE SAMURAI?
23.

FORGET ABOUT THAT *RONIN*! HE'S JUST SOME HIRELING WHO BEGGED ME FOR A JOB.
YES, MOTHER.

DON'T GIVE HIM ANY MONEY, THOUGH. HE'S AN INCOMPETENT WORKER, AND HE'S RUDE!
YES, MOTHER.

HURRY! KEEP UP! YOU ALWAYS WERE SO SLOW. WHO KNOWS WHAT THAT INCOMPETENT WIFE OF YOURS IS DOING!
YOUR HOUSEHOLD NEEDS TO BE ORGANIZED LIKE A BUSINESS. I'LL HAVE EVERYTHING IN ORDER IN NO TIME!
YES, MOTHER.

WALK FIVE PACES BEHIND ME.
YES, MOTHER.
POOR HARUMI.

THE END

DREAMS AND NIGHTMARES

SLASH!

ZIP!

SLASH!
ZWIT!

HYAAH!!

TANGG!!
2.

YOU--!
WHO ARE YOU?
Heh, heh, heh!
Me...?

I am your destiny.

I MAKE MY OWN DESTINY!

WHO ARE YOU?!
TANG!
TANG!
TANG!
TANG!
TANG!
TANG!
You know who I am!

YOU REEK OF EVIL!

Hee, hee, hee!

FOUL DEMON!
3.

--DIE!
SHOONK!

Grahh--!!

Hauk! Hauk!
GO BACK TO HELL WHERE YOU BELONG, DEMON!

Hauk!
Aheh... heh...
!

Heh, heh, heh, heh, heh, heh!
WH-WHAT'S HAPPENING?
WHY CAN'T I DRAW OUT MY BLADE?!

I--I CAN'T LET GO!
4.

TH-THERE'S A SHADOW CONSUMING MY BLADE!

I-IT'S TRAVELING UP MY ARM!

Aheh, heh, heh, heh!

.....

N-NO!

.....

EYAHH!
5.

YAAHHH!!

GASP! GASP! GASP!
A DREAM-- IT WAS ONLY A NIGHTMARE...!
AUNTY... AUNTY, ARE YOU ALL RIGHT?

AUNTY?
WHERE IS AUNTY?
SHE WAS HERE A SECOND AGO.
WHO ARE YOU?

ANSWER ME--WHO ARE YOU?

WH-WHAT AM I D-DOING h--

Hee hee hee hee!
6.

Why, my innocent, I'm right here. Can't you see me?
OH, THERE YOU ARE, AUNTY!

We must be going. Thank our host for his hospitality.
YES, AUNTY.

THANK YOU, SIR!

YOU LOOK CHILLY. ALLOW ME TO COVER YOU WITH THIS MAT, SIR.
7.

Come, my innocent, we have a long way to travel.
YES, AUNTY.
THE END

GEN and the DOG
EEP!

HEY, INNKEEPER-- SAKE*!
SURE, SAMURAI. YOU WANT THE CHEAP STUFF--OR THE GOOD STUFF?
THE GOOD STUFF... ALWAYS THE GOOD STUFF.
*RICE WINE

HERE YOU ARE, SAMURAI.
THANKS.

SLAM!

A SILVER COIN?!! I--I CAN'T MAKE CHANGE FOR THAT!
THEN KEEP IT.

THANKS, SIR!
BUT, FIRST, I NEED YOU TO ANSWER A FEW QUESTIONS.
SIP!
2.

HAVE YOU SEEN THIS WOMAN?

OH, YEAH. HER. I SAW HER A COUPLE OF DAYS AGO.

SHE AND THAT LITTLE GIRL WALKED THROUGH TOWN... GAVE ME THE CHILLS AS THEY PASSED.
LITTLE GIRL?

INAZUMA HAS ALWAYS TRAVELED ALONE.
ARE YOU SURE THIS IS THE ONE YOU SAW?

WELL, SHE LOOKED DIFFERENT, ALL RIGHT--A LOT SCARIER--BUT THERE'S NO MISTAKING THAT LIGHTNING BOLT IN HER HAIR.

THE ENTIRE TOWN CLEARED THE STREETS. IT WAS LIKE, YOU KNOW, THE PLAGUE WAS COMING THROUGH, OR SOMETHING.
THESE COUNTRY BUMPKINS--ALWAYS EXAGGERATING!
3

WHICH WAY DID SHE GO?

LIKE I TOLD THE OTHER GUY-- CHECK THE FOOTHILLS TO THE EAST.
OTHER GUY?

YEAH. HE CAME IN ABOUT AN HOUR AGO...SHOWED ME THE SAME WANTED POSTER.
WHAT DID HE LOOK LIKE?

I DON'T KNOW IF I SHOULD SAY. HE GAVE ME A GOLD COIN.
OKAY. HERE. YOU'LL MAKE MORE OUT OF THIS THAN I WILL.

HE WAS BIG AND MEAN-LOOKING, WITH A CIRCLE AROUND HIS LEFT EYE. OH, YEAH, AND HE HAD ONE BLACK EAR.

IS HE A FRIEND OF YOURS, SIR?
YEAH.
4.

-UY BOOK 9: DAISHO

TO THE EAST, HUH? HOPEFULLY OTHERS HAVE SEEN HER TOO. I'VE GOT TO GET TO INAZUMA BEFORE STRAY DOG DOES.

HEY, YOU-- UGLY PEASANTS!
YES, SAMURAI?

HAVE YOU SEEN THIS WOMAN?
HER? UH... WELL, I DON'T KNOW...

MAYBE THIS WILL JOG YOUR MEMORY.
IT SURE DOES!
SHE WAS HEADED TOWARDS THE EASTERN FOOT-HILLS.

BE CAREFUL OF HER--SHE LOOKED CREEPY!
THANKS.

HE GAVE US A SILVER COIN!
WHAT A CHEAPSKATE! THE OTHER GUY GAVE US **TWICE** AS MUCH!
?
6

THROUGHOUT THE DAY...
THIS IS COSTING ME A FORTUNE.
OVER IN THE EAST FOOTHILLS.
YEAH, I KNOW.
HEY, SAMURAI, I HEARD YOU'RE BUYING INFORMATION!
THE OTHER GUY GAVE ME TWO GOLD COINS.
BAH! ANOTHER DEAD END.
YOW!
7

THERE'S ANOTHER ONE.
I MUST HAVE ALREADY INVESTIGATED A HALF DOZEN OF THESE MOUNTAIN HUTS.
BUT... I'VE GOT A FEELING ABOUT THIS ONE! SHE'S THERE, ALL RIGHT.
I'D BETTER BE CAUTIOUS, THOUGH. THE LAST TIME I MET INAZUMA,* SHE MANAGED TO GET AWAY--BUT NOT THIS TIME.
*UY BOOK 12: GRASSCUTTER

I'LL CHECK OUT THE PERIMETER BEFORE GOING INTO THE HUT.

AH... FOOTPRINTS-- AN ADULT'S AND A CHILD'S. IT COULD BE INAZUMA AND THE GIRL. WHY IS SHE TRAVELING WITH A KID, ANYWAY?

ANOTHER SET OF FOOTPRINTS.

THEY PROBABLY BELONG TO THAT SCUM, STRAY DOG. SO THAT MEANS I'M AT THE RIGHT PLACE.
8.

STRAY DOG IS NOT GOING TO CLAIM MY REWARD-- NOT THIS TIME.
IT'S EASY ENOUGH TO FOLLOW HIS FOOTPRINTS...
...BUT THEN, WHY SHOULD HE MAKE AN EFFORT TO HIDE THEM? HE DOESN'T KNOW I'M ON HIS TRAIL.
QUIETLY, GEN-- ANY NOISE WILL NOT ONLY ALERT STRAY DOG, BUT INAZUMA AS WELL.
THERE HE IS--TOO INTENT ON STAKING OUT THAT HUT EVEN TO BE AWARE THAT I'M BEHIND HIM.
9.

SMOKE IS COMING OUT OF THE VENT. THOSE PEASANTS WERE RIGHT-- SOMEONE IS IN THERE, BUT IT'S NOT THE OWNER.

AT THIS TIME OF DAY, A PEASANT WOULD BE TOILING OUTSIDE.

BY HER REPUTATION, INAZUMA IS TOO SKILLED A SWORDSWOMAN TO CONFRONT IN A FAIR FIGHT.

IT'S A GOOD THING I'VE GOT THE ELEMENT OF SURPRISE ON MY SIDE.

SNAP!
EH--?
10.

GEN?!

UH--!
CHOK!

THIS WILL TEACH YOU TO CHEAT ME!
KRAK!
WOOK!

SOME BOUNTY HUNTER YOU ARE! ONLY AN AMATEUR WOULD ALLOW HIMSELF TO BE TAKEN UNAWARES!
11.

JUDGING BY THE LUMP ON HIS HEAD, I'D SAY STRAY DOG WILL BE UNCONSCIOUS FOR A WHILE.

I SHOULD CUT OFF HIS EARS FOR WHAT HE DID TO ME, BUT I'M TOO NICE A GUY.
THUD!

BESIDES, I'M CASTING FOR BIGGER FISH.

THE LAST TIME I FOUGHT HER, INAZUMA ALMOST BEAT ME.

SHE WON'T GET AWAY THIS TIME...
...ESPECIALLY WHEN I TAKE HER BY SURPRISE.

I'LL QUICKLY SLIDE THE DOOR OPEN, RUSH IN, AND CORNER HER BEFORE SHE EVEN HAS A CHANCE TO DRAW HER SWORD.
12.

HYAHH!
CHUK!

NGGH!

I CAN'T BELIEVE IT-- THE DOOR'S STUCK!

NGGGH! SOMETHING MUST BE JAMMED UP AGAINST IT!

I SHOULD HAVE DONE THIS IN THE FIRST PLACE.
NOTHING BEATS THE DIRECT APPROACH!
BAM! BAM! BAM!

CRASH!

DON'T MOVE!
THIS IS A SURPRISE RAID!
13.

DESERTED.
I GUESS IT'S JUST AS WELL.

OR MAYBE THIS PLACE ISN'T AS DESERTED AS I THOUGHT.

COLD AS ICE. THIS GUY'S BEEN DEAD FOR A WHILE.

LET'S TAKE A LOOK AT YOU.

¡GASP!

14.

POOR FOOL.
I'VE SEEN THIS LOOK OF DEATH BEFORE...

...INFLICTED BY THE SAME FIEND WHO WOUNDED MY SHOULDER.

BUT JEI IS DEAD! DID INAZUMA KILL THIS OLD FOOL?

JEI WAS A DEMON. WHAT WAS HIS RELATIONSHIP TO INAZUMA?

I'D HATE TO BE MIXED UP WITH JEI AGAIN.

MAYBE I SHOULD CUT MY LOSSES AND ABANDON MY SEARCH FOR INAZUMA.

AFTER ALL, I'M NOT IN THIS TOO DEEPLY...
...YET.
15.

GEN--YOU FILTHY POND SCUM BUCKET OF SCUMMY POND FILTH!
UH-OH.

I'LL TEACH YOU TO AMBUSH ME AND TRY TO STEAL MY REWARD!
IT LOOKS LIKE HIS HEAD IS EVEN HARDER THAN I THOUGHT.

I'M GOING TO START WITH YOUR EARS, AND WORK MY WAY DOWN TO YOUR TOES.
LOOK, STRAY DOG, IT WAS JUST A JOKE. I DON'T EVEN WANT INAZUMA ANYMORE.
YOU CAN TAKE A JOKE--
GRR--!
--CAN'T YOU?

THE END

WHEN RABBITS FLY!
EEP!
EEP! EEP!
HURRY! FASTER! FASTER!
I NEED MORE SPEED!
FASTER! FASTER!
1

HUFF! HUFF! HUFF!

HIYAHHH!

FLAP! FLAP!

CRASH!

ARE YOU ALL RIGHT?
THAT WAS A NASTY FALL!
HMM... I NEED MORE HEIGHT... MAYBE IF I JUMPED FROM SOMEPLACE HIGHER.
SENSEI*!
*TEACHER
TIE THE WINGS ONTO THE CART, HASU.
YES, TAKENOKO-SENSEI. WE'VE GOT LOTS OF ROPE.
"WINGS"?
OF COURSE. I WOULDN'T BE ABLE TO FLY WITHOUT THEM.
"FLY"? YOU MEAN LIKE THE KOMORI NINJA?
BAH! THEY'RE MURDEROUS BRIGANDS! I MEAN FLIGHT FOR DECENT PEOPLE!
OH, EXCUSE ME. I AM CALLED MIYAMOTO USAGI.
I AM TAKENOKO. HASU HERE IS MY HELPER.
PLEASED TO MEET YOU, USAGI-SAN.
3.

WHAT IS IT THAT PEOPLE YEARN FOR?
A BOWL OF HOT NOODLES?

NO, NO, NO! **KNOWLEDGE** IS WHAT WE QUEST FOR...AND THE ULTIMATE KNOWLEDGE IS **FLIGHT**!

I FLEW ON A KITE ONCE. I DIDN'T MUCH LIKE IT-- ESPECIALLY THE LANDING.
I WRENCHED MY SHOULDER.
HMM...
YES...

...BUT TO GLIDE ON A KITE IS ONE THING. TO ACTUALLY FLY IS ANOTHER.
THAT IS WHAT I DREAM TO DO SOMEDAY.

YOU'RE NOT LAUGHING!
SHOULD I BE?

YOU ARE OBVIOUSLY AN INTELLIGENT PERSON. COME AND HAVE A MEAL WITH ME. I WILL ENJOY THE CONVERSATION.
THANK YOU.
4.

HOW WONDERFUL TO MEET SOMEONE AS ENLIGHTENED AS YOU ARE, USAGI!
WALKING, TAKENOKO? I WOULD HAVE EXPECTED YOU TO FLY INTO TOWN! SNIGGER!
HA! HA! HA! HA! HA!
PAY HIM NO MIND, USAGI. THAT'S UDON. HE'S AN IGNORANT BULLY.
HA! HA! HA! HA! HA! HA! HA! HA!
FUME!
HERE IS MY HOME. PREPARE A MEAL, HASU. I WANT TO SHOW USAGI MY WORKSHOP.
IT'S JUST OUT IN THE BACK, USAGI.
5

COME ON IN, USAGI, AND BE MY GUEST.
THANK YOU.
!
AMAZING!
OH, IT'S NOTHING MUCH, REALLY.
SUCH WONDERS!
6.

STEAM IS MAKING THIS WHEEL SPIN?
FWEEEE

THIS IS THE SECOND BIGGEST HEAD BONE I'VE EVER SEEN!

WHAT MARVELOUS THINGS.
THERE IS SO MUCH TO LEARN. I AM A DOCTOR. I HEAL THE SICK AND INJURED, BUT I WANT TO DO SO MUCH MORE!

HERE, LOOK AT THIS SCROLL.

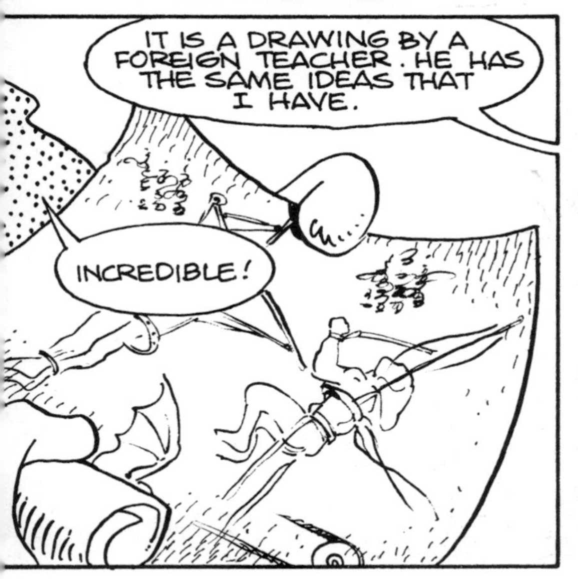
IT IS A DRAWING BY A FOREIGN TEACHER. HE HAS THE SAME IDEAS THAT I HAVE.
INCREDIBLE!

WHO KNOWS HOW MUCH MORE ADVANCED THEY ARE! ONE DAY, FOREIGNERS COULD COME SWOOPING INTO EDO.
7.

I DESPISE THE POLITICS THAT SEPARATE US FROM THE FOREIGNERS. THINK OF HOW MUCH MORE WE COULD LEARN IF WE FREELY EXCHANGED KNOWLEDGE.

BUT NOT ALL KNOWLEDGE IS GOOD.
NONSENSE.

THE MORE WE LEARN, THE MORE WE KNOW. KNOWLEDGE IS NEITHER GOOD NOR EVIL.

YES, BUT THE WAY THAT KNOWLEDGE IS APPLIED CAN BE.
HMM... I NEVER THOUGHT ABOUT THAT.

A MEAL IS READY, TAKENOKO-SENSEI.
THANK YOU, HASU.

YOU HAVE GIVEN ME MUCH TO PONDER, USAGI. PLEASE SPEND THE NIGHT HERE, AND WE CAN TALK SOME MORE.
THANK YOU.

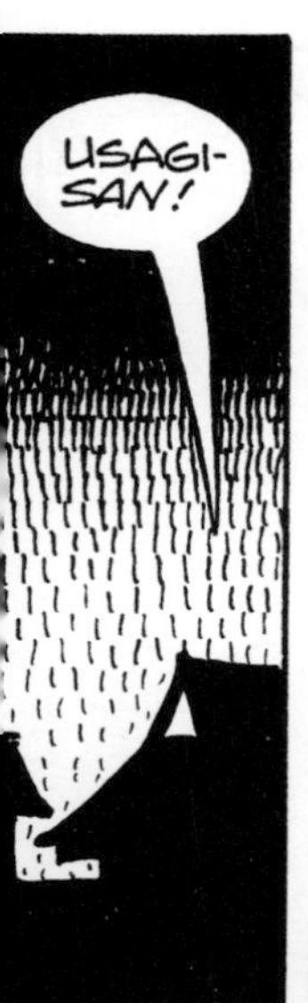
USAGI-SAN!

MMM--?

GOOD MORNING, TAKENOKO-SENSEI. YOU'RE UP EARLY.
I NEVER WENT TO SLEEP, USAGI. I'VE BEEN WORKING ALL NIGHT. I THINK I'VE SOLVED THE PROBLEM WITH MY WINGS.

YOU MEAN THEY'LL FLY?
I WOULDN'T BE SURPRISED IF THEY FLEW OFF ON THEIR OWN!
YAWN!

BUT I STILL NEED MORE HEIGHT! I AM GOING TO JUMP FROM THE TOP OF THE WATERFALL.

THE FALLS? ARE YOU SURE THAT'S SAFE?
OF COURSE! YOU DON'T THINK I WOULD DO ANYTHING DANGEROUS, DO YOU?

HASU--! GET THE CART READY! WE'RE GOING OUT!
9.

STILL TRYING TO FLY, TAKENOKO? IT'S A GOOD THING YOU'RE A DOCTOR. YOU'RE GOING TO HAVE TO HEAL YOUR OWN BROKEN BONES! HAW!
DOESN'T HE HAVE BETTER THINGS TO DO THAN TAUNT YOU?

DO NOT BOTHER WITH HIM, USAGI-SAN. HE IS NOT WORTH ARGUING WITH.
I DOUBT HE HAS BRAINS ENOUGH TO KNOW HE IS BEING ARGUED WITH.

HUH? WHAT DO YOU MEAN BY THAT?
THAT'S RIGHT! HE WOULDN'T KNOW.
HA! HA! HA! HA! HA! HA! HA! HA! HA! HA! HA! HA! HA! HA! HA! HA! HA! HA! HA! HA! HA!

STOP LAUGHING AT ME!
SHUT UP, YOU!
GAKK!
WHAP!
OW!

GRR! I'LL TEACH HIM TO MAKE A FOOL OF ME!
OOO--!
GAK!
COME ON-- WE'LL FOLLOW HIM!

LATER...
SHRAA!

IT'S PRETTY HIGH.
GOOD. I'LL BE ABLE TO FLY FOR SURE FROM WAY UP HERE.

I'LL GET A GOOD RUNNING START ALONG THE CLIFF...
...AND THEN SOAR OFF THE EDGE.

USAGI--YOU AND HASU WAIT BELOW, AND I'LL SWOOP DOWN TO YOU.
SHOULDN'T WE STAY UP HERE WITH YOU?
NONSENSE. WHAT COULD HAPPEN TO ME HERE?
11.

AREN'T YOU WORRIED ABOUT TAKENOKO-SENSEI, HASU?
OF COURSE NOT. WHY SHOULD I BE?
HE IS THE SMARTEST PERSON I'VE EVER MET. IF HE SAYS HE WILL FLY, HE **WILL** FLY.

LET'S WATCH HIM FROM THIS LEDGE.

IT'S STILL A LONG WAY TO THE BOTTOM, BUT THERE'S NO BETTER VANTAGE AREA THAN RIGHT HERE.

AH, GOOD. THEY'RE IN POSITION.

I CAN GET A RUNNING START ALONG HERE.
NOW WE'LL SEE HOW MY WINGS OF BAMBOO AND SILK WILL DO.
AH, THEY WORK PERFECTLY!
I WONDER HOW FAR I'LL ACTUALLY FLY.
STRAIGHT TO THE BOTTOM!
HUH?
HEH, HEH, HEH, HEH, HEH.
UDON-- WHAT ARE YOU DOING HERE?!
SO, YOU'RE ALONE, HUH? CAUGHT WITHOUT THAT ASSISTANT OF YOURS--OR THAT SWORDSMAN.
13.

YOU LIKE TO LEARN, DON'T YOU? WELL, I'M HERE TO TEACH YOU A LESSON.
HEH HEH.
HEH HEH.
HEH HEH.

I DON'T WANT LESSONS IN STUPIDITY!

HA HA HA HA HA! THAT JOKE WAS EVEN FUNNIER THAN HIS LAST ONE!
HA HA HA HA!

SHUT UP!
I TOLD YOU NOT TO LAUGH AT ME!
OUCH!
YAH!
OW!

YAHH! HE'S GONE CRAZY!
I'LL SHOW YOU WHO'S STUPID!
I'M GOING TO RIP YOUR WINGS TO SHREDS!
OW!
OW!
KEEP AWAY FROM ME!
14.

USAGI-SAN-- LOOK!
THAT BULLY IS BACK!
THERE'S NOT ENOUGH TIME TO RUN UP THERE TO HELP TAKENOKO.
THERE'S NOTHING I CAN DO!
I'M GOING TO--
HE'S GOING TO JUMP!
15

--FLY!
I'M DOING IT! I'M FLYING! I'M--
ZIP!
UH-OH!
SENSEI--!
WHAT CAN I DO? WHAT CAN I--
!
HOLD ONTO THIS!
?
16.

YAHH!

I HOPE I'VE TIMED THIS RIGHT.

SENSEI--!
USAGI?!
17

GOT YOU!
UMPH!

UGH!
TWANG!

I-- CAN'T-- KEEP A-- GRIP!
HOLD ON, HASU!

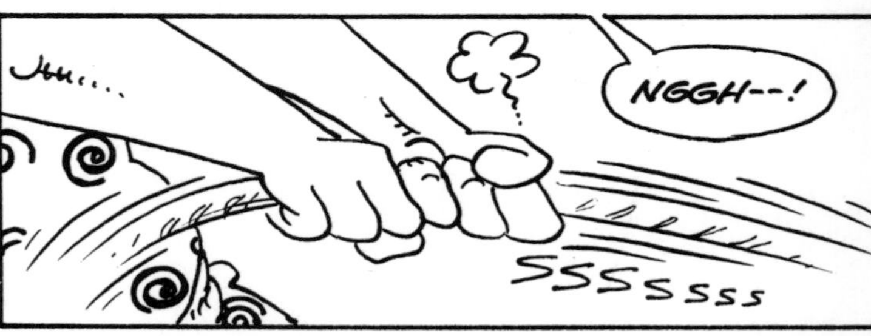
NGGH--!
SSSSSSS

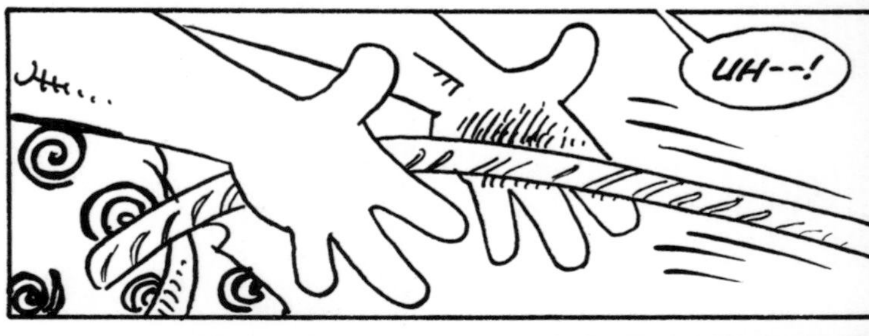
UH--!

SENSEI--!

THE WALL!

UH--!
SWAM!

I--I DIDN'T THINK HE WOULD ACTUALLY JUMP!

I DON'T SEE HIM. THAT ASSISTANT OF HIS IS LOOKING OVER THE EDGE. THAT LITTLE GUY MUST HAVE PLUMMETED LIKE A ROCK!

I'D BETTER GET OUT OF HERE. AS FAR AS ANYONE KNOWS, TAKENOKO DIED BECAUSE OF HIS CRAZY EXPERIMENTS.

THE ONLY ONE WHO MIGHT KNOW I HAD A HAND IN HIS DEATH IS THAT ASSISTANT OF HIS--AND HE WON'T TALK... I'LL SEE TO THAT.

SENSEI! SENSEI!

WE'RE ALL RIGHT, HASU! THROW DOWN THE EXTRA ROPE--AND HURRY!
19.

JUST A LITTLE MORE, USAGI-SAN.
THANK YOU, HASU.
ARE YOU ALL RIGHT, TAKENOKO-SENSEI?
THE WINGS DIDN'T WORK! HMMM...
THAT'S DISAPPOINTING.
WHAT HAPPENED UP THERE?
HMM... HEIGHT IS NOT THE ANSWER. THE PROBLEM MUST BE WITH THE WINGS THEMSELVES. HMM...
HASU, GET THE CART. WE'RE GOING BACK TO TOWN.
?
YES, SENSEI.
AND SO...
AREN'T YOU GOING TO REPORT UDON TO THE AUTHORITIES?
MAYBE IF I MADE THE WINGS LONGER...
HE'S DEEP IN HIS OWN THOUGHTS, USAGI-SAN.
20

LOOK-- IT'S THAT CRAZY DOCTOR!
WHAT?! I-IT CAN'T BE!

HE'LL REPORT US!
BUT... HOW--?
WE'VE GOT TO GET OUT OF HERE!
WE'VE GOT TO LEAVE THE PROVINCE!

TAKENOKO'S WINGS MUST HAVE WORKED-- THAT'S THE ONLY EXPLANATION!

IMAGINE ARMIES SWOOPING DOWN FROM THE SKIES. THEY WOULD BE UNBEATABLE! A LORD WOULD PAY ANYTHING TO GET THOSE WINGS!

TAKENOKO COULD MAKE A *FORTUNE*...

...OR *I* COULD!
21.

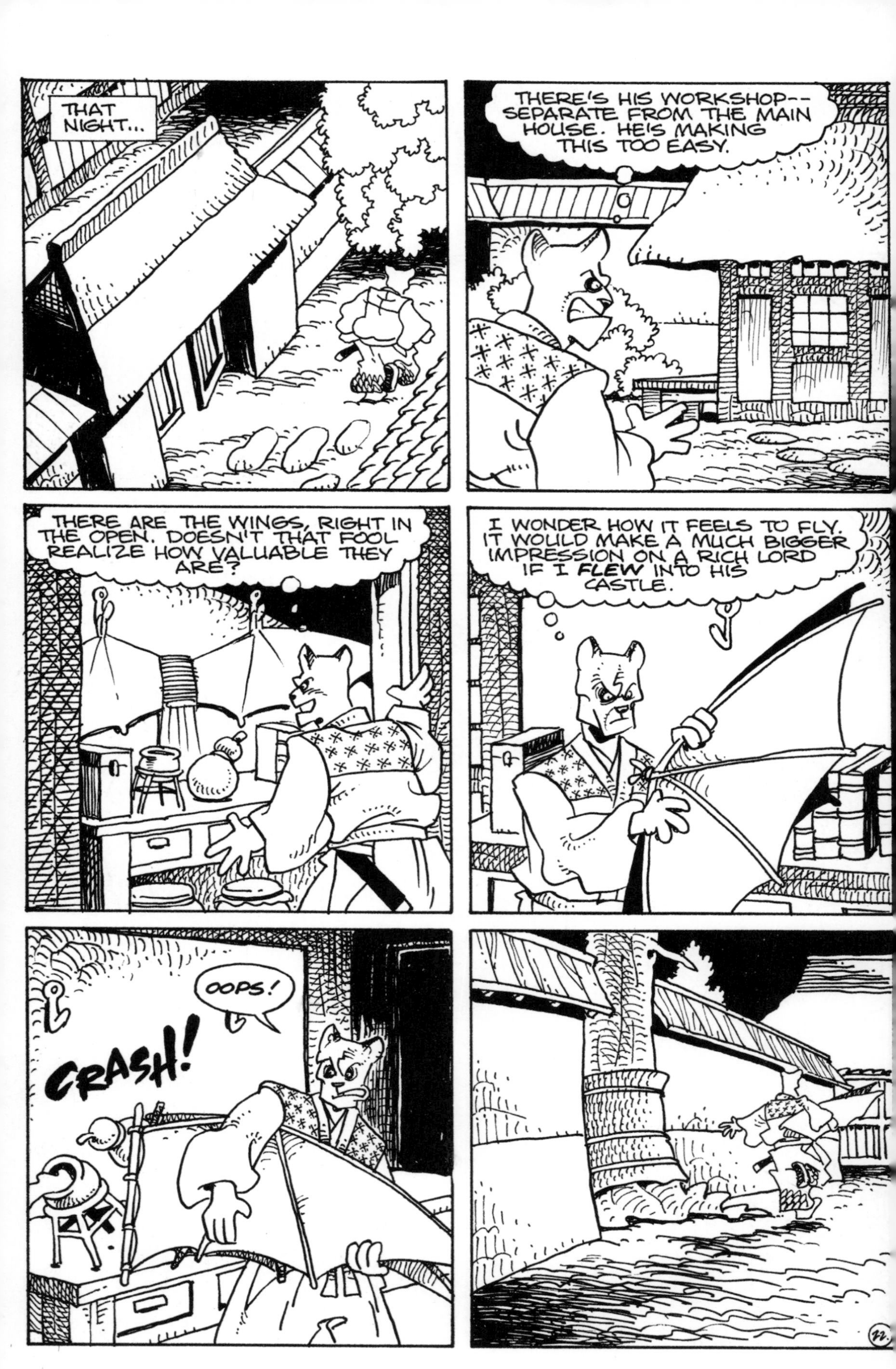
THAT NIGHT...
THERE'S HIS WORKSHOP-- SEPARATE FROM THE MAIN HOUSE. HE'S MAKING THIS TOO EASY.
THERE ARE THE WINGS, RIGHT IN THE OPEN. DOESN'T THAT FOOL REALIZE HOW VALUABLE THEY ARE?
I WONDER HOW IT FEELS TO FLY. IT WOULD MAKE A MUCH BIGGER IMPRESSION ON A RICH LORD IF I **FLEW** INTO HIS CASTLE.
OOPS!
CRASH!
22.

WHO'S OUT THERE?
LOOK-- THE WORK-SHOP DOOR IS OPEN!

WHAT A MESS! SOMEONE WAS IN HERE, ALL RIGHT.

MY WINGS ARE GONE! WHY WOULD ANYONE STEAL THEM? THEY DON'T WORK AT ALL!

WHO CAN FATHOM THE MIND OF A CRIMINAL?

AH... MY HORSELESS CART--NOW THIS WILL WORK!
23

MORNING...

GOOD-BYE, TAKENOKO-SENSEI! GOOD-BYE, HASU! THANK YOU FOR YOUR HOSPITALITY!
COME BACK AGAIN ANYTIME, USAGI!

THE WATERFALL IS SOMEWHERE UP IN THOSE MOUNTAINS.

IMAGINE BELIEVING THAT PEOPLE COULD EVER FLY!

THE END

KEEE--!

KEEEEE--!
KEEEE--!

KEEEE--!

FLAP! FLAP!

INTO THE MIST
EXCELLENT, LORD NORIYUKI! SUCH A FINE BIRD!
YOU CERTAINLY HAVE A WAY WITH HIM!
THANK YOU, LORD HORIKAWA. ECHIZO IS ONE OF MY BEST BIRDS.
1.

KEEE--! KEEE--!
FLY, ECHIZO!

LET'S SEE WHO CAN RETRIEVE WHATEVER GAME ECHIZO FLUSHES OUT OF HIDING.
YES, TONO*!
*LORD

HORIKAWA IS IN A HURRY. AREN'T YOU GOING, TOMOE?
MY DUTY IS TO STAY BY YOUR SIDE, TONO.
YOU ARE SUCH A MOTHER HEN. IF I AM NOT SAFE IN MY OWN LANDS, WHERE AM I SAFE?
BUT, TONO...
GO.

I'LL EXPECT YOU TO BRING BACK A PHEASANT FOR OUR DINNER, TOMOE.
HA HA HA! YES, TONO!

HORIKAWA IS SUCH A SYCOPHANT.

HE'S BEEN TRYING TO DRIVE A WEDGE BETWEEN LORD NORIYUKI AND ME FOR YEARS.
I CAN'T LET HIM GET TO THE QUARRY FIRST!

STRANGE--IT'S SUCH A CLEAR DAY, BUT WHERE IS THIS MIST COMING FROM?
IT'S ROLLING IN QUICKLY.
2.

I CAN'T SEE A THING!
LORD NORIYUKI--?!

WHERE ARE YOU?

ANYBODY?

AH, THE MIST IS LIFTING AT LAST.

WHAT THE--?!
WHERE DID THAT ARMY COME FROM?
THEY FLY THE DRAGONFLY BANNER. WHAT CLAN IS THAT?

WHAT IS THIS?! WHERE AM I?

THE GEISHU ARMY--BEHIND ME!
GENERAL AME--? ARE YOU ALL RIGHT?
3

ATTACK!
!
CLOPCLOPCLO

WHAT ARE YOUR ORDERS, GENERAL AME?
WHAT?

GENERAL-- YOUR ORDERS!
UH?
GENERAL!
THEY'RE ATTACKING!

RAVEN'S WING FORMATION! THE CENTER WILL RETREAT ON MY COMMAND, THEN THE WINGS WILL ATTACK ON EITHER SIDE, TRAPPING THE ENEMY! TIMING IS ESSENTIAL!
YES, GENERAL AME!

NOW, CHARGE!
4.

I DON'T KNOW WHAT'S GOING ON, BUT IT'S BETTER TO ACT FIRST, AND FIGURE IT OUT LATER!

URK!

YAGH!

FLOO!

FALL BACK! FALL BACK!

NOW--SIGNAL THE WINGS TO ATTACK!

FALL BACK! FALL BACK! LURE THE ENEMY INTO OUR TRAP!

THE ENEMY IS IN POSITION! WHERE ARE THE WINGS? IF THE TRAP IS NOT SPRUNG NOW, IT WILL BE OUR LOSS!

GENERAL HORIKAWA IS HOLDING BACK HIS FORCES!
WHAT--?! HORIKAWA--? THAT IS LUNACY!
HE HAS ALWAYS BEEN ENVIOUS OF YOUR POSITION WITH OUR LORD!

HERE COME THE WINGS!
IT'S TOO LATE! THEY'VE FIGURED OUT OUR PLAN! WE'RE BEING OVERWHELMED!

THEY'RE MASSACRING OUR MEN!
BACK--! WE'VE GOT TO COUNTERATTACK BEFORE IT BECOMES A TOTAL ROUT!

COME ON!
COVER THEIR RETREAT!

OOK!
7.

BRING HER DOWN!
.....
UH--!
I'VE GOT HER!

LET GO!
GRAB HER!
PULL HER DOWN!

GHAA!

THE GEISHU ARMY IS ON THE RUN! I'VE GOT TO GET OUT OF HERE!
HAUK!

HYAAHH!
GAK!
URK!
8

THERE'S ANOTHER GEISHU WARRIOR!
AN OFFICER, BY THE LOOK OF HER ARMOR!
A REWARD TO THE ONE WHO BRINGS ME HER HEAD!

SHE CAN'T GET AWAY!

I'M EXHAUSTED.
I WON'T BE ABLE TO RUN MUCH FARTHER.

OH, NO-- NOT THE MIST AGAIN!
I CAN'T SEE A THING!

UH--!
SHE'S OVER HERE!

I SEE HER--THERE SHE IS!
9.

I FOUND HER!

YOU WON'T TAKE ME WITHOUT A FIGHT!
WUFF!

LADY TOMOE-- *STOP!*
IT'S ME-- NOBU!

NOBU...? AND OTHER GEISHU *SAMURAI?*
WHEN YOU DID NOT RETURN, LORD NORIYUKI SENT US TO LOOK FOR YOU.

WHAT OF MY HORSE?
HE RETURNED HOURS AGO.
LORD NORIYUKI IS IN HIS PAVILION!

...AND IT WAS A TERRIBLE DEFEAT FOR THE GEISHU CLAN.
AH, LADY TOMOE IS BACK!
THERE YOU ARE, TOMOE. WE WERE GETTING CONCERNED.
MY APOLOGIES, LORD NORIYUKI.
10

YOU MISSED AN EXCELLENT PHEASANT MEAL, LADY TOMOE. IT'S A PITY YOU COULD NOT FIND YOUR WAY BACK.

YES, TOMOE. IT IS NOT LIKE YOU TO GET LOST. WAS THERE SOME DIFFICULTY?
I WAS DISORIENTED BY SOME MISTS, TONO.

MIST? WHAT MIST? IT HAS BEEN CLEAR ALL DAY-- A PERFECT DAY FOR FALCONING. I MUST SAY, LADY TOMOE, YOUR EXCUSE LEAVES MUCH TO BE DESIRED.
WHAT ARE YOU ACCUSING ME OF?

ER...UH... LORD HORIKAWA WAS RELATING TO US A STORY FROM GEISHU HISTORY.
I'M SURE TOMOE WOULD LIKE TO HEAR IT.
OF COURSE, TONO.

IT WAS TWO HUNDRED YEARS AGO TO THIS DAY, AND NOT VERY FAR FROM THIS EXACT SPOT THAT THE GEISHU CLAN SUFFERED A DEFEAT BY THE HOKI CLAN.

IN FACT, IT IS WRITTEN IN MY FAMILY RECORDS THAT ONE OF YOUR ANCESTORS HAD A PIVOTAL ROLE IN THAT DISGRACE.
DID THE HOKI WEAR THE DRAGONFLY CREST?
SO, YOU HAVE HEARD OF THEM.
11.

YOUR ANCESTOR ORDERED A WEAK OFFENSIVE, AND THE GEISHU TROOPS WERE OVERWHELMED.

THE GEISHU EVENTUALLY WON THE WAR, OF COURSE, AND THE HOKI CLAN WAS ABOLISHED.

BUT IT MIGHT EASILY HAVE BEEN THE GEISHU CLAN WHO LOST THE WAR, BECAUSE OF GENERAL AME'S STRATEGY.

NO, LORD HORIKAWA. THE STRATEGY WAS SOUND. IT WAS ***YOUR ANCESTOR*** WHO DELAYED THE ATTACK, COSTING US THE BATTLE!

H-HOW DARE YOU SLANDER MY FAMILY?! WHERE DID YOU READ OF SUCH AN ACCOUNT?!

NOT ALL TRUTHS ARE WRITTEN IN YOUR BOOKS, LORD HORIKAWA.
NOW EXCUSE ME, *TONO*, I'VE BEEN OUT ALL DAY AND I'M HUNGRY FOR SOME OF THAT PHEASANT.

DID YOU HEAR WHAT SHE SAID, *TONO*?! I DEMAND SHE BE REPRIMANDED!

THE END

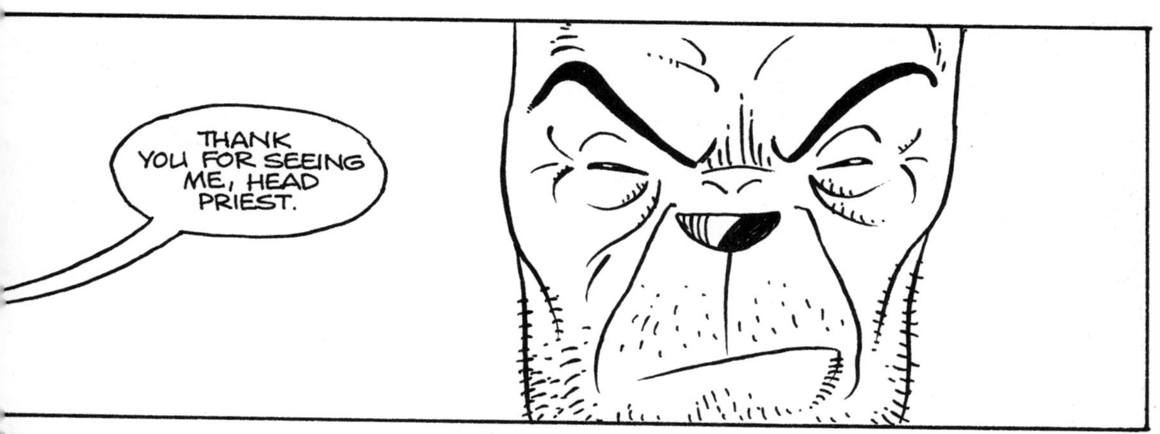
THANK YOU FOR SEEING ME, HEAD PRIEST.

NOCTURNAL

I'VE COME TO YOU FOR COUNSEL.
YOU ARE ONE OF OUR MOST PROMISING ACOLYTES, KENJI. I UNDERSTAND YOU WILL TAKE YOUR FINAL VOWS SOON.
THAT IS WHAT I MUST SPEAK TO YOU ABOUT, SANSHOBO.
OH?

YOU LOOK HAGGARD, KENJI. HAVE YOU NOT BEEN SLEEPING WELL?
YOU MUST TAKE BETTER CARE OF YOURSELF.

I MUST ADMIT THAT MY SLEEP THE PAST TWO NIGHTS HAS BEEN PLAGUED WITH NIGHTMARES...
...PERHAPS BROUGHT ON BY... GUILT.

OH?
WHAT HAVE YOU DONE THAT CAUSES SUCH INNER TURMOIL?

I WAS TO BE WED TO HARUKO, THE CARPENTER'S DAUGHTER.
BUT THE TEMPLE CALLED TO ME, AND I BROKE OFF THE ENGAGEMENT.
SHE WAS DEVASTATED AND ANGRY. I HAD HUMILIATED HER AND HER FAMILY.

I HAVE NOT SEEN HER IN YEARS. IT IS NOW TIME TO ACCEPT MY VOWS, BUT I AM FILLED WITH GUILT AND DOUBT. WHAT SHOULD I DO?

IT IS GOOD THAT YOU HAVE COME TO ME. IT IS NATURAL TO HAVE SUCH FEELINGS NOW. THE MATTER BETWEEN YOU AND HARUKO IS STILL UNRESOLVED. GO INTO TOWN AND TALK TO HER.
2.

ONLY WHEN THIS HAS BEEN SETTLED IN YOUR HEART, CAN YOU LEAVE THE WORLD BEHIND AND ENTER INTO CONTEMPLATION.
THANK YOU, HEAD PRIEST. I WILL FOLLOW YOUR ADVICE. I...I...
...I...
.....
UH...
SENZO-- COME HERE!
THUD!
HE'S COLD AND CLAMMY. HE'S IN WORSE CONDITION THAN I FIRST THOUGHT.
YOU CALLED FOR ME, HEAD PRIEST?
SUMMON THE DOCTOR!
HURRY!
3.

IT IS A MYSTERY. THERE IS MORE TO HIS CONDITION THAN JUST TWO NIGHTS OF REST-LESS SLEEP.
HE HAS ALSO BEEN PLAGUED BY GUILT AS HE NEARS HIS VOWS.
HE WAS BETROTHED TO HARUKO, BUT ABANDONED HER TO JOIN THE TEMPLE.

HARUKO, YOU SAY? SHE HAS BEEN MISSING FOR THREE DAYS, NOW.
A STRANGE COINCIDENCE.

I CAN GIVE HIM A DRINK WITH CRUSHED POPPY SEEDS TO HELP HIM SLEEP...
...BUT FINDING A CURE FOR HIS GUILT FALLS UNDER YOUR EXPERTISE, PRIEST SANSHOBO.

BUT SOLVE THAT PROBLEM LATER. RIGHT NOW HE NEEDS TO SLEEP.

GOOD NIGHT, SANSHOBO. PLEASE SEE THAT KENJI SLEEPS UNDISTURBED.
YES, DOCTOR.
4.

WATCH YOUR STEP IN THE DARK, DOCTOR.
THANK YOU. I'LL BE BACK IN THE MORNING.

I CAN RELATE TO KENJI'S RESTLESS NIGHTS.
DO YOU SUFFER FROM NIGHTMARES, SENZO?

YES...
EVER SINCE THE NIGHT THAT MOST OF OUR PRIESTS WERE MURDERED.*
*UY BOOK 12: GRASS-CUTTER

SUCH A MEMORY WOULD GIVE ANYONE NIGHTMARES.
THEY WILL FADE OVER TIME.
I HOPE SO.

LOOK--WHO IS THAT?
A WOMAN!
5

SHE RAN INTO THE PRIESTS' QUARTERS!

WHAT IS THAT WOMAN DOING HERE?

WHERE IS SHE? HOW COULD SHE HAVE DISAPPEARED SO QUICKLY?

WHERE COULD SHE HAVE GONE?
CHOKE!
KENJI!

HISSSS--!
HANNYA!

GET AWAY FROM HIM!

GYAHHHH!!
FLOOOOOO

UH--!
¡GAG!
¡CHOKE!
7.

GRAW!

SLASH!
OW!

NO MORE! STOP! ST--

.....

GYAHH!

WOP!
GET BACK, SENZO!
8.

SENZO--
ARE YOU ALL
RIGHT?
UH...UH...
YEAH, I'M
OKAY, HEAD
PRIEST.

FOUL DEMON--
I COMMAND YOU
TO RETURN TO THE
PIT YOU CRAWLED
OUT OF!

ABANDON
YOUR REASON
FOR BEING
HERE!
I
COMMAND
YOU TO
DEPART!
NNGHH...!
UHH...

WHAT'S
GOING
ON?
ARR!
UH--!
SHRAAAN!
9.

TWO OF YOU-- LOOK AFTER KENJI! THE REST WILL FOLLOW US!
COME ON, SENZO, AFTER HER!

WE'VE GOT HER NOW!

HURRY-- WE CAN'T LET HER GET AWAY!

HOW CAN WE DEFEAT SOMETHING LIKE ***THAT***?
YOU MUST HAVE FAITH, SENZO! COME ON!
10.

SHE'S GOING DEEPER INTO THE WOODS!
WE CAN'T KEEP UP WITH HER!
WHAT IS THAT?

WHICH WAY DID SHE GO?

HUFF! HUFF! GASP!
I-I CAN'T RUN ANY FARTHER!

IT'S NO USE. WE'VE LOST HER.
NO...

...WE'VE FOUND HER.
11.

WH-WHO IS SHE?
HER NAME IS HARUKO. SHE HAD BEEN MISSING FOR THREE DAYS.

KENJI SAID SHE WAS HEARTBROKEN WHEN HE LEFT HER. IN HER DESPAIR, SHE HUNG HERSELF JUST BEFORE HE WAS TO TAKE HIS VOWS.

HER ANGRY SPIRIT RETURNED AS A DEMON *HANNYA* TO EXACT HER VENGEANCE, EACH NIGHT DRAINING A PART OF HIS LIFE SPIRIT.

BRING HER DOWN.
WE'LL CHANT THE SUTRAS OVER HER BODY BEFORE WE CREMATE IT.
POOR SOUL.

THE END

TANG!

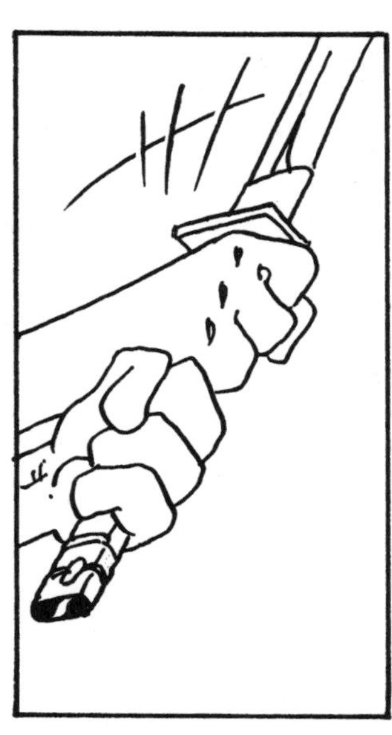

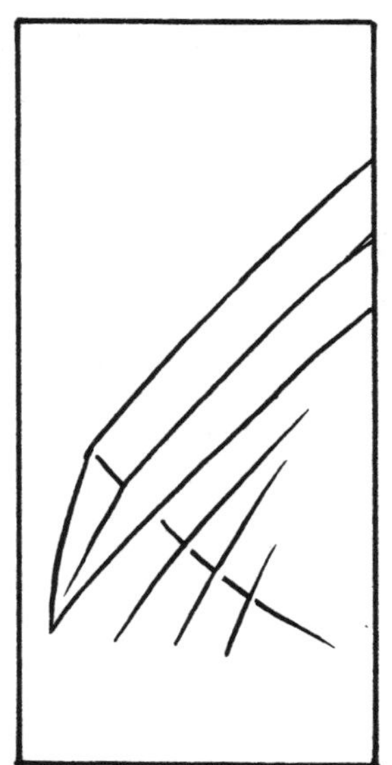

!

Vendetta's end

URK!
HYAHH!
EEE--!
GYAH!
.....
HIYAHHH!
UH--!
2

FWTT!

ARE YOU ALL RIGHT?
Y-YES, SAMURAI.
WE'RE UNHURT.
PLOP!

ER... THANK YOU FOR COMING TO OUR RESCUE, SAMURAI. WE ARE UNHURT.

BUT YOU ARE INJURED, SAMURAI.

IT'S A MINOR WOUND-- BARELY MORE THAN A SCRATCH.
3

WE ARE IN YOUR DEBT. YOU MUST ALLOW US TO HELP YOU.
YES. PLEASE.

PRIEST HIROSHI IS MAKING HIS ROUNDS THROUGH OUR VILLAGE TODAY. HE CAN TREAT YOUR WOUNDS. COME ON--IT'S NOT TOO FAR.

PRIEST HIROSHI?
YES. HE HAS NOT BEEN IN THIS AREA LONG, BUT HE IS TRULY A GODSEND.

HE HAS ORGANIZED THE VILLAGES, AND HAS DRIVEN OUT THE BANDITS IN THIS AREA... WELL, MOST OF THEM, ANYWAY.

HE GOES FROM VILLAGE TO VILLAGE, TENDING TO THE SICK AND INJURED.

TRULY, HE IS ONE WHO WALKS WITH THE BUDDHA.
4.

HOI! IS PRIEST HIROSHI STILL HERE?
YEAH! HE'S OVER AT JIRO'S HOUSE. JIRO FELL OFF THE ROOF AND BROKE HIS LEG, THAT CLUMSY CLOD!
YOW! YOW! YOW! OW!
!
COME ON, USAGI-SAN, THIS WAY.
5.

HOLD STILL. THIS MAY HURT A BIT.

NNNGGH...

OW OW OW OW OW!

THIS SHOULD HOLD IT. YOU'LL NEED TO STAY OFF YOUR FEET FOR A FEW WEEKS.
IT HURTS.

GOOD. THAT WILL REMIND YOU TO RELAX FOR A BIT.

I'LL BE BACK TOMORROW WITH MORE HERBS TO HELP EASE THE PAIN.
6.

PRIEST HIROSHI.
EH?

AH, GON, HARU... AND A SAMURAI? WHAT CAN I DO FOR YOU?

USAGI-SAN SAVED US FROM BANDITS, BUT SUSTAINED AN INJURY HIMSELF.

LET'S TAKE A LOOK AT IT, SHALL WE?
IT'S NOTHING SERIOUS--REALLY.

HMM... IT'S NOT TOO BAD. I SUSPECT YOU'VE SUFFERED WORSE INJURIES.

COME ON BACK TO THE TEMPLE AND I'LL BANDAGE YOU UP. YOU CAN STAY THERE THE NIGHT AS WELL, IF YOU WISH.
THANK YOU.
7.

YOU ARE HIGHLY REGARDED IN THIS AREA.
WE ALL DO WHAT WE CAN TO EASE SUFFERING, USAGI-SAN.
JUST AS YOU DID WHEN YOU CAME TO GON AND HARU'S RESCUE.

IT IS NO MERE CHANCE THAT BROUGHT YOU TO THIS AREA.

YOU MEAN KARMA BROUGHT ME HERE TO RESCUE GON AND HARU?
PERHAPS... OR MAYBE FOR ANOTHER REASON.

I DON'T BELIEVE THAT. IT WAS JUST A COINCIDENCE.

PERHAPS. WE'LL SEE.

THIS IS MY TEMPLE. IT IS SMALL AND IN POOR CONDITION, BUT THEN I HAVE NOT BEEN HERE VERY LONG.
THAT IS WHAT HARU SAID. WERE YOU AT ANOTHER TEMPLE?

NO.

IT WAS ANOTHER LIFE.

SIT. I WILL GET WATER AND BANDAGES.

9.

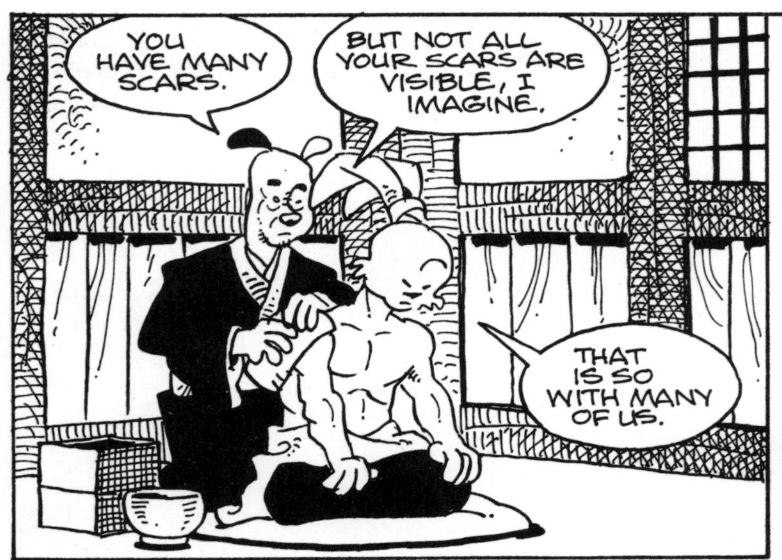
YOU HAVE MANY SCARS.
BUT NOT ALL YOUR SCARS ARE VISIBLE, I IMAGINE.
THAT IS SO WITH MANY OF US.

YES.

YOU REMIND ME MUCH OF A FRIEND OF MINE--A PRIEST LIKE YOURSELF, NAMED SANSHOBO.

A PRIEST LIKE ME, YOU SAY?
THEN I WILL PRAY FOR HIS SOUL.

THERE. THAT WASN'T TOO BAD.
IT'S A VERY GOOD FIELD DRESSING.

WHAT YOU NEED NOW IS REST. I WILL BREW SOME HERBS TO HELP YOU SLEEP.
NO, THANKS. I DON'T LIKE TO SLEEP TOO SOUNDLY.

PARDON MY INTERRUPTION, BUT I NEED SOME INFORMATION.
WHAT CAN WE DO FOR YOU, SIR?
ANOTHER SAMURAI? THE SECOND ONE TODAY!
COME IN, COME IN.
11.

I AM LOOKING FOR A TEMPLE IN THIS AREA.
A TEMPLE, YOU SAY?

THERE IS A TEMPLE NOT TOO FAR AWAY, BUT THE PATH TO IT CAN BE DANGEROUS AT THIS TIME OF NIGHT.

THE MOON WILL BE OUT IN A COUPLE OF HOURS. WE'VE GOT SOME BARLEY RICE--IT IS POOR FARE, BUT YOU ARE WELCOME TO SHARE OUR MEAL.
THANK YOU. YOU ARE VERY KIND.

THINK NOTHING OF IT, *SAMURAI*. THE PRIEST WOULD BE DISAPPOINTED IF WE DID NOT OFFER YOU OUR HOSPITALITY. HE IS THAT KIND OF PERSON.

UH... EXCUSE ME FOR BEING SO NOSY, SIR, BUT WHAT IS THAT WRITING ON YOUR HEAD-BAND?

IT READS "*FUKUSHU*."
GULP!
"*REVENGE*"?

I AM SANCTIONED BY THE *SHOGUN* TO TRACK DOWN THE KILLERS OF MY FATHER.

I HAVE TRACED THE LAST OF THEM TO THIS AREA. HIS NAME IS IKKAI.

"IKKAI," YOU SAY? I HAVEN'T HEARD OF ANYONE AROUND HERE BY THAT NAME. HOW ABOUT YOU, HUSBAND?
NO, I DON'T KNOW ANYONE BY THAT NAME. BUT THEN, WE DON'T GET AROUND MUCH.

WHAT ABOUT THE PRIEST?

PRIEST HIROSHI? THAT'S A GOOD IDEA. IF THIS *IKKAI* PERSON IS IN THE AREA, PRIEST HIROSHI WOULD KNOW HIM.
THAT'S RIGHT!

GO AND SEE PRIEST HIROSHI. HE'S A TERRIFIC PERSON. HE'LL HELP YOU FOR SURE.
13.

OLD HABITS ARE DIFFICULT TO BREAK.

I THOUGHT YOU WERE RESTING.
YOU KNEW SOMEONE WAS BEHIND YOU, AND REACHED FOR A SWORD.
YOU USED TO BE A SAMURAI.

YES... NOT LONG AGO, IN MY EARTHLY LIFE... BUT IT WAS TRULY A LIFETIME AGO.

"I ASSOCIATED WITH OTHER THUGS, BULLIES LIKE MYSELF.

"AFTER A NIGHT OF CAROUSING, WE WERE CONFRONTED BY A LONE *SAMURAI*--A *HATAMOTO** IN OUR LORD'S EMPLOY.

"HE ADMONISHED OUR DRUNKEN BEHAVIOR AS BEING UNWORTHY OF *SAMURAI*--AND A BAD REFLECTION ON OUR LORD.

"ANGERED, WE ATTACKED HIM.

"THE ENORMITY OF WHAT WE HAD DONE SOBERED US--IMMEDIATELY. WE WOULD BE EXECUTED.

"SO WE RAN AWAY.

"WE LIVED AS PETTY ROBBERS, PREYING ON POOR PEASANTS AND TRAVELING MERCHANTS.

"WE ACCOSTED TWO TRAVELERS ON A PILGRIMAGE--A FATHER AND HIS DAUGHTER.

"WHEN THEY DIDN'T HAVE AS MUCH AS WE EXPECTED, MY COMPANIONS KILLED THE PAIR. EVEN I WAS APPALLED BY SUCH BRUTALITY.

"I STOOD THERE, STUNNED. THE ONLY THING I WAS AWARE OF WAS THE SOUND OF THE RIVER FLOWING UNDER THE BRIDGE.

"I LOOKED AT MY REFLECTION AND SAW HOW LOW I HAD SUNK.

"I BELIEVE THE GODS STRIPPED ME OF MY SANITY THAT DAY.

"I RAN AS FAST AND AS FAR AS I COULD.

"I WANDERED IN A DAZE FOR MONTHS. I HAVE NO REMEMBRANCE OF HOW I SURVIVED DURING THAT TIME.

"WHEN I CAME TO MY SENSES, I CUT OFF MY TOPKNOT AND JOINED THE PRIESTHOOD."

I KNOW I SHOULD BURN IT, BUT I KEPT THAT CHONMAGE AS A REMINDER OF WHO I WAS, AND IT HELPS ME STRIVE TO DO BETTER.

TO JUDGE BY THE VILLAGE FOLK, YOU TRULY REFLECT BUDDHA'S TEACHINGS.
I HAVE MUCH TO ATONE FOR.
17

KOYAMA MATABEI!

I AM SURPRISED TO SEE YOU HERE, USAGI.

ARE YOU STILL ON THE TRAIL OF THE LAST OF YOUR FATHER'S KILLERS?

YES. I HAVE LEARNED THAT THE FOURTH KILLER CUT OFF HIS CHONMAGE AND BECAME A PRIEST.

!
18

IT'S TRUE, MATABEI. I AM ONE OF THOSE WHO MURDERED YOUR FATHER.

ONCE I PLACE YOUR SEVERED HEAD ON MY FATHER'S GRAVE, MY VENDETTA WILL FINALLY BE OVER AND HE CAN REST PEACEFULLY.

I WILL NOT RESIST.
WHAT?

MY QUEST COMES TO AN END AT LAST!

STOP!
19.

PRIEST HIROSHI IS A GOOD PERSON. IT WOULD BE A SIN TO DEPRIVE THE PEOPLE OF HIS WORK!
IKKAI IS A KILLER!

THE SAMURAI YOU SEEK NO LONGER EXISTS!

I SEEK JUSTICE!
NO, YOU SEEK VENGEANCE!

YES.
NOW STAND ASIDE, USAGI. I WILL SLAY YOU TO GET TO HIM.

I DON'T WANT TO FIGHT YOU, MATABEI.
I'LL TELL YOU AGAIN-- STAND ASIDE.

DO AS HE SAYS, USAGI. I DO NOT WANT YOUR BLOOD ON MY HANDS AS WELL.

YOU'RE MAKING A MISTAKE, MATABEI.
NO. HE IS THE ONE WHOM I HAVE BEEN AFTER FOR SO LONG.

I MUST PLACE A TROPHY ON MY FATHER'S GRAVESITE. I WILL TELL YOU FOR THE LAST TIME--STEP ASIDE.

YOU ARE AN HONORABLE *SAMURAI*, MATABEI. IF YOU WERE NOT, YOU WOULD NOT HAVE UNDERTAKEN THIS VENDETTA. BUT WOULD YOU ROB THE PEOPLE HERE OF THE PRIEST THEY LOVE?

IS THIS WHAT YOUR FATHER WOULD HAVE WANTED?

21.

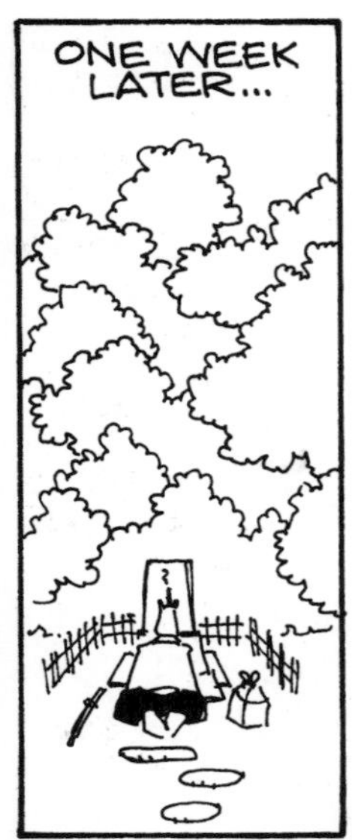
ONE WEEK LATER...

MY VENDETTA IS FINALLY OVER, FATHER. I FOUND THE LAST OF YOUR MURDERERS, AND HAVE BROUGHT HIS TROPHY. I APOLOGIZE THAT IT TOOK SO LONG.

BUT PLEASE KNOW THAT I HAVE BEEN A GOOD AND FAITHFUL SON.

HIS *CHONMAGE*...

...THE LAST REMNANT OF THE FOURTH *SAMURAI* WHO COWARDLY KILLED YOU.
22

YOUR LEG IS HEALING NICELY, JIRO.
REMEMBER TO KEEP YOUR BANDAGES CLEAN.

YOU'LL SOON BE OUT WORKING THE FIELDS AGAIN, SO ENJOY YOUR SHORT HOLIDAY.
AND REMEMBER TO STAY OFF THE ROOF.
HA HA!

PLEASE SUMMON ME IF YOU NEED ANY MORE HELP.
PRIEST HIROSHI.

THANK YOU, PRIEST HIROSHI. I DON'T KNOW WHAT WOULD BECOME OF OUR VILLAGE IF IT WERE NOT FOR YOU.

NOR I WITHOUT YOU, JIRO.
23.

AH...
THE GEISHU PROVINCE.
THE END

THE MOTHER OF MOUNTAINS

I GREW UP IN West Los Angeles, California. As a kid, I could take a bus all the way from Sepulveda down Wilshire Boulevard to La Brea Avenue, where for many years there was a movie theater called the Toho La Brea. The Toho La Brea screened only Japanese films in their original versions, with English subtitles. There were Japanese-owned nurseries all over West LA then, and many of my schoolmates were Japanese-American. And it was those kids who introduced me to the Toho La Brea theater and the samurai movie!

While most of the population of the United States was first introduced to Japanese cinema by the bastardized *Godzilla, King of the Monsters*, I had already seen the glories of Kurosawa and the magnificent Toshiro Mifune!

So, many, many years later, when I was with my (then little) son Max at the legendary Golden Apple comic book store on Melrose, my eye was naturally drawn to the colorful cover of a comic featuring what appeared to be a samurai rabbit! After leafing through just a few pages, I was hooked. *Yojimbo* is now not just the title of one of my favorite movies, but *Usagi Yojimbo* has become the title of one of my favorite comics too!

I hold Stan Sakai right up there with Winsor McCay, Chester Gould, Art Spiegelman, Jack Davis, Wally Wood, Al Capp, Charles Schulz, Robert Crumb, Jules Feiffer, Will Eisner, and all the others who can move me and tell such wonderful stories with just drawings on the page.

This collection of *Usagi Yojimbo* tells the epic tale of two cousins and a lost mine. The evil Noriko can hold her place among the great villainesses—like Cruella De Vil, but with deadly martial arts skills! This whole saga reminds me again of how close the samurai stories are to our westerns. If Italians can make westerns in Spain, why can't Stan Sakai make realistic samurai tales about a brave and accomplished and honorable rabbit? Stan can, and he does!

The similarities between comics and film are well known. Movie storyboards—illustrated shot lists—are just comics, after all. When a movie—or play or book or graphic novel or painting—succeeds, it's called "suspension of disbelief." Simply, you believe it.

You're there. Stan's work does that. In some weird feudal Japan where these strange lizards run around and anthropomorphic warriors and peasants live, I lose myself entirely.

I love this stuff!

John Landis
Los Angeles, CA
March 2007

KLAK!

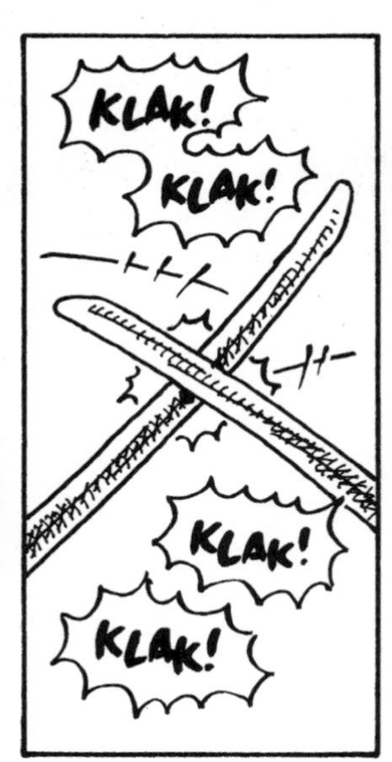
KLAK!
KLAK!
KLAK!
KLAK!

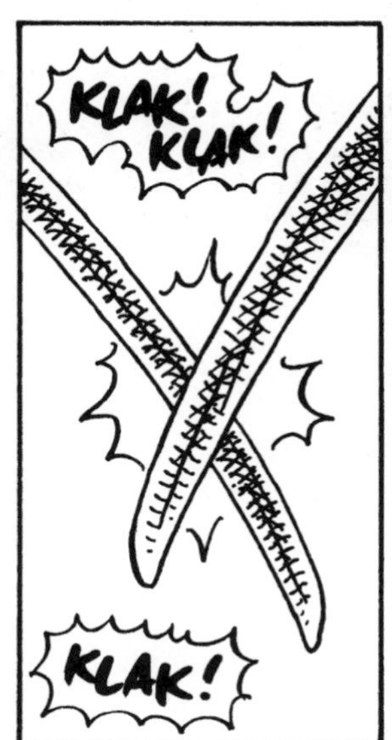
KLAK! KLAK!
KLAK!

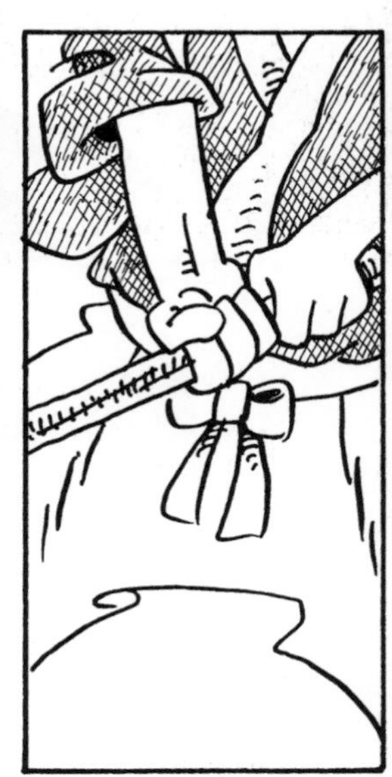

HIIIYAHHHHHHH

KIAHHHHHHHH

KLAK!

KLAK!
KLAK!
KLAK!
KLAK!
KLAK!
KLAK!
KLAK!

KLAK!
KLAK!
KLAK!
KLAK!

KLAK!

KLAK!
KLAK!
KLAK!
KLAK!

KLAK!

UH--!
KLAK!

I CONCEDE, NORIKO. THE MATCH IS YOURS.

HIIYAAHH!
!

STOP, NORIKO!

OW--!

UH--!

I DECIDE WHEN THE MATCH IS OVER...
...COUSIN.
5.

THE TREASURE OF THE MOTHER OF MOUNTAINS

THE GEISHU SIDE OF THE MOUNTAINS IS USUALLY BETTER FOR HUNTING...

...BUT I HAVEN'T SEEN ANY GAME SO FAR.

TODAY IS SUCH AN UNLUCKY DAY.

AH... I SPOKE TOO SOON... MEAT FOR THE COOKING POT!
ZZZ ZZZZ...

TWANG!!

EEP?
EEP?
EEP?
EEP?
EEP?
THOK!
7.

GRR... I'LL GET YOU THIS TIME!

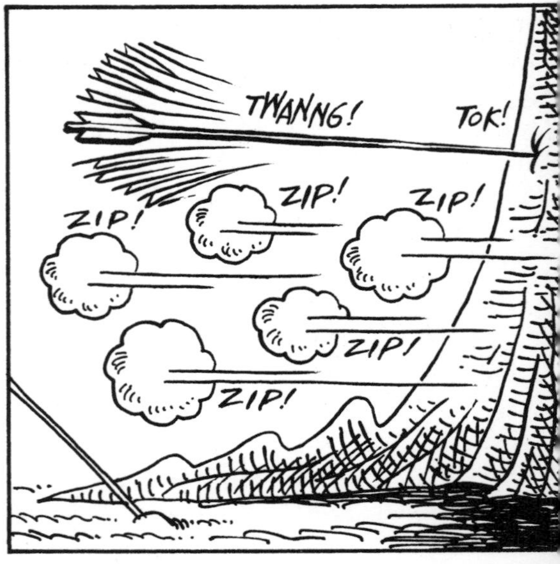
TWANNG!
TOK!
ZIP!
ZIP!
ZIP!
ZIP!
ZIP!

COME BACK HERE, YOU!
EEP!
EEP!
EEP!
!!!
EEP!
EEP!

HUFF! PUFF! THOSE STUPID TOKAGÉ-- THEY'RE GETTING AWAY!

BUT I SWEAR-- MY FAMILY WILL NOT GO HUNGRY TONIGHT!

ULP!

YAHHHHHHHHHHH

OOK!

OOOOOHHH... THIS IS THE WORST DAY OF MY LIFE. MY BOW IS BROKEN... I'VE LOST ALL MY ARROWS... I THINK I BROKE MY... MY...

WHAT'S THIS?!

I-I CAN'T BELIEVE IT! A GROMWELL BUSH!

HOORAY! THIS IS THE BEST DAY OF MY LIFE!

OOOOOHHH...
9

TWO MONTHS LATER...

HEY--! GET BACK TO WORK! WHAT ARE YOU LOOKING AT, ANYWAY?

HAVE YOU NOTICED ALL THE DUST CLOUDS ON THAT TALL PEAK?

THE ONE WE CALL "THE MOTHER OF MOUNTAINS"? YEAH, NOW THAT YOU MENTION IT, THERE IS A LOT OF DUST UP THERE.

WHAT DO YOU THINK CAUSES IT?
I DON'T KNOW. MAYBE IT WAS KICKED UP BY AN EARTHQUAKE.

DON'T BE RIDICULOUS! I HAVEN'T FELT ANY EARTHQUAKES IN A WHILE.
YEAH, I GUESS YOU'RE RIGHT.

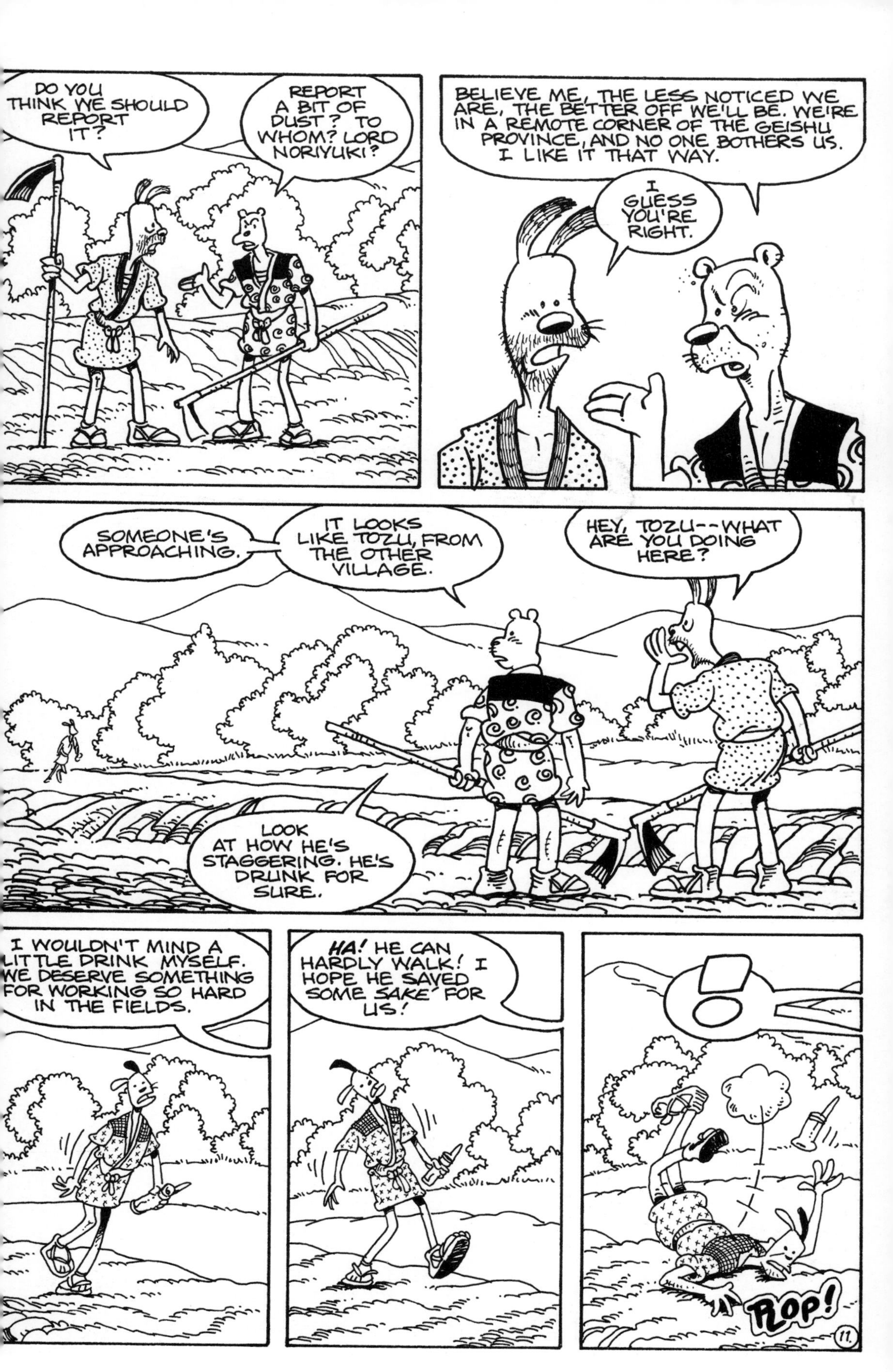
DO YOU THINK WE SHOULD REPORT IT?
REPORT A BIT OF DUST? TO WHOM? LORD NORIYUKI?
BELIEVE ME, THE LESS NOTICED WE ARE, THE BETTER OFF WE'LL BE. WE'RE IN A REMOTE CORNER OF THE GEISHU PROVINCE, AND NO ONE BOTHERS US. I LIKE IT THAT WAY.
I GUESS YOU'RE RIGHT.
SOMEONE'S APPROACHING.
IT LOOKS LIKE TOZU, FROM THE OTHER VILLAGE.
HEY, TOZU--WHAT ARE YOU DOING HERE?
LOOK AT HOW HE'S STAGGERING. HE'S DRUNK FOR SURE.
I WOULDN'T MIND A LITTLE DRINK MYSELF. WE DESERVE SOMETHING FOR WORKING SO HARD IN THE FIELDS.
HA! HE CAN HARDLY WALK! I HOPE HE SAVED SOME SAKE' FOR US!
!
PLOP!
11.

HA HA HA!
TOZU, YOU OLD DRUNKARD--!
IT WOULD SERVE HIM RIGHT IF HE HAD A HANGOVER FOR A WEEK!

I'LL FLIP HIM OVER.
HEY--THIS IS JUST PLAIN WATER!

GASP!
HE'S DEAD!
WHAT?!

L-LOOK AT HIS FACE!
IT'S THE PLAGUE FOR SURE!

EYAHH!
YOW!

A MONTH LATER...

...AND I DEMAND THAT LADY TOMOE EITHER PRESENT PROOF OF HER ALLEGATIONS...

...OR APOLOGIZE.

LORD HORIKAWA, BE REASONABLE.
"REASONABLE"? SHE ALL BUT ACCUSED MY ANCESTOR OF INCOMPETENCE... OF BEING RESPONSIBLE FOR OUR CLAN'S DEFEAT IN A BATTLE TWO HUNDRED YEARS AGO.
I FEEL I AM BEING VERY REASONABLE.

NOW SHE MUST OFFER EITHER HER EVIDENCE...OR AN APOLOGY AND ADMIT HER ERROR.

VERY WELL, TO MAINTAIN PEACE WITHIN OUR CLAN...
TOMOE...?
13

I...
I HAVE NO PROOF THAT YOU WOULD ACCEPT.

AN APOLOGY THEN.

I--
I APOLOGIZE, HORIKAWA-SAMA.

NOW THAT THE ISSUE IS SETTLED, LET US PUT IT BEHIND US AND WORK TOGETHER.
OF COURSE, LORD NORIYUKI.
I AM NOT ONE TO BEAR GRUDGES FOR INCOM-PETENCE.

MY LORD, A MESSENGER HAS ARRIVED.

THANK YOU. SHOW HIM IN, MOTOKAZU.

LORD NORIYUKI, I BRING NEWS REGARDING THE PLAGUE AT OUR SOUTHERN BORDER.
ENTER, SAMURAI, AND REPORT.
14

THE ENTIRE AREA HAS BEEN QUARANTINED. NO ONE IS ALLOWED IN, AND ALL WHO LIVED THERE ARE DEAD OR HAVE BEEN EVACUATED.

FORTUNATELY, IT IS A REMOTE PART OF OUR PROVINCE-- JUST A COUPLE OF VILLAGES-- SO IT WAS AN EASY TASK TO CONTAIN THE OUTBREAK.

OUR NEIGHBOR, LORD SANADA, HAS WISELY MADE NO AGGRESSIVE MOVES AGAINST THAT PART OF OUR LANDS, NOR DO WE EXPECT HIM TO.

THAT REGION MUST BE INVESTIGATED THOROUGHLY BEFORE WE CAN EVEN CONSIDER LIFTING THE QUARANTINE.
I AGREE, TOMOE.
THEN, MY LORD, I HAVE A SUGGESTION.

YOU MUST SEND SOMEONE YOU TRUST COMPLETELY TO INVESTIGATE THE SOUTHERN BORDER. WHO BETTER THAN LADY TOMOE TO JUDGE WHETHER THAT AREA IS SAFE OR NOT?

AN EXCELLENT SUGGESTION, LORD HORIKAWA. TOMOE, YOU WILL LEAVE AT ONCE.

AS YOU COMMAND, LORD NORIYUKI.

15

WHY IS LORD NORIYUKI SENDING YOU AWAY, LADY TOMOE? IS THIS MISSION A REPRIMAND FOR YOUR ACCUSATIONS AGAINST LORD HORIKAWA?
THE REASONS ARE UNIMPORTANT, MOTOKAZU. IT IS OUR LORD'S COMMAND.
I DO NOT TRUST LORD HORIKAWA.
HUSH. SUCH WORDS CAN BE CONSIDERED TREASON AGAINST OUR CLAN.

FORGIVE ME, LADY TOMOE. I AM STILL GETTING USED TO LIVING IN A CASTLE IN THE HEART OF THE GEISHU CLAN.
THERE IS NO HARM DONE, MOTOKAZU. BESIDES, I SHARE YOUR FEELINGS... JUST DO NOT VOICE THEM ALOUD.

IS-- IS IT DANGEROUS, WHERE YOU ARE GOING?

NO, IT IS A ROUTINE ASSIGNMENT. I MAY BE GONE A WHILE, THOUGH.
CAN I COME WITH YOU?
NO. I HAVE SOMETHING I NEED YOU TO DO HERE.

PROMISE ME THAT YOU WILL LOOK OUT FOR LORD NORIYUKI.

ME? BUT I AM ONLY A PAGE.
YOU ARE HIS **PERSONAL** PAGE. YOU ARE ALWAYS BY HIS SIDE.
16

I WILL DO MY BEST, LADY TOMOE. YOU CAN DEPEND ON ME.
I KNOW I CAN, MOTOKAZU.

YOU HAVE BEEN WORKING HARD AND DOING WELL. YOUR FATHER WOULD BE PROUD OF YOU.

I HOPE SO, BUT TO THINK THAT HE WAS GENERAL IKEDA, LORD NORIYUKI'S ONETIME SWORN ENEMY.

BUT, IN THE END, HE SERVED LORD NORIYUKI AS A FAITHFUL AND LOYAL VASSAL. HE WAS A TRUE SAMURAI.
AS I HOPE TO BE.

I WILL NOT LET YOU DOWN-- BUT, PLEASE, BE CAREFUL, LADY TOMOE.

DON'T WORRY ABOUT ME. IT IS A ROUTINE MISSION. I SHOULD RETURN IN A FEW WEEKS.
FAREWELL, LADY TOMOE.
17.

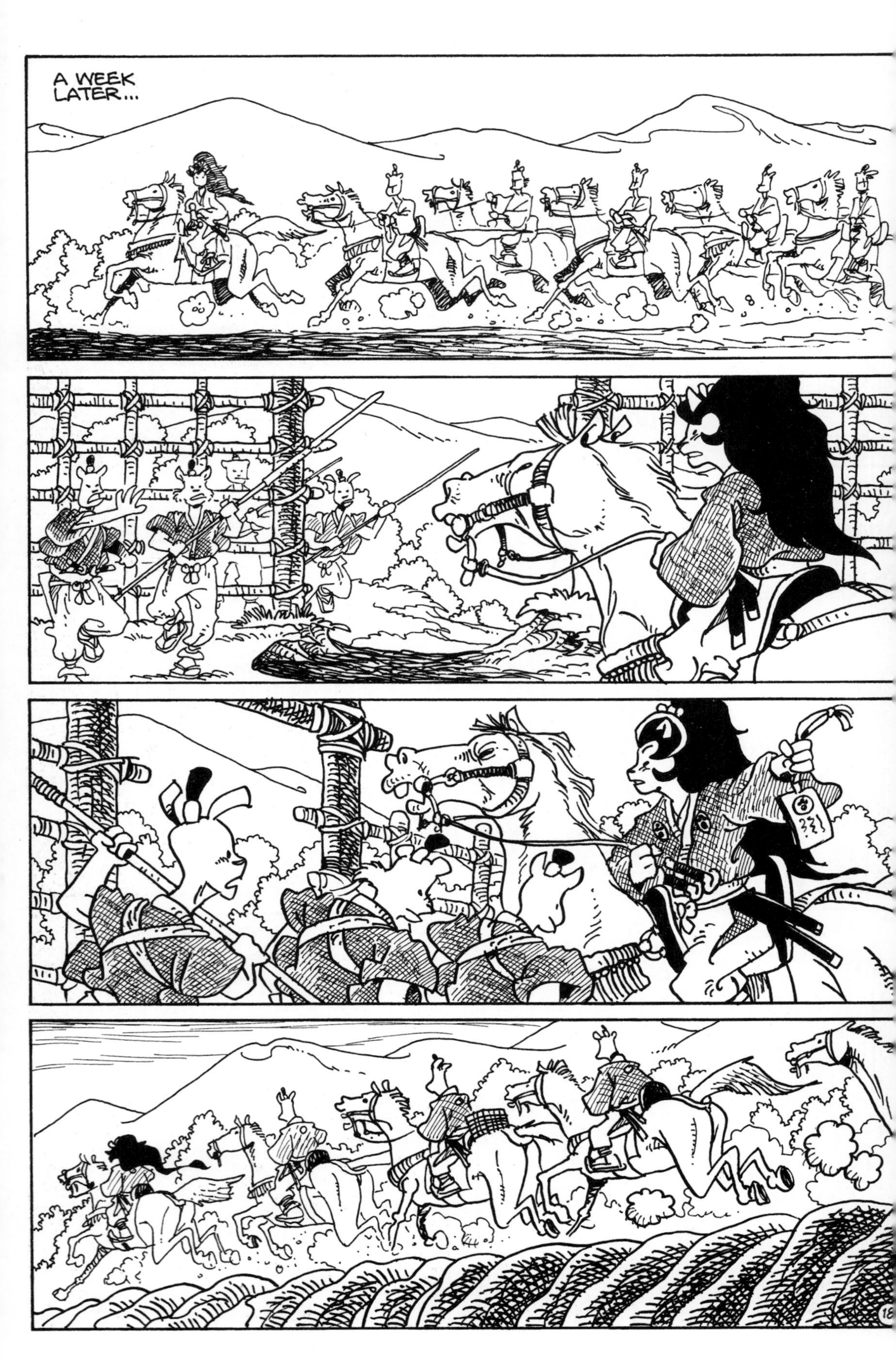
A WEEK LATER...

¡GULP!

A-ARE YOU SURE IT'S SAFE ?

WE'LL FIND OUT SOON!

BE CAREFUL !
DON'T TOUCH ANY-THING.
19

WHEW! WHAT A LONG RIDE THAT WAS.

HOW TERRIBLE THIS PLAGUE IS.
IT KILLS EVERY-THING.

GULP! GULP! GULP!

GULK!

.....
20

IT'S THE WATER-- IT MUST BE POISONED!
SO...IT MAY NOT BE A PLAGUE AFTER ALL!

WHO HAS THE MESSENGER PIGEON?
SEND A MESSAGE OF OUR SUSPICIONS TO THE WHITE HERON CASTLE.
I DO.
YES, LADY TOMOE!

ARH--!

CRASH!
THUD!
21.

WHAT--?!
GEISHU WARRIORS! TAKE COVER!
UGH!
ARGH!
ZWIP!
FLIT!
VWIT!
VWIP!
FWIPP!
FWIPT!
TAK!
TAK!
TAK!
TAK!
HIYAAHHHH!
22

LADY TOMOE--GRAB MY HAND! I CAN TAKE YOU TO SAFETY!
NO--I'LL HOLD THEM BACK! RIDE OUT OF HERE! REPORT THIS TO LORD NORIYUKI!
BUT YOU--!
GO!

I WILL DO AS YOU ORDER, LADY TOMOE!
GOOD LUCK!
HURRY!

TWANG!

TOK!
URK--!

23.

WHO ARE THEY?
THERE'S ONLY ONE OF THEM LEFT!
SLAY HER!

HIIIYAAAAAAAAAHHHH

THE TREASURE of the MOTHER of MOUNTAINS

THE GEISHU PROVINCE ALWAYS LOOKS SO WELCOMING.
THERE'S A VILLAGE IN THE DISTANCE. I HOPE I CAN FIND A WELCOME THERE.
I WONDER WHY THERE'S A DUST CLOUD AT THE TOP OF THAT MOUNTAIN.
MAYBE I'LL SEE TOMOE WHILE I'M VISITING THIS AREA.
BUT I HOPE SHE DOESN'T ASK IF I TOLD JOTARO I'M HIS REAL FATHER.
I WOULD HATE TO TELL HER I'M REALLY A COWARD.
THAT VILLAGE SHOULDN'T BE TOO FAR AWAY NOW.
THAT HORSEMAN LOOKS LIKE HE'S IN A HURRY.
2.

HEY! LOOK OUT, YOU IDIOT!

UH--!

WHAT'S YOUR HURRY?! YOU DON'T OWN THE ROAD, YOU KNOW!
IDIOT!

!
WHINNY!

IT'S A GEISHU SAMURAI!
WHAT HAPPENED TO YOU?
3.

GEISHU-- YOUR WOUNDS ARE FATAL.
TELL ME WHAT HAPPENED!
UHH... AMBUSH IN VILLAGE... LADY TOMOE... YOU'VE GOT TO HELP... UH...
UH...
UH... UH... NGGHHH--!
TOMOE?
.....
TOMOE!
4

FLOO--!
GOOGH!
GYAH!

EGH!

PANT! PANT!

SHE'S TIRING! PRESS IN ON HER! SHE CAN'T DEFEAT ALL OF US!

HE'S RIGHT. I'VE FAILED YOU, LORD NORIYUKI.

KILL HER!
FLOOK!
GYAA--!
UH!
LOOK OUT--SHE'S STILL A WILDCAT!

BUT EVEN WILDCATS CAN BE CAUGHT FROM BEHIND!

?
GURK!

USAGI?!

!
ZWIT!

WHP! WHP! WHP!

THOK!
EYAH!

THUD!

ARE YOU INJURED?
NO. YOU ARRIVED JUST IN TIME.
7.

I WANT ONE OF THEM ALIVE.
THERE'S ONLY ONE LEFT.
STAY BACK, YOU TWO!
THEY CALL ME THE ORPHAN MAKER...
...BECAUSE I'M SO DEADLY WITH A BLADE!
EEP--!

EEYAHHHH--!
8

WHAT'S GOING ON?
I DON'T KNOW.

I WAS SENT BY LORD NORIYUKI TO INVESTIGATE THE SUDDEN OUTBREAK OF A PLAGUE IN THIS AREA.

BUT THE PLAGUE WAS A SHAM--A CONSPIRACY TO KEEP PEOPLE AWAY FROM HERE.

I HAVE NOT YET DISCOVERED THE REASON FOR THIS RUSE. THAT IS WHY I NEEDED ONE OF THEM ALIVE TO INTERROGATE.

NOW WILL YOU REPORT BACK TO LORD NORIYUKI?
AND TELL HIM WHAT? MY INVESTIGATION IS STILL NOT COMPLETE.

THE ORPHAN MAKER RAN IN THAT DIRECTION. THAT'S AS GOOD A WAY AS ANY TO GET TO THE BOTTOM OF THIS.
SPEAKING OF ORPHANS...DID YOU TELL JOTARO THAT YOU ARE HIS FATHER?

WELL... I... ER...
HA! COWARD!
9.

SOON...
WAGON TRACKS.
JUDGING BY THEIR DEPTH, THEY WERE FULLY LOADED WHEN THEY PASSED THROUGH.

THEY WERE GOING UP THE MOUNTAINSIDE, TO THAT PEAK. I SAW A LARGE DUST CLOUD UP THERE EARLIER.
THAT TALL PEAK IS CALLED **THE MOTHER OF MOUNTAINS.**

THAT'S WHERE WE'LL FIND THE ANSWER TO THIS MYSTERY.
HOLD IT!
LET'S GET OFF THE TRAIL.

GUARDS... BUT THEY'RE NOT GEISHU *SAMURAI*.
THEY DO NOT BEAR ANY CLAN CREST AT ALL, BUT THEY'RE NOT FILTHY ENOUGH TO BE *RONIN*.*
*MASTERLESS SAMURAI

I'M A *RONIN*, AND I'M NOT FILTHY.
SNIFF! SNIFF!
WELL, MAYBE I AM.

WE'LL CIRCLE AROUND THEM AND SEE JUST WHAT THEY'RE GUARDING.

THERE'S AN OVER-LOOK.

GODS--!
WHAT IS IT?

A SECRET MINING OPERATION!
THAT'S WHY THEY NEED TO KEEP THIS AREA ISOLATED.
11.

IT LOOKS LIKE THEY'VE GOT SLAVES TO DO THE LABOR.

WHAT COULD THEY BE MINING AROUND HERE?
I DON'T KNOW.
THIS AREA IS FAIRLY REMOTE...

...BUT THEY SHOULD KNOW THEY CANNOT KEEP SUCH AN OPERATION SECRET FOR LONG.

THIS IS A LARGE-SCALE PROJECT--
--WHO COULD BE BEHIND THIS?

OH, NO--!

NORIKO-SAN!
EH?

WE AMBUSHED A GROUP OF GEISHU SAMURAI WHO WERE INVESTIGATING THIS AREA.
DID ANY OF THEM ESCAPE?
ER... JUST TWO.

WHAT?!

IF NEWS OF OUR ACTIVITIES REACHES THAT GEISHU BRAT, OUR WORK WILL BE IN VAIN.

INCREASE PATROLS IMMEDIATELY!

I DON'T WANT ANYONE ESCAPING FROM THIS AREA.
IN FACT, I EXPECT TO HEAR NEWS OF THEIR CAPTURE OR DEATH BY DAY'S END.
YES, NORIKO-SAN.
13

THEY WILL NOT GET AWAY. THE GEISHU WARRIORS ARE ALL INCOMPETENTS.

MAYBE WITH ONE EXCEPTION.

WE'RE BEHIND SCHEDULE. WORK THE SLAVES HARDER.
THEY'RE ALREADY WORKING AS HARD AS THEY CAN.

THEN YOU'VE GOT TO GIVE THEM A BETTER MOTIVATION TO WORK HARDER.
BUT HOW?

WE'LL FIND SOME INCENTIVE.
HEY, LOOK OUT, YOU!
UH...

GET UP!
PANT! PANT! GASP!

I SAID, GET UP!
UH... UH...

SLASH!

DID YOU SEE THAT? THAT IS WHAT WILL HAPPEN TO EACH ONE OF YOU LAZY PEASANTS IF YOU DO NOT WORK HARDER.
H-HIS HEAD--!
UH...
GULP!
GASP!
JIRO--!
YAHH!
SOB!

YOU'LL GET A GREATER EFFORT OUT OF THEM NOW.
Y-YES, NORIKO-SAN!

D-DID YOU SEE THAT? SHE KILLED HIM AS IF HIS LIFE MEANT NOTHING.
THAT IS WHY SHE IS NICKNAMED THE BLOOD PRINCESS.
15

WHY THAT--!
STOP, TOMOE!

DON'T THINK WITH YOUR EMOTIONS. WE DON'T STAND A CHANCE AGAINST ALL OF THEM.
YOU'RE RIGHT. MY FIRST DUTY IS TO REPORT THIS TO LORD NORIYUKI.

IF I DO NOT RETURN, HE WILL BELIEVE I FELL VICTIM TO THE PHONY PLAGUE.

IT MAY BE WEEKS BEFORE HE SENDS OUT ANOTHER PARTY TO INVESTIGATE THIS AREA.

BUT I SWEAR THAT I WILL SOON RETURN AND AVENGE THOSE INNOCENT LIVES.

COME ON.
YEAH. I'M RIGHT BEHIND YOU.
WHO IS SHE?

THE WHITE HERON CASTLE OF LORD NORIYUKI...
GLUUUUUUU
THANK YOU FOR AGREEING TO THIS INFORMAL AUDIENCE, LORD NORIYUKI. WHAT I WISH TO DISCUSS IS A DELICATE MATTER, WHICH I DID NOT WANT TO BRING UP AT A COUNCIL MEETING.
FORGIVE ME FOR BEING SO BLUNT, BUT THE GEISHU CLAN HAS BECOME A LAUGHINGSTOCK BECAUSE WE HAVE A WOMAN IN TOO EXALTED A POSITION.
I, OF COURSE, SPEAK OF LADY TOMOE.
17.

BUT SURELY, LORD HORIKAWA, TOMOE HAS PROVEN HER LOYALTY AND ABILITIES TIME AND AGAIN.
THE POSITION SHE NOW HOLDS HAS BEEN WELL EARNED!
I WILL NOT HAVE HER MALIGNED.
OF COURSE, LORD NORIYUKI.
I MEANT NO OFFENSE.

I DO NOT DOUBT HER LOYALTY OR HER SWORDSMANSHIP, MY LORD.

IT PAINS ME TO SAY THIS, MY LORD, BUT IT IS HER EMOTIONAL AND MENTAL HEALTH THAT I AM CONCERNED ABOUT.
OH?

HER FALSE ACCUSATIONS AGAINST MY FAMILY WERE JUST ONE SYMPTOM OF HER FRAIL EMOTIONAL HEALTH.

AND, AFTER ALL, WHAT OTHER CLAN HAS A WOMAN IN SUCH AN ELEVATED POSITION AS LADY TOMOE?

OUR NEIGHBOR, LORD SANADA, EMPLOYS A FEMALE WARRIOR.

YES, BUT SHE IS A DEADLY, BLOODTHIRSTY DEVIL. YOU CANNOT COMPARE LADY TOMOE TO SOMEONE LIKE NORIKO.

BESIDES, THE BLOOD PRINCESS KNOWS HER PLACE.

SHE IS TOLERATED BY LORD SANADA BECAUSE HE VALUES HER EXPERTISE WITH THE SWORD. SHE DOES NOT INFLUENCE HIS POLICY MAKING.

MY OWN MOTHER INFLUENCED MANY OF MY FATHER'S DECISIONS.
TRUE, BUT SHE DID SO BEHIND THE SCENES. MOST PEOPLE DID NOT EVEN KNOW OF HER INVOLVEMENT. LADY TOMOE OPENLY GIVES HER OPINIONS.

ARE YOU IMPLYING THAT IT IS TOMOE, AND NOT I, WHO DETERMINES THE WORKINGS OF THE GEISHU CLAN?!
19.

OH, NO, THAT IS NOT WHAT I MEANT AT ALL. HOWEVER, IN THE RIGHT CIRCUMSTANCES, LADY TOMOE CAN BE AN EVEN MORE EFFECTIVE VASSAL FOR OUR CLAN.

OH? WHAT DO YOU SUGGEST?
?

ITO NOREN, A VASSAL OF LORD KOJIMA OF THE WEST, HAS SEEN LADY TOMOE AND HAS BECOME QUITE SMITTEN WITH HER.

A MARRIAGE WOULD UNITE BOTH OUR CLANS. I DON'T HAVE TO TELL YOU WHAT A POWERFUL ALLY LORD KOJIMA WOULD BE.

AND ITO IS INVOLVED IN THE HERB TRADE WITH THE COUNTRY OF THE DRAGONS ACROSS THE SEA.

A MARRIAGE TO SUCH A VASSAL IS MORE THAN LADY TOMOE COULD HOPE FOR. IT WOULD BE A HAPPY UNION. DON'T YOU THINK SHE DESERVES IT?

HMM... I NEVER THOUGHT OF IT LIKE THAT. TOMOE HAS GIVEN MUCH TO THE GEISHU CLAN. IT'S ABOUT TIME SHE RECEIVED SOME HAPPINESS FOR HERSELF...

YOU MAY BE RIGHT. PERHAPS TOMOE SHOULD GET MARRIED.

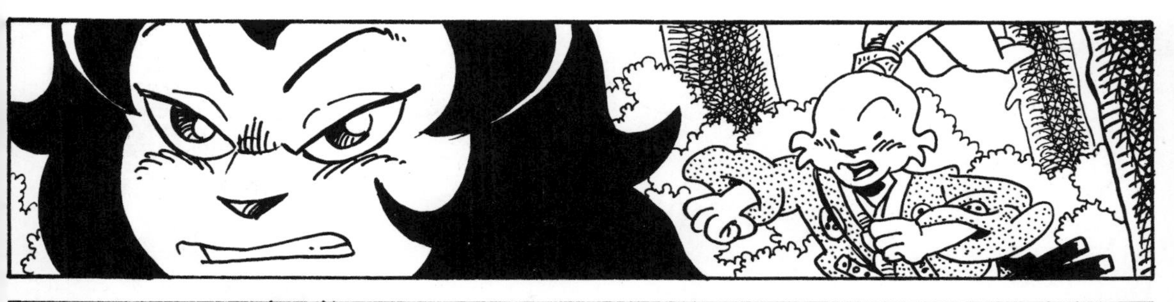

HOLD IT!

ANOTHER PATROL--THIS WAY IS BLOCKED AS WELL!

WE CAN FIGHT OUR WAY THROUGH THEM!
ONCE WE SHOW OURSELVES, THEY'LL SIGNAL FOR A DOZEN HORSEMEN TO COME CHARGING DOWN ON US.

WE'LL NEVER ESCAPE THAT WAY.
IF NOTHING ELSE, NORIKO IS VERY EFFICIENT.
21.

WHO IS NORIKO?
YOU SEEM TO HAVE SOME ANIMOSITY TOWARD HER.

NORIKO IS MY COUSIN--THE DAUGHTER OF MY MOTHER'S YOUNGER SISTER.

AUNT HARUKO MARRIED THE SWORDMASTER OF THE SANADA CLAN.

"THEY HAD A DAUGHTER THEY NAMED NORIKO.

"WE PLAYED TOGETHER AS CHILDREN, BUT SHE HAD A MEAN STREAK IN HER."

IT WAS NOT ENOUGH TO DEFEAT HER OPPONENT, SHE HAD TO HUMILIATE HIM OR HER AS WELL.
22.

IT SOUNDS LIKE SHE IS ADEPT WITH A BLADE.
SHE IS THE DAUGHTER OF A SWORDMASTER...

...AS AM I.

HMM... I WONDER WHO WOULD WIN YOUR DUELS NOW.

GULP!

COME ON. LET'S GET OUT OF HERE.
23.

HURRY--!
COME ON!
THIS WAY LOOKS CLEAR!

THE TREASURE of the MOTHER of MOUNTAINS

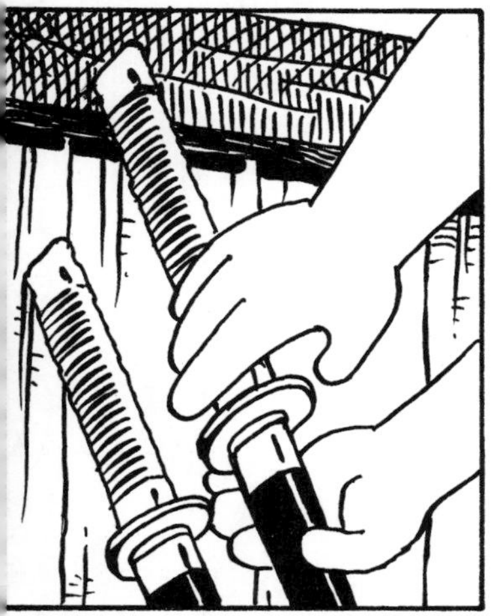

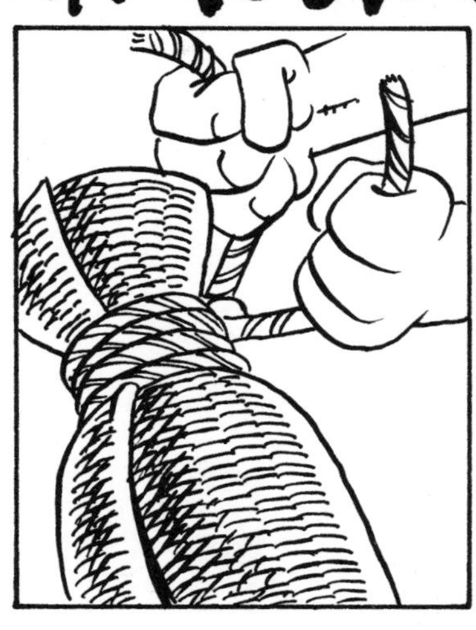

EXCUSE ME.
3

WHAT DO YOU WANT, KID?
I AM HERE TO SEE LADY TOMOE.

HA HA HA! EVEN I WOULD NOT BE ABLE TO SEE LADY TOMOE! WHY WOULD SHE TAKE TIME TO SEE A KID?

SHE GAVE ME THIS LETTER INSTRUCTING ME TO COME TO THE WHITE HERON CASTLE.

GULP! YES, SIR! I'LL SUMMON AN ESCORT IMMEDIATELY!

PLEASE, SIR. RIGHT THIS WAY.

I AM GLAD TO SEE YOU AGAIN, MOTOKAZU...

...BUT I AM SADDENED TO HEAR OF THE DEATH OF YOUR FATHER.
THANK YOU, LADY TOMOE.

GENERAL IKEDA WAS A GOOD AND HONORABLE *SAMURAI.*

YES, MA'AM. I HOPE TO BRING HONOR TO HIS MEMORY.

AND YOUR MOTHER-- IS SHE WELL?

YES. THE MONEY THAT A PRIEST NAMED SANSHOBO LEFT US WILL SUPPORT MY MOTHER AND SISTER FOR A WHILE.* THERE IS EVEN ENOUGH TO HIRE LABORERS FOR THE FARM.

AH, GOOD. I SUSPECT YOU ARE HERE TO ENTER INTO LORD NORIYUKI'S SERVICE, AS YOUR FATHER WANTED.
YES, MA'AM.
5

YOU WILL BE SCHOOLED IN THE MILITARY ARTS. IF YOU HAVE ANY PROBLEMS, PLEASE COME TO ME.
THANK YOU, LADY TOMOE.

COME. I WILL INTRODUCE YOU TO THE INSTRUCTOR OF PAGES.

SEIBO-*SENSEI* WILL OVERSEE YOUR EDUCATION, INCLUDING SWORDSMANSHIP IN THE AME-*RYU*, HEADED BY MY BROTHER.
I WARN YOU, THOUGH, SEIBO-*SENSEI'S* ONLY SON WAS KILLED IN THE REVOLT LED BY YOUR FATHER. BUT HE IS A FAIR AND HONORABLE *SAMURAI*.
YES, MA'AM.

SEIBO-*SENSEI*, I'VE BROUGHT YOU A NEW STUDENT.
THIS IS IKEDA MOTOKAZU. HE COMES FROM A NOBLE BACKGROUND. PLEASE WORK HIM HARD.
WITH PLEASURE, LADY TOMOE.

I WILL LEAVE YOU IN SEIBO-*SENSEI'S* CARE, MOTOKAZU. PLEASE DO YOUR BEST.
I WILL NOT DISAPPOINT YOU, LADY TOMOE.

SO, YOU ARE GENERAL IKEDA'S SON.
Y-YES, SIR.

I KNEW YOUR FATHER. HE WAS A FINE WARRIOR.
!

WE'LL BEGIN YOUR TRAINING IMMEDIATELY.
Y-YES, SIR.

THE MONTHS PASSED UNDER THE TUTELAGE OF SEIBO-*SENSEI*.
HOWEVER, MOTOKAZU'S RELATIONSHIP WITH THE OTHER STUDENTS WAS NOT AS SMOOTH.
IN FACT, SOMETIMES IT WAS VERY BAD.
7.

ONE DAY...
THERE--I WANT THE BEAM ON THAT SECTION OF THE GATE REINFORCED.
YES, TOMOE-SAN. I'LL HAVE THAT TAKEN CARE OF.
HURRY, STUDENTS--DON'T DAWDLE.

EH...? MOTOKAZU. HOW ARE YOU?
YOU LOOK VERY SMART IN THE GEISHU LIVERY.
ER... THANK YOU, MA'AM.

HMM... A BRUISED EYE.
I FELL. I'M VERY CLUMSY.

YES, *SAMURAI* TRAINING CAN BE DIFFICULT.
EXCUSE ME. I SHOULD NOT KEEP SEIBO-*SENSEI* WAITING.
OF COURSE.

SHALL WE CONTINUE WITH THE INSPECTION OF THE GROUNDS, LADY TOMOE?
ER... LADY TOMOE?

POUNCE!
POUNCE!

YOU SENT FOR ME, TOMOE?
YES, SEIBO. I WOULD LIKE TO HAVE AN INFORMAL DISCUSSION.
OH?
ABOUT MOTOKAZU.

TO BE HONEST, HE IS HAVING A DIFFICULT TIME. AFTER ALL, HE IS THE SON OF IKEDA, A TRAITOR TO THE CLAN.

BUT GENERAL IKEDA SAVED OUR LORD'S LIFE. LORD NORIYUKI HIMSELF PRAISED HIM.

EVEN SO, MOTOKAZU HAS SUFFERED MUCH BULLYING. JUST YESTERDAY HE FOUGHT THREE BOYS OLDER THAN HE.

THAT IS HOW HE RECEIVED HIS BRUISED EYE... BUT TWO OF THE BOYS ARE IN THE INFIRMARY.
HE HAS SPIRIT, THAT ONE... AND GREAT POTENTIAL.

ALL THIS TROUBLE, AND HE HAS NEVER COME TO ME FOR HELP.
I AM IMPRESSED WITH HIS CHARACTER.
I AM, AS WELL.
9.

TAK
TAK
TAK

OW!
KLAK!

MOTOKAZU, COME WITH ME.
YES, SEIBO-SENSEI.

LADY TOMOE HAS SUMMONED YOU.
OH?

YOU ARE TO BE LORD NORIYUKI'S PERSONAL PAGE.
WHAT?
DID YOU HEAR THAT?
WOW!

MOTOKAZU!

MOTOKAZU! DAYDREAMING AGAIN?
HUH?

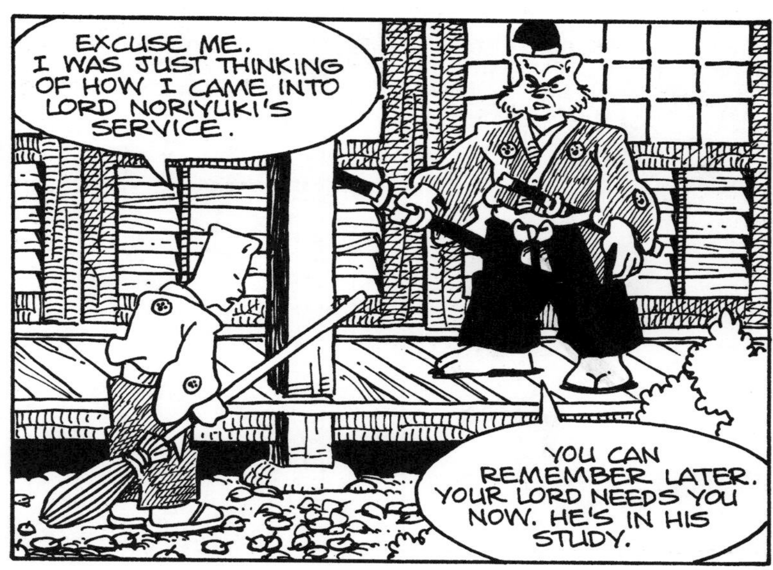
EXCUSE ME. I WAS JUST THINKING OF HOW I CAME INTO LORD NORIYUKI'S SERVICE.
YOU CAN REMEMBER LATER. YOUR LORD NEEDS YOU NOW. HE'S IN HIS STUDY.

THAT AFTER-NOON...
WHAT? THE CARRIER PIGEON RETURNED WITHOUT A MESSAGE FROM TOMOE?
IT MUST HAVE FALLEN OFF DURING FLIGHT. SHE PROBABLY DID NOT SECURE IT PROPERLY.
I'M SURE IT'S NOTHING TO BE CONCERNED ABOUT.

BUT SHE DID GO TO INVESTIGATE A PLAGUE. WHAT IF SHE ENCOUNTERED SOME OTHER DANGER?
AFTER ALL, THAT PART OF OUR LAND BORDERS LORD SANADA'S PROVINCE.

NONSENSE. WE HAVE BEEN AT PEACE WITH LORD SANADA FOR YEARS. WHAT REASON HAS HE TO START TROUBLE NOW?
YOU'RE PROBABLY RIGHT.
11.

TOMOE WAS JUST TO CHECK THAT OUR SOUTHERN SECTION IS QUARANTINED. THAT'S NOT A DANGEROUS ASSIGNMENT, IS IT?
NO. SHE PROBABLY SENT A ROUTINE MESSAGE TO SAY THAT ALL IS GOING WELL.
TO ACT ON YOUR FEAR WOULD SHOW A LACK OF FAITH IN HER.
IT IS BEST TO DO NOTHING. YES, NOTHING IS THE BEST COURSE OF ACTION TO TAKE.
NOW, LET US HAVE SOME TEA, LORD NORIYUKI.
BOY, BRING US SOME TEA.
BOY?
EH?
MOTOKAZU? HE WAS HERE JUST A MOMENT AGO.
BAH! GOOD HELP IS SO DIFFICULT TO GET NOWA-DAYS.

HURRY-- THIS IS THE FASTEST WAY DOWN THE MOUNTAIN.
WATCH OUT FOR THE LOW BRANCHES.
OOP!
TOMOE...
YES, WE WERE TOO ANXIOUS.
SLAY THEM!
HA! THEY'LL RUN RIGHT INTO US!
13

BE CAREFUL, USAGI!
YOU SHOULD KNOW BY NOW THAT I'M THE MOST CAUTIOUS PERSON THERE IS.
GET READY-- THEY'RE RUNNING STRAIGHT INTO US!
HA! THEY WON'T GET AWAY!

LOOK OUT!

UGH!
GET OUT OF HER WAY!

OOG!

UGH!
YAHH!

OOK!
GYAH!

ULK!
GLUK!

WE BROKE PAST THEM! ARE YOU OKAY?
YEAH. COME ON.

DON'T LET THEM GET AWAY!
AFTER THEM!
WHERE ARE OUR ARCHERS?!
15

THERE'S ANOTHER GROUP OF THEM COMING UP THE MOUNTAIN...
...AND WE'RE CAUGHT IN THE MIDDLE!

COME ON--THIS WAY!
CIRCLE AROUND THEM!

NOW HEAD DOWN-HILL!

I'LL GET THEM!

UH--!

HA!
THOK!

WHAP!
OW--!

UH--!
WE'VE GOT HIM NOW!

USAGI!
HERE I COME, USAGI!

NO!

RUN, TOMOE!
.....
RUN!
17.

USAGI!
NO, TOMOE-- GO--GET BACK TO LORD NORIYUKI!
WATCH OUT! HE'S STILL A WILDCAT!
URK--!
THOOK!
OOF!

TOMOE-- GET AWAY! RUN!

UH--!
WHAK!

.....
18

USAGI?!
AFTER HER!
HERE COME OUR ARCHERS!
GET HER!
19.

UH...

SPLASH!
GLUG!

YOU DO NOT WEAR THE GEISHU CREST. WHO ARE YOU?
BE CAREFUL. HE FIGHTS LIKE A DEMON--
--HE AND THE OTHER ONE.
COUGH! COUGH! SPUT! GAG!

I--COUGH! I'M A WANDERER WHO BLUNDERED ONTO THIS LAND. I COUGH!--I MEAN YOU NO TROUBLE.

A LONG-EARED WANDERER, EH? I HAVE HEARD OF SUCH A PERSON. HE IS A FRIEND OF MY COUSIN AND THAT BRAT SHE SERVES.
20

DID YOU CAPTURE THE OTHER ONE?
NO, NORIKO-SAN. SHE ESCAPED.

A WOMAN, EH? I THINK I KNOW WHO SHE IS.

TIE HIS SWORD ARM TO A BOARD.
WITH PLEASURE, NORIKO-SAN!

I'LL TEACH YOU TO MAKE A FOOL OF THE ORPHAN MAKER!
NGGH--!

NOW YOU'RE THE ONE-EYED ORPHAN MAKER!
GYAHH!
GOUGE!

EEYAHH! MY EYE!
FOOL!
SUBDUE HIM--QUICKLY!
COUGH! GAG!
21.

SOON...
LET ME GO, YOU WITCH!
MY, MY, SUCH LANGUAGE. BUT IT'S NOT YOU I'M AFTER.

TOMOE-- I KNOW IT'S YOU OUT THERE!
TURN YOURSELF IN TO ME!

IF YOU WON'T COME OUT, I'LL START CHOPPING OFF HIS FINGERS...

...THEN A HAND...

...THEN WHO KNOWS WHERE I'LL STOP!
22

SO, COME OUT, TOMOE, BEFORE I START CUTTING!

SHE CAN'T HEAR YOU. SHE'S TOO FAR AWAY, ON HER WAY BACK TO LORD NORIYUKI!

I KNOW MY COUSIN. SHE'S TOO SOFT HEARTED, AND WOULD NOT LEAVE A COMRADE IN PERIL.

AM I RIGHT, TOMOE? STEP ON OUT!
THIS LONG-EARS IS A *RONIN*. HE HAS NO STAKE IN THIS!
LEAVE NOW! THE GEISHU ARMY WILL SOON ARRIVE!
QUIET, RONIN!

GIVE YOURSELF UP, COUSIN, AND I WILL RELEASE HIM UNHARMED! YOU HAVE MY WORD OF HONOR!
YOU HAVEN'T MUCH TIME!

YOU KNOW HOW VERY IMPATIENT I AM, TOMOE!
NGGH--!
23

HMM...

HOW DISAPPOINTING.
I TOLD YOU--SHE'S GONE!
I THINK YOU'RE RIGHT.

I GUESS I MISJUDGED HER, RONIN.
TOO BAD.

NOW, WHICH FINGER SHOULD I START WITH?

CLOPCLOPCLOPCLOP

THE TREASURE of the MOTHER of MOUNTAINS

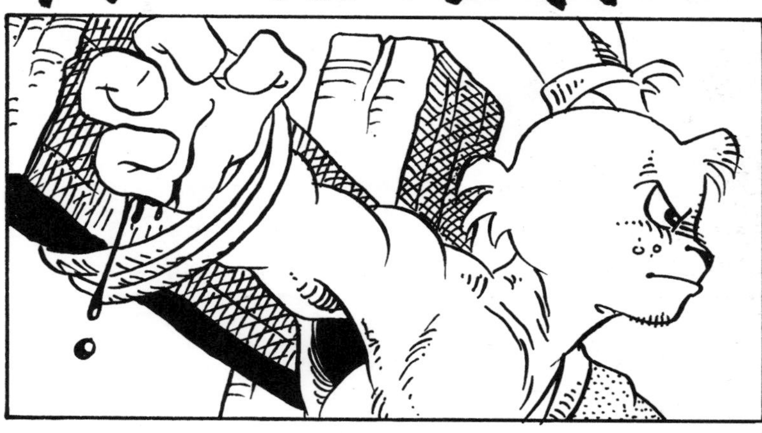

MAYBE I'LL TAKE YOUR ENTIRE HAND!
HA! HA!

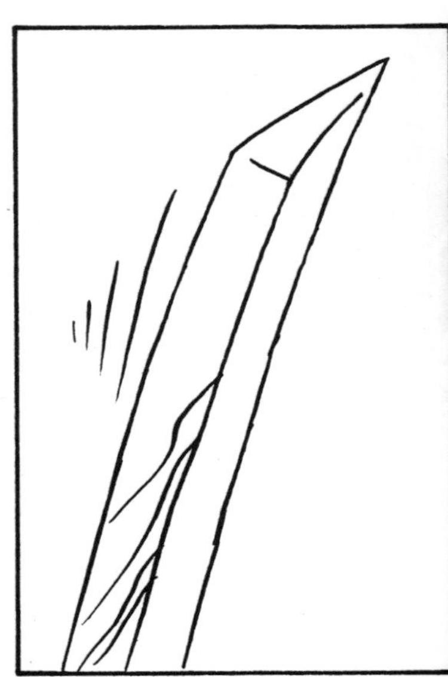

STOP!
EH--?

AH, TOMOE, DEAR COUSIN. SO, I WAS RIGHT. YOU DID NOT LEAVE, AFTER ALL.
TAKE HER SWORDS.

RELEASE USAGI, NORIKO.
IT'S A GOOD THING FOR THE RONIN THAT YOU CAME OUT OF HIDING.
WHEW!
BUT YOU TOOK LONGER THAN I EXPECTED.

AND I DON'T LIKE TO BE KEPT WAITING!

HIYAHH!
CHOP!
NO!

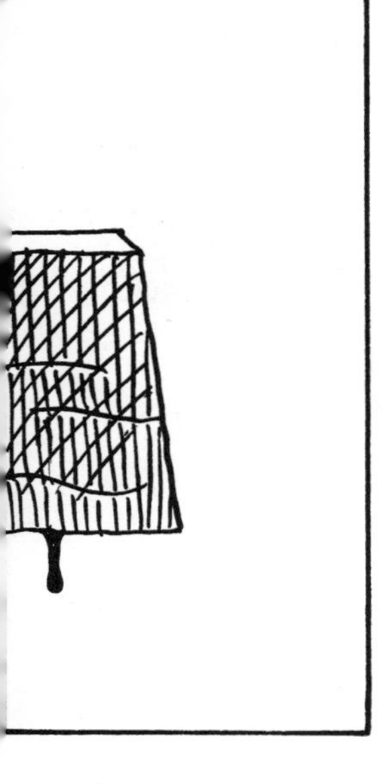

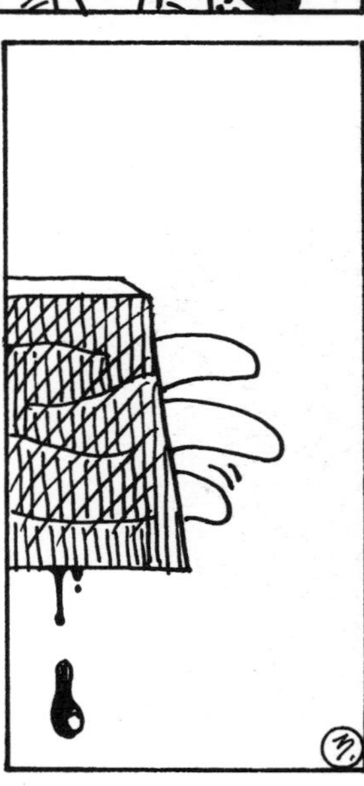

ANY SLOWER IN CLOSING YOUR FIST, AND YOU WOULD HAVE LOST ALL YOUR FINGERS, RONIN. I'M IMPRESSED WITH YOUR REFLEXES.
YOU'RE CRAZY.
YOU PROMISED TO RELEASE USAGI IF I TURNED MYSELF OVER TO YOU, NORIKO.
DON'T BE AN IDIOT. GUARDS-- LOCK THEM AWAY. WE HAVE TWO MORE LABORERS.
BUT... YOU GAVE YOUR WORD AS A SAMURAI!
AND YOU BELIEVED ME? YOU TRULY ARE A FOOL, TOMOE.
WHAT ARE YOU LOOKING AT?! GET BACK TO WORK, SLAVES.
4.

YOU CAN'T GET AWAY WITH THIS. LORD NORIYUKI WILL SOON SEND A PARTY TO INVESTIGATE MY DISAPPEARANCE, AND YOUR MINE WILL BE DISCOVERED.
YOU'RE RIGHT, TOMOE.
THAT IS WHY I'LL HAVE ONE OF MY MEN DRESS IN A DEAD GEISHU'S LIVERY.

I'LL SEND A MISSIVE TO NORIYUKI BY WAY OF HIS BORDER GUARDS.

"THIS AREA IS STILL CONTAMINATED WITH PLAGUE. I WILL SEND WORD WHEN IT IS CONTAINED." I WILL SIGN YOUR NAME TO IT.

THAT SHOULD BUY US A FEW MORE WEEKS...AND THAT IS ALL THE TIME WE WILL NEED.

CUT HIM DOWN, AND THROW THEM BOTH INTO THE CAGE WITH THE OTHER SLAVES.
YES, NORIKO-SAN.
5

GO ON, GEISHU--TOWARDS THE SLAVE PENS.
NO SUDDEN MOVES, *RONIN*, OR I'LL SLAY YOU AT ONCE.

GET IN THERE.

THIS WILL BE YOUR HOME UNTIL YOUR DEATH, GEISHU...
...AND THAT WON'T BE LONG.

THANK YOU FOR COMING BACK.
DON'T THANK ME. I SHOULD HAVE LEFT YOU AND REPORTED TO LORD NORIYUKI. I'VE BETRAYED HIS TRUST IN ME.

YEAH. BUT, WELL... I'VE STILL GOT MY HAND.
6.

WE'VE GOT TO BIDE OUR TIME AND WAIT FOR AN OPPORTUNITY TO ESCAPE.
WE DON'T EVEN KNOW WHAT'S GOING ON. WHAT ARE THEY MINING?

GOLD.
EH--?

HOW COULD THEY KNOW OF GOLD IN THESE MOUNTAINS? EVEN WE, THE GEISHU, DO NOT KNOW OF IT.
IT WAS MY FAULT.

I AM--OR WAS--A HUNTER FROM SANADA PROVINCE. I WAS POACHING GAME IN THE GEISHU LANDS WHEN I FELL UPON A GROMWELL BUSH.

ACCORDING TO LOCAL FOLKLORE, THAT PLANT GROWS ONLY IN THE PRESENCE OF GOLD.

I BELIEVED I WOULD BE HANDSOMELY REWARDED, SO I REPORTED MY DISCOVERY TO MY VILLAGE HEADMAN... FOOL THAT I AM!
7.

OUR HEADMAN TOLD THE AREA MAGISTRATE, WHO INFORMED LORD SANADA.

THEN THE DEVIL WOMAN-- NORIKO-SAN-- ARRIVED.

SHE POISONED THE WELLS AND SPREAD RUMORS OF A PLAGUE, TO ISOLATE THIS PORTION OF THE GEISHU PROVINCE. IT'S PRETTY REMOTE, ANYWAY.
SIP!

THEN SHE CONSCRIPTED ALL THE SANADA VILLAGES ALONG THE BORDER.

NOW WE WORK AS SLAVES, DIGGING EVERY DAY, SEARCHING FOR THE GOLD. I WISH I HAD NEVER FOUND THAT BUSH.

YOU HAVE NOT YET DISCOVERED THE GOLD?
NOT YET.

SURELY LORD SANADA CANNOT IMAGINE HIS OPERATIONS WILL GO UNNOTICED.
THAT IS A MYSTERY.
8

AT THE BARRICADE...
SOMEONE'S COMING FROM THE QUARANTINE AREA.
HE MUST BE FROM THAT GROUP OF OUR *SAMURAI* WHO CAME THROUGH EARLIER.

YEAH, IT'S ONE OF OUR GUYS, ALL RIGHT.
HEY--! WHAT'S GOING ON?

A MESSAGE FROM LADY TOMOE! SEND IT ON THROUGH TO LORD NORIYUKI. IT'S URGENT!
ARE YOU ALL RIGHT? THERE'S BLOOD ON YOUR CLOTHES.

THE PLAGUE IS STILL DEADLY. I MIGHT HAVE CONTRACTED IT.
GASP!

MAKE SURE THAT NO ONE COMES THROUGH THOSE GATES.
Y-YES, SIR!
GULP!

UH... HERE. **YOU** TAKE THE MESSAGE.
OH, NO! I'M NOT TOUCHING THAT THING! DROP IT IN A POUCH AND SEND IT TO THE CAPITAL.
9.

EXCUSE ME.
EH? WHO COULD IT BE AT THIS TIME OF NIGHT?
IT'S PROBABLY THAT GOOD-FOR-NOTHING, LAZY BROTHER OF YOURS. HE'S ALWAYS LOOKING FOR A HANDOUT. HE'S SUCH A LEECH.
IT CAN'T BE. HE'S STILL IN PRISON.

PHAUGH! HE SHOULD ROT IN THERE.

MY HORSE IS EXHAUSTED. WOULD YOU ALLOW ME TO REST HERE AWHILE?
OF -- OF COURSE, YOUNG LORD.

YOU SHALL HAVE OUR FINEST, YOUNG MASTER. TIE YOUR HORSE IN THE BACK, WHILE WE PREPARE A MEAL FOR YOU.
THANK YOU.

WHAT'S WRONG WITH YOU? WE CAN'T AFFORD TO SHARE OUR MEAL WITH HIM! WE HAVE BARELY ENOUGH FOR SECONDS FOR OURSELVES!

DID YOU SEE HOW WELL HE'S DRESSED AND HOW HANDSOME THAT HORSE OF HIS IS?

WE'LL KILL HIM AS HE SLEEPS, AND TAKE HIS HORSE AND WHATEVER IS IN THAT PURSE OF HIS.
IT WON'T BE DIFFICULT -- AFTER ALL, HE'S JUST A CHILD.

THERE'S HARDLY ANYTHING LEFT-- JUST HALF A POT.
NOW GET HIM SOMETHING TO EAT.

EXCUSE ME...

AH, YOUNG MASTER, COME IN, COME IN. OUR HOUSE IS YOURS.
SIT. SIT AND EAT.
THANK YOU.
11.

LATER...
HE'S ASLEEP. HE MUST HAVE BEEN RIDING ALL DAY. HE MUST BE DEAD TIRED.

BUT SOON, HE'LL JUST BE DEAD. NOW GO ON-- KILL HIM.
DON'T RUSH ME! DON'T RUSH ME!
ZZZZ....

IT WILL BE LIKE FILLETING A FISH.

JUST THINK OF HOW MUCH MONEY HE COULD BE CARRYING.
YEAH. YEAH.

GO ON. GO ON.

HEH, HEH, HEH.

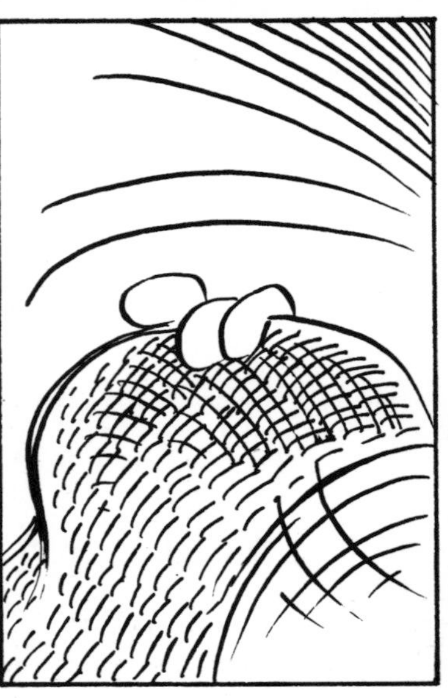

YAHHHHHH!

YOW!
WHAT ARE YOU UP TO?!

A MISTAKE, MY LORD! MY-- MY WIFE PUT ME UP TO IT! SHE'S A WICKED, EVIL WOMAN!
SPARE ME!

HOW DARE YOU PLACE THE BLAME ON ME! IT WAS ALL YOUR IDEA!
OW! OW!

THAT'S ENOUGH! IF I DID NOT HAVE URGENT BUSINESS FOR LORD NORIYUKI, I WOULD HAND YOU OVER TO THE AUTHORITIES.

HE'S ON LORD NORIYUKI'S BUSINESS. IT WOULD HAVE BEEN AWFUL IF SOMETHING BAD HAD HAPPENED TO HIM.
YEAH, WE'D BETTER GET OUT OF THIS AREA IN CASE HE REPORTS US.
WE'LL GO SOMEPLACE YOUR BROTHER WON'T BE ABLE TO FIND US.
13.

ALL RIGHT, WAKE UP, YOU LAZY SCUM!

WAKE UP, TOMOE.
HMM...?

I WON'T FORGET THAT YOU TOOK MY EYE, *RONIN*.
IF NORIKO-*SAN* HAD NOT ORDERED US NOT TO KILL YOU, YOU'D BE DEAD ALREADY.

LINE UP, YOU PATHETIC PIECES OF FILTH! YOU'LL PUT IN A HARD DAY'S LABOR TODAY!
COME ON, KEEP MOVING!

YOU'VE BEEN DIGGING FOR WEEKS, AND YOU HAVE YET TO FIND MY GOLD!

THAT IS BECAUSE YOU HAVE NOT BEEN WORKING HARD ENOUGH.

YOUR FOOD RATIONS WILL BE CUT BY A QUARTER, AND AN HOUR WILL BE ADDED TO YOUR WORKDAY UNTIL THE GOLD IS FOUND.
GROANNNN

FOUR OF YOUR FELLOW SLAVES DIED LAST NIGHT.

FORTUNATELY, WE HAVE TWO MORE LABORERS. THEY WILL MORE THAN MAKE UP FOR THE DEAD.
19.

PICK UP YOUR TOOLS AND GET TO WORK!

GIVE THAT TO ME!
OH!

PICK UP THE BASKET, TOMOE. YOU WILL LABOR IN THE MINE LIKE THE OTHER PEASANTS.

KILL ME IF YOU WANT TO, NORIKO, BUT I WILL NOT LIFT A FINGER TO HELP LORD SANADA.

PICK UP THE BASKET.

NO.

.....
16

HIYAHH!
!

PICK UP THE BASKET, COUSIN, OR I'LL KILL ANOTHER, THEN ANOTHER, THEN ANOTHER, UNTIL YOU COMPLY!
.....

PICK IT UP! DO YOU WANT TO BE RESPONSIBLE FOR ANOTHER DEATH?
DO YOU?!
WELL?

SOFT-HEARTED FOOL.
SHE WAS ONLY A PEASANT.
17.

HOURS LATER...
OHHH, MY BACK.

TODAY I USED MUSCLES I NEVER KNEW I HAD.
A LITTLE MORE TO THE LEFT.
THE FOOD TASTES LIKE VILE SWILL.
YEAH, AND SUCH SMALL PORTIONS.

DID YOU NOTICE ANY WEAK AREAS IN THEIR SECURITY?
NO. THERE ARE AT LEAST TWO GUARDS WITH EACH OF US AT ALL TIMES.
TAN-TON-TAN

DID YOU SEE THE ARCHERS ON TOP OF THE CLIFFS?
YEAH. IT'S NOT GOING TO BE EASY TO ESCAPE.
THAT FEELS GOOD.
TAN TON TAN

IF NOTHING ELSE, NORIKO IS EFFICIENT AT WHAT SHE DOES.
IT'S MY TURN TO GET A MASSAGE.
AHH...!

SOMEONE'S COMING.
RATS!
18

WHERE IS THE GEISHU WOMAN?
WHAT DO YOU WANT?
HELLO, ONE-EYE.

GRR... I'LL KILL YOU YET, *RONIN*.
COME OUT, WOMAN. NORIKO-SAN WANTS TO TALK TO YOU ALONE.

AND SO...
I COULD NOT SLEEP, COUSIN.
LET US GET TO KNOW EACH OTHER.
WE'VE KNOWN EACH OTHER OUR ENTIRE LIVES.

AH, BUT THERE ARE ALWAYS SECRETS--**FAMILY** SECRETS.
SAKÉ?
I WON'T DRINK WITH THE LIKES OF YOU.

AS YOU WISH. YOU WERE ALWAYS TOO EMOTIONAL FOR YOUR OWN GOOD, TOMOE.
SLURP!

THAT IS WHY I ALWAYS BEAT YOU DURING SWORD PRACTICE-- YOUR EMOTIONS OVERCAME YOUR SKILLS.
AHH...
19.

DO YOU EVER THINK OF YOUR FATHER, TOMOE?
OF COURSE.

I THINK ABOUT MINE CONSTANTLY-- MY **REAL** FATHER, NOT THAT DOLT WHO RAISED ME.
WHAT ARE YOU TALKING ABOUT? I DON'T UNDERSTAND.

MY PARENTS HAD AN ARRANGED MARRIAGE, DID YOU KNOW THAT? IT WAS A UNION TO STRENGTHEN THE TIES BETWEEN TWO CLANS.
SLURP!

AN ARRANGED MARRIAGE IS NOT UNCOMMON. MY OWN PARENTS HAD ONE.
A MARRIAGE IS OFTEN MORE ABOUT POLITICS THAN LOVE.

BUT LOVE CAN COMPLICATE A UNION. MOTHER DETESTED THE ONE SHE CALLED HUSBAND. SHE LOVED ANOTHER, AND HE LOVED HER.

HER HEART BELONGED TO THE ONE WHO MARRIED HER OLDER SISTER.
"*OLDER--*"? B-BUT THAT WAS **MY FATHER!**
20

DID YOU EVER WONDER WHY, AFTER MOTHER DIED, I SPENT SO MUCH TIME WITH YOU AND YOUR FAMILY IN THE GEISHU PROVINCE?

MY FATHER COULD NOT BEAR THE SIGHT OF ME, SO HE SENT ME TO MY **REAL** FATHER.

"**REAL** F-FATHER"? BUT... BUT... THAT WOULD MEAN THAT YOU-- WE'RE... WE'RE...

SISTERS, TOMOE, WE ARE SISTERS, NOT COUSINS.

BUT YOUR FATHER NEVER ACKNOWLEDGED ME, AND YOUR MOTHER LOATHED ME.

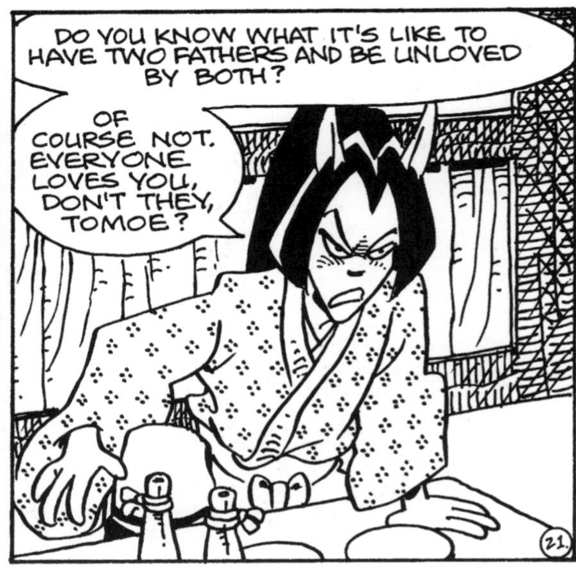
DO YOU KNOW WHAT IT'S LIKE TO HAVE TWO FATHERS AND BE UNLOVED BY BOTH?
OF COURSE NOT. EVERYONE LOVES YOU, DON'T THEY, TOMOE?
21

BUT I SETTLED THE SCORE.
MY OWN FATHER, I KILLED WITH POISON.

DO YOU REMEMBER HOW YOUR FATHER DIED?

HE-HE WAS AMBUSHED WHILE RETURNING TO THE *DOJO* LATE ONE NIGHT. HE WAS STRUCK FROM BEHIND. HIS SWORD NEVER EVEN LEFT ITS SCABBARD.

WHO WOULD HAVE SUSPECTED HIS KILLER TO BE A GIRL?
NO...
YOU KILLED...

HIYAHHH!!
YOU KILLED HIM!

AFTER YEARS OF DENYING ME, I CONFRONTED HIM ONE LAST TIME. I NEEDED HIM TO ACKNOWLEDGE ME AS HIS DAUGHTER.
HIYAH!

UH--!

HE REFUSED ME. HE SAID CLAIMING ME WOULD DISHONOR MY FATHER, AS WELL AS HIMSELF.
UHK!

HE SAID HE ALREADY HAD A DAUGHTER, THEN TURNED AWAY.
HE TURNED HIS BACK ON ME!
OOF!

HOW COULD HE HAVE CAST ME ASIDE SO CASUALLY?! THAT WAS WHEN I STRUCK. I KILLED HIM, TOMOE. IT WAS ME! I DID IT!

HE DENIED ME BECAUSE OF YOU, AND I KILLED HIM FOR IT!
NO. NO. NO. NO. NO.
23

IT WAS BECAUSE OF YOU THAT YOUR FATHER DIED, TOMOE! DO YOU HEAR ME?! IT WAS YOUR FAULT! YOU KILLED HIM!
GUARDS!
SOB! SOB!

TAKE THIS GEISHU SLIME BACK TO THE SLAVE PENS.
YES, LADY NORIKO.
SOB! SOB!

GLUB! GLUB!

THE TREASURE of the MOTHER of MOUNTAINS

YOU HEARD ME--
GET BACK TO YOUR
DIGGING!

DON'T TRY ANYTHING, *RONIN*, OR EVERY SLAVE HERE WILL BE KILLED--BEGINNING WITH THIS ONE!
OKAY. CALM DOWN, AND PUT AWAY YOUR SWORD.
GET BACK TO WORK!

CHUNK!

WAIT A MINUTE!
HUH?

WHY ARE YOU STOPPING NOW?! GET BACK TO WORK!
I WARNED YOU! THIS TIME SOMEONE DIES!

WE'VE FOUND THE GOLD.
DO YOU SEE THE VEINS IN THE ROCK?

THE G-G--?

NORIKO-SAN! NORIKO-SAN! I'VE FOUND IT! I'VE FOUND THE GOLD!
!
3.

THE GOLD-- WHERE IS THE GOLD?
THIS WAY, NORIKO-SAN, THIS WAY!

AH... A VERY RICH VEIN, BY THE LOOKS OF IT!

YES, THIS IS WORTH DIGGING OUT.
GOOD WORK, TOMOE. YOU AND THE *RONIN* HAVE ONLY BEEN HERE A WEEK, AND YOU'VE DISCOVERED MY GOLD.

HMM... WHERE IS THAT DRAFT COMING FROM?

IT'S FROM THE BELLOWS. THEY FORCE FRESH AIR INTO THE MINE SHAFT THROUGH THOSE BAMBOO PIPES. YOU WOULDN'T WANT THE SLAVES TO SUFFOCATE IN HERE, WOULD YOU?
OF COURSE NOT. HEH HEH.

NOW, EVERYBODY OUT!
I WANT THIS MINE CLEARED AT ONCE!

WHY IS SHE ORDERING US OUT OF THE MINE?
IT DOESN'T MAKE ANY SENSE.

YOU WOULD THINK NOW THAT THE GOLD IS FOUND, WE WOULD HAVE TO DIG **HARDER**.
WHAT IS SHE PLANNING?

HURRY-- COME ON OUT! STOP LOITERING!

BRING THE WAGONS HERE!

CARRY THOSE KEGS INTO THE MINE ENTRANCE!
HURRY! IT'S ALMOST DARK!
WHAT COULD BE IN THEM?

BE CAREFUL WITH THIS.

OH--!
FOOL!
CRAK!

NO--! NO--! GYAHH!

THIS IS WHAT WILL HAPPEN TO ANYONE WHO DROPS A KEG.

THE FOREIGN BLACK POWDER!
EXPLOSIVES!

HEY, *RONIN*-- *CATCH!*
!

OOF!

GOOD CATCH, *RONIN*.
TOO BAD.

WELL, IT WON'T MATTER TOMORROW, ANYWAY.
7.

GET BACK TO WORK!
WHAT HAPPENS TOMORROW, ONE-EYE?

GRR... YOU PEASANTS--CARRY THESE KEGS INTO THE MINE SHAFT!

I CAN WAIT ONE MORE DAY, RONIN.
YOU HEARD HIM. GET BACK TO WORK!

NORIKO MEANS TO SEAL UP THE MINE!
BUT WE'VE JUST DISCOVERED THE GOLD. WHY LOSE IT AGAIN?

AS YOU SAID, LORD SANADA IS A SUPPORTER OF LORD HIKIJI, WHOSE AMBITION IS TO TAKE CONTROL OF OUR COUNTRY. THEY WILL FIND SOME WAY TO CREATE A BORDER DISPUTE.

EVENTUALLY, THIS REGION WILL BE GIVEN TO LORD SANADA. THEN HE CAN MINE THE GOLD IN THE OPEN.
BRING UP THE NEXT CART!

SURELY THE *SHOGUN* WILL NOT TURN AGAINST THE GEISHU CLAN!

THE ***SHOGUN'S PEACE*** IS STILL NEW, AND LORD HIKIJI'S POWER IS GREAT. THE *SHOGUN* WOULD GO TO GREAT LENGTHS TO AVOID CONFLICT. BESIDES, AS FAR AS EVERYONE IS CONCERNED, THIS IS A REMOTE, INCONSEQUENTIAL AREA OF OUR COUNTRY. WHAT WOULD IT MATTER IF SANADA OR THE GEISHU CONTROLLED IT?
WHAT GOLD IS TAKEN OUT OF THESE MOUNTAINS WILL BE ADDED TO LORD HIKIJI'S WAR CHEST.

AND WHEN THE EVIL LORD COMES INTO POWER, THE REMAINDER OF THE GEISHU PROVINCE WILL BE GIVEN TO LORD SANADA.

IT'S AN AUDACIOUS PLAN, BUT THE REWARDS ARE GREAT.
BUT WHAT WILL HAPPEN TO THE LABORERS?

NORIKO CANNOT AFFORD ANY WITNESSES. NO DOUBT WE WILL ALL BE KILLED.
THAT IS WHAT ONE-EYE MEANT.

YEAH.
"TOMORROW."
LEAVE YOUR KEGS HERE.
9.

;YAWN!; IT'S BEEN A WEEK SINCE ANYONE'S COME ALONG!
WELL, THAT MAKES OUR JOB OF GUARDING THE QUARANTINED AREA THAT MUCH EASIER.
YEAH, BUT IT'S SO BORING.
WHAT PERSON IN HIS RIGHT MIND WOULD ENTER A PLAGUE AREA?
HEY, SOMEONE IS COMING!
IT LOOKS LIKE A KID.
WHAT COULD HE WANT HERE?
WHAT ARE YOU DOING HERE, KID?
GET OFF YOUR HORSE.
UH-OH.
10.

I AM IKEDA MOTOKAZU, PERSONAL PAGE TO OUR LORD NORIYUKI! LET ME THROUGH.

WE WERE ORDERED TO LET NO ONE THROUGH THESE GATES.

I AM HERE ON LORD NORIYUKI'S BUSINESS--I MUST FIND LADY TOMOE! NOW LET ME THROUGH!

IF YOU ARE HERE ON OUR LORD'S BEHALF, WHERE IS YOUR AUTHORIZATION?
I HAVE IT RIGHT HERE.

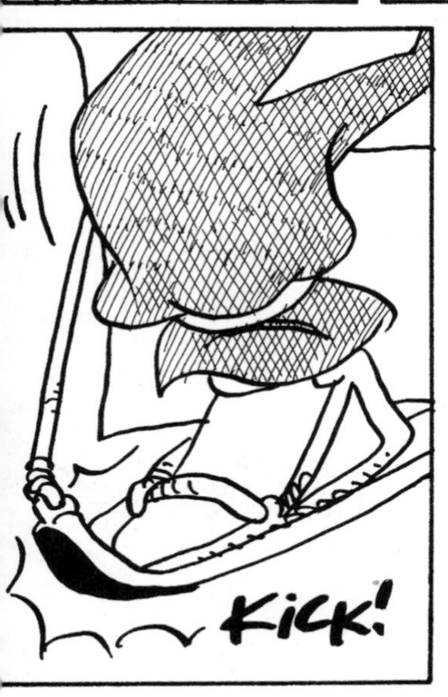
KICK!

HYAHHH!
LOOK OUT! HE'S BREAKING THROUGH!
HE'S CRAZY!
11.

HURRY--! GET A HORSE AND RIDE AFTER HIM!
UH-UH, NOT ME.

WHAT?!
THERE'S A PLAGUE BEYOND THAT GATE! I'M NOT GOING IN THERE! YOU DO IT!

I'M NOT GOING THROUGH THOSE GATES. HE'LL BE DEAD SOON ANYWAY. I'M NOT GOING AFTER A DEAD KID!

WE WERE ORDERED NOT TO LET ANYONE THROUGH THOSE GATES, WEREN'T WE? THEN WE WOULD BE GOING AGAINST ORDERS IF WE WENT IN THERE.
YEAH. YOU'RE RIGHT.

12

LATER...
THERE'S A VILLAGE. I HOPE I CAN FIND SOME TRACE OF TOMOE-SAN THERE.
EEP! EEP!
?
¡GULP!¡
G-GEISHU SAMURAI--!
THEY'RE ALL DEAD, BUT NOT FROM THE PLAGUE.
WHAT COULD HAVE HAPPENED HERE?!
13.

THEY WERE ALL KILLED BY ARROWS OR SWORDS.

I DON'T SEE LADY TOMOE'S BODY... THANK THE GODS.

WHERE CAN SHE BE?

ALL THE GEISHU DEAD ARE IN THE VILLAGE SQUARE...

...BUT A TRAIL OF ENEMY DEAD LEADS THIS WAY.
14.

ALMOST ALL THE KEGS OF BLACK POWDER ARE IN THE MINE, NORIKO-SAN, AND THE SLAVES ARE RETURNING TO THEIR PENS.

EXCELLENT.

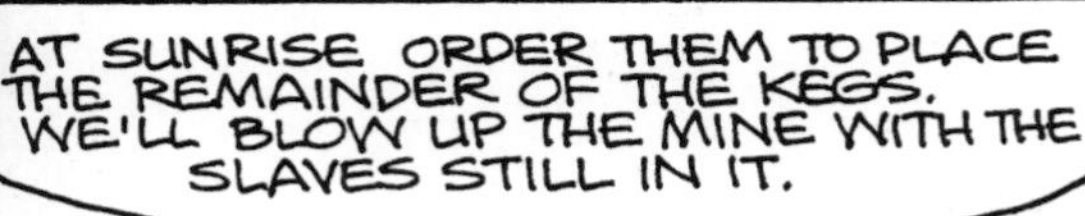
AT SUNRISE ORDER THEM TO PLACE THE REMAINDER OF THE KEGS. WE'LL BLOW UP THE MINE WITH THE SLAVES STILL IN IT.

WHAT OF THE *SAMURAI?* SURELY THEY WON'T BE KILLED WITH THE PEASANTS.

NO, THAT WOULD BE TOO QUICK AND PAINLESS. WE WILL TAKE THEM WITH US. I HAVE SOMETHING **SPECIAL** PLANNED FOR MY GEISHU "COUSIN."

BUT I HAVE NO USE FOR THE *RONIN.* DO YOU WANT HIM? HE'S YOURS.
THANK YOU, NORIKO-SAN, THANK YOU.
15

THE ROAD HERE LOOKS PRETTY WELL TRAVELED. I'D BETTER LOOK AROUND ON FOOT FOR A WHILE.

I'LL TIE YOU HERE. THERE IS PLENTY TO EAT, AND YOU CAN REST FROM OUR TRAVEL.

MAYBE I CAN GET AN OVERVIEW OF THE AREA FROM THE TOP OF THIS HILL.

THERE'S A LIGHT UP AHEAD.

A SENTRY. BUT WHAT IS HE GUARDING?
I'D BETTER GET TO ANOTHER OVERLOOK.

UH-OH!
NUDGE

WHO'S THERE?!
¡GULP!

WHO'S THERE?!
UH...
UH...

EEP! EEP!

STUPID TOKAGE' LIZARDS!
WHEW!

SCUTTLE! SCUTTLE!

SOON...
IT'S AN ARMED CAMP DOWN THERE!
WHO COULD THEY BE?
IS LADY TOMOE DOWN THERE?
17.

WHO ARE THOSE SAMURAI? THEY'RE NOT WEARING ANY CLAN CRESTS.
EVERYTHING IS GOING ACCORDING TO PLAN, NORIKO-SAN. THE SLAVES WILL BE DEAD IN THE MORNING, AND WE SHOULD BE OUT OF HERE BY EVENING.
GOOD.

IS SOMETHING WRONG?
SOMEONE IS WATCHING US!
HUH?

THERE!
18.

THERE IS NO ONE THERE, NORIKO-SAN!
IT WAS PROBABLY MY... IMAGINATION.

PHEW! I GOT AWAY JUST IN TIME!

THE GUARDS HAVE BEEN WATCHING US TOO CLOSELY. WE HAVEN'T HAD AN OPPORTUNITY TO GET AWAY.

WE DON'T HAVE MUCH TIME. I'M SURE THEY'LL KILL US ALL TOMORROW.
THEN WE'LL HAVE TO MAKE A MOVE WHETHER WE'RE READY OR NOT!
WHAT ABOUT THE OTHERS?

I-I DON'T WANT THEM TO GET HARMED...

...BUT MY FIRST DUTY IS TO GET MY INFORMATION BACK TO LORD NORIYUKI!
IF I CAN ESCAPE ON MY OWN, I WILL.
I-IT WAS A MISTAKE TO RETURN FOR YOU.
19

HEY--
QUIET IN
THERE!

GET
SOME
SLEEP!
YOU GEISHU
SCUM TALK TOO
MUCH!

"GEISHU"!

UHH--!
BONK!

LADY TOMOE--? ARE YOU IN HERE?

MOTOKAZU! AM I GLAD TO SEE YOU! WHERE IS THE REST OF LORD NORIYUKI'S ARMY?
THERE IS NO ONE ELSE. I-I'M ALONE.
WHAT?!

I LEFT WITHOUT LORD NORIYUKI'S PERMISSION. I DESERTED MY DUTIES.
WE CAN DISCUSS THAT LATER. RIGHT NOW, GET US OUT OF HERE.

THE GUARD DOESN'T HAVE THE KEY.

USE THE HOE TO BREAK THE LOCK!

21.

NNGGH!

POP!

EH--? WHAT WAS THAT?

IT CAME FROM THE SLAVE PENS.

!

BONK!

GOOD WORK. NOW WE HAVE *TWO* SETS OF SWORDS.

HEY, HUNTER, WAKE UP!
HMM...?

SHH...
QUIETLY WAKE THE OTHERS. WE'RE ALL GOING TO ESCAPE.
HUH? WHAT? NOW?

BE PATIENT. YOU'LL HAVE TO STAY IN HERE JUST A LITTLE WHILE LONGER, BUT YOU'LL BE SAFE TOMORROW.

DON'T WORRY. WE'LL BE BACK SOON.
WE'RE GETTING OUT OF HERE.
SHH--!
MMPH!
23.

STAY WITH THE PRISONERS, MOTOKAZU.
BUT I CAN HELP YOU!

NO. I NEED YOU TO STAY HERE AND KEEP THE PRISONERS CALM, AND HIDE THE UNCONSCIOUS GUARDS... AND MAKE SURE THEY STAY QUIET.
WHERE ARE YOU GOING?

WE'RE GOING TO EVEN THE ODDS A BIT.
HAVE THE PRISONERS READY TO LEAVE WHEN WE RETURN.

I THOUGHT YOU SAID YOU WERE GOING TO LEAVE WITHOUT THE OTHERS.
OH, SHUT UP.
HA HA!

READY?
YEAH. LET'S GO.

THE TREASURE OF THE MOTHER OF MOUNTAINS

COME ON! WAKE UP!
HEY-- WHAT IS THAT?

WHERE?
THERE-- ON HIS NECK.

IT'S WET AND STICKY.

BLOOD.
WHAT?!

¡KLIK!¡
EH--? SOMEONE BEHIND--

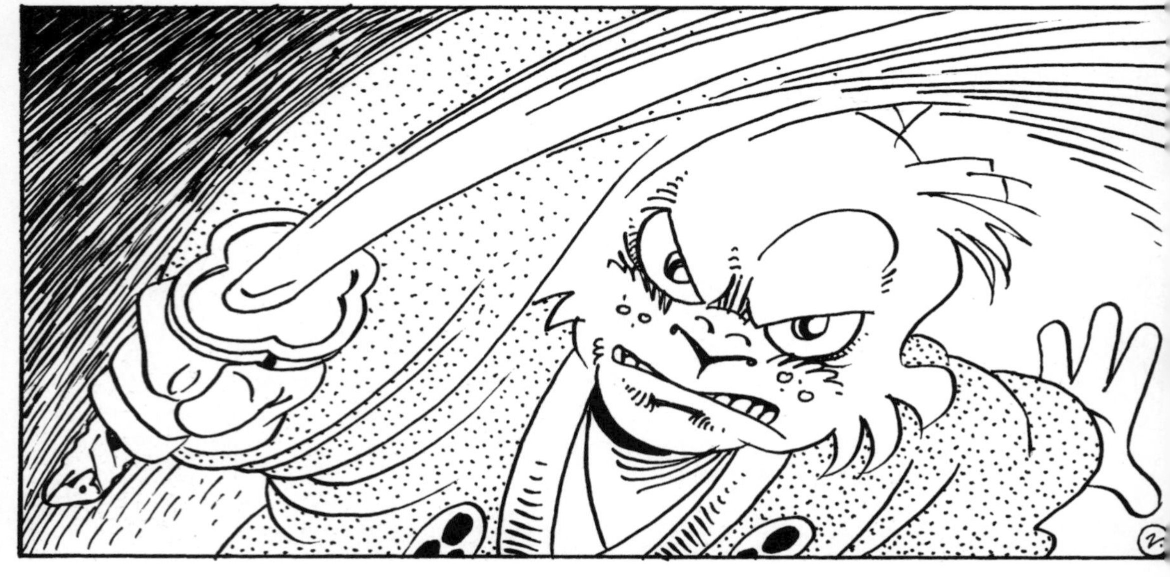

WHERE IS THE FOOL WHO'S SUPPOSED TO BE GUARDING THE SLAVE PENS?

NORIKO-SAN WILL HAVE HIS HEAD IF HE HAS ABANDONED HIS POST.

ZZZZZZZZZZZZZZZZZZZZZ
......

WELL, THE PRISONERS ARE SOUND ASLEEP.

EH--?

THE *LOCK*--!
3.

ALER--

URK!

.....

MOTOKAZU?

I'M HERE. ARE YOU ALL RIGHT, TOMOE-SAN?
I'M FINE. IS EVERYONE READY?

YES, TOMOE-SAN, THEY ALL KNOW THE PLAN.
GOOD.
WHAT IS KEEPING USAGI? HE SHOULD HAVE BEEN BACK BY NOW.

I AM BACK. I HAD A LITTLE TROUBLE WITH A COUPLE OF THE SENTRIES.
WE STARTED THE ESCAPE WITHOUT YOU.
THANK YOU, SAMURAI. I THOUGHT WE WOULD ALL DIE IN THERE.
SHH... SILENCE IS OUR GREATEST ALLY.

THE PERIMETER GUARDS ARE STILL ALIVE. THERE IS VERY LITTLE CHANCE OF US ESCAPING COMPLETELY UNDETECTED.
I KNOW.

WE'LL LEAD THEM OUT OF THE ENCAMPMENT, AND THEN WE'LL ALL SCATTER.
MANY WILL BE HUNTED DOWN AND SLAIN.
IF ONLY WE HAD A DIVERSION TO KEEP THE GUARDS OCCUPIED.

I'M HOPING THAT NORIKO WILL COME AFTER THE TWO OF US-- AND IGNORE THE PEASANTS.

THAT IS THE BEST THAT WE CAN DO FOR THEM.
COME ON!
5.

YAWN! I HATE NIGHT SENTRY DUTY. I'LL BE GLAD WHEN THIS IS ALL OVER.
YAWN!

THIS COLD NIGHT AIR IS TERRIBLE FOR MY JOINTS. IT GIVES ME A STIFF NECK TOO.
RUB! RUB!

HMMM... THAT'S STRANGE.

THE CAMPFIRES AROUND THE SLAVE PENS ARE NOT BURNING.

HUH?
ANOTHER FIRE HAS GONE OUT!

SOMETHING WEIRD IS GOING ON DOWN THERE!
THE SLAVES MAY BE ATTEMPTING AN ESCAPE!

ALERT! ALERT!

ALERT! ALERT! THE SLAVES ARE ESCAPING!
WHAT?

HEH! IT'S PROBABLY HIS IDEA OF A JOKE!
IT'S NO JOKE!
HUH?

WE REALLY ARE ESCAPING!

HURRY! THERE'S NO NEED FOR SECRECY NOW! STAY TOGETHER FOR NOW, BUT DISPERSE ONCE WE'RE OUTSIDE THE MINE AREA!
FIND A WEAPON--A SWORD, A HOE--ANYTHING! WE OUTNUMBER THEM, BUT YOU HAVE ALL GOT TO FIGHT OR WE WON'T GET AWAY!

YOUR WAKIZASHI IS TOO SHORT AGAINST SWORDS, MOTOKAZU! FIND A SPEAR, BUT STAY OUT OF THE FIGHTING IF YOU CAN!
YES, TOMOE-SAN!

MANY OF US WILL BE SLAIN. THE SAMURAI ASKED FOR A DIVERSION. MAYBE I CAN GIVE HIM ONE.
7.

NO ONE WILL BE MADE TO SLAVE IN THE MINE AGAIN!

WOW.

GYAH!
UL~K!
OOK!

!
EEGH!
KILL THEM ALL! DON'T LET THEM GET AWAY!

NYAKK!
GARK!
KEEP TOGETHER! THERE'S GREATER SAFETY IN A GROUP!

EEE!
HA HA!

HAUGH!

WE'RE ALMOST OUT OF THE COMPOUND!
BUT THEY'VE GOTTEN OVER THEIR SURPRISE AT OUR ESCAPE!
9.

WHAT'S GOING ON?
IT'S THE SLAVES-- THEY'RE ESCAPING, NORIKO-SAN!

WHAT?!

I'LL KILL ALL OF YOU IF EVEN ONE OF THEM GETS AWAY!
Y-YES, MA'AM!

NOW QUIT DAWDLING, AND STOP THEM!
Y-YES, NORIKO-SAN!
I KNOW YOU'RE BEHIND THIS, TOMOE!

WHERE IS SHE?!
YIKES!

WHERE IS TOMOE?!
GYAH!

STAY CLOSE TO MY SIDE, MOTOKAZU!
YES, TOMOE-SAN!

WHERE IS USAGI?
I THINK HE'S COVERING OUR RETREAT.

HURRY! HURRY!

!
YARK!

VWIT!

I'LL GET THAT LONG-EARED VERMIN!
TCHAK!
11.

RYAAAAAAAAAAAAAA
.....
YARG!

GURK!
GAHH!

SWIT!

SO, ONE-EYE, ARE YOU READY TO TAKE YOUR REVENGE?!
I'LL KILL YOU, RONIN!

WE'LL NOT DIE IN THE MINE.

SOON, THERE WON'T EVEN BE A MINE.

AND ITS DESTRUCTION WILL DISTRACT THE GUARDS SO WE CAN GET AWAY.

I NEED A TORCH.

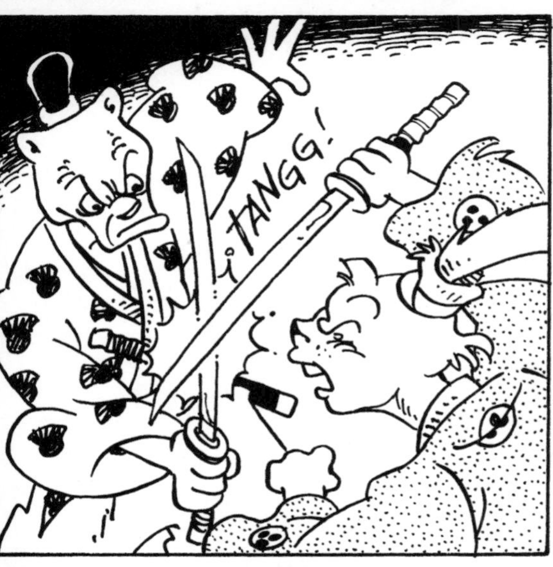
TANGG!

OOK!

HOLD STILL, YOU!
HEY--! WATCH OUT! ARE YOU TRYING TO KILL ME?!

STOP HIDING BEHIND THE OTHERS, ONE-EYE!
ULK!
13.

I'LL KILL YOU!
YOU WERE THE WORST OF THE LOT IN MISTREATING THE PEASANTS.
KILL YOU!
YAR!
ZWIT!
A QUICK DEATH IS TOO GOOD FOR YOU!
YAHH!
MY EYE!
MY GOOD EYE!
YAHH! I'M BLIND!
BLIND!
14

AHHK!

TOMOE!
AND WHO IS THIS YOUNG WARRIOR?
?

STAY OUT OF THE WAY, MOTOKAZU.

MOTOKAZU, IS IT? A FRIEND OF YOURS? I'LL MAKE SURE TO DEAL WITH HIM... AFTER I SLAY YOU.

I'LL SEE TO IT THAT YOU WON'T LAY A FINGER ON HIM!

SUCH CONFIDENCE, TOMOE, BUT YOU'VE NEVER BEATEN ME BEFORE.

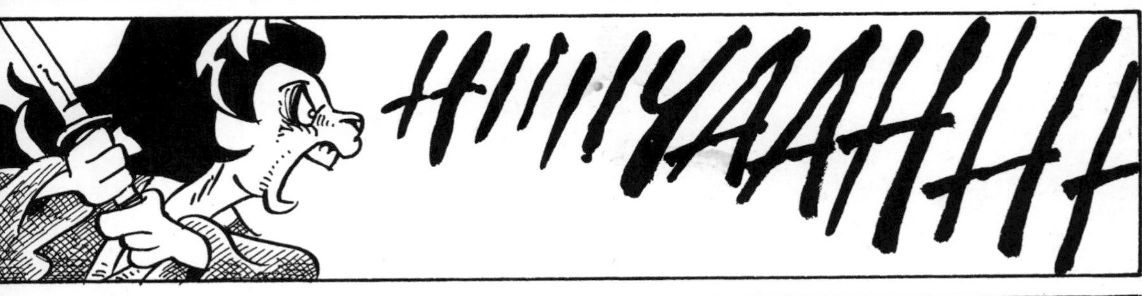
HIIIYAAHHH

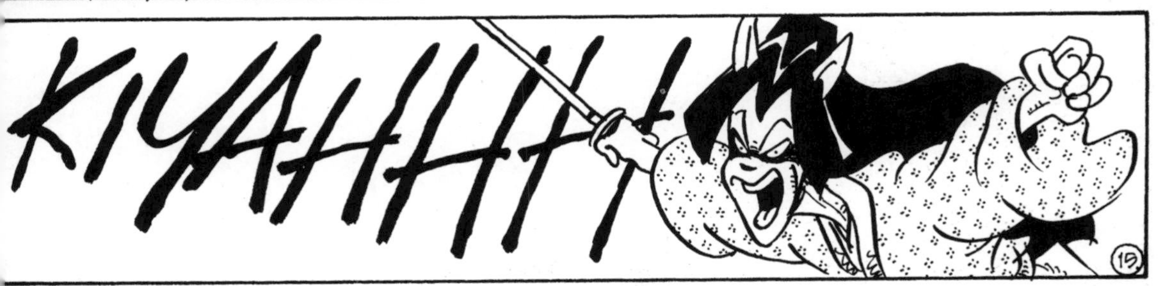
KIYAHHHH
15

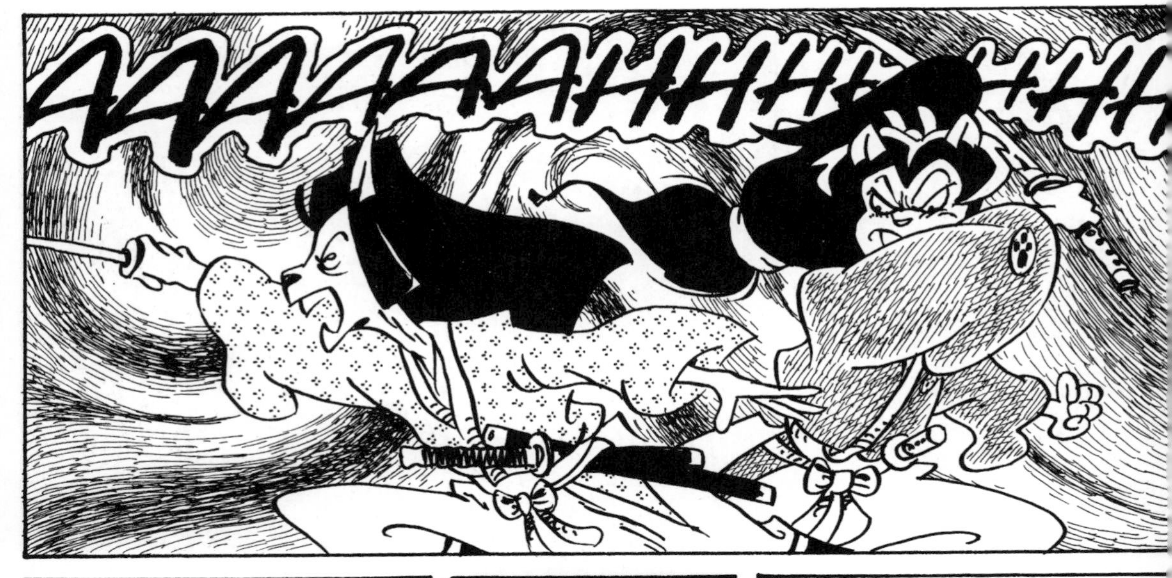
AAAAAAAAHHHHHHHHHH

TANG!

.....

SNIT!

HA!
YOUR HAIR WAS TOO LONG, ANYWAY.
CHOP!

I'LL CUT MORE THAN YOUR HAIR!
TANG!
16

UH--!
TANG!

I HAVE SAID IT BEFORE, TOMOE-- YOU ARE MUCH TOO EMOTIONAL. YOU ALLOW YOUR ANGER TO GET THE BETTER OF YOU.
TANG! TANG! TANG! TANG! TANG! TANG! TANG!

TANG! TANG! TANG! TANG! TANG! TANG! TANG!
YOU TIRE. I'M WEARING YOU DOWN, TOMOE.

HIIIII--!

UHH--!
STAY BACK, MOTOKAZU!
WHAK!
HIYAH!

UH--!
HIYAH!
TANG!
17

NO! NO! DON'T KILL ME!

PLEASE--
--SISTER!

SIS--?!

HA! SENTIMENTAL FOOL!
UH--!

NORIKO!
HA HA HA! YOU CAN NEVER DEFEAT ME, TOMOE!
I'LL GET HER!
THIS WILL PROVIDE THE DIVERSION WE NEED.
18

YOW!
FFFFSSSHHH

YAHHH!
FFSSHHH

I SHOULD HAVE TAKEN YOUR HAND WHEN I HAD THE CHANCE, *RONIN*!
GIVE YOURSELF UP, NORIKO!

SO... TOMOE BEHIND ME, AND THE *RONIN* IN FRONT...

IT SEEMS THERE IS JUST ONE VIABLE OPTION LEFT TO ME.
I WILL NOT BE HUMILIATED BY CAPTURE.
FFSSS SHH
19.

YOU WON'T GET AWAY FROM ME, NORIKO!
YES, FOLLOW ME, TOMOE. YOUR ANGER STILL BLINDS YOU!
TOMOE!

TOMOE-- STOP!
LET ME GO, USAGI! SHE'S GOT TO PAY FOR WHAT SHE'S DONE!

LET-- GO!
IT'S GOING TO EXPLODE!

FSSTT!

WHAT?

GET DOWN!

BAKA-DOON!
21.

ULF--!
THUD!
STAY DOWN!
AND PRAY WE DON'T GET COVERED BY AN AVALANCHE!
TOMOE-SAN!
AH--!
ARE YOU ALL RIGHT?
Y-YES. WE'RE BOTH UNHURT.
UH... YEAH.
22

SAMURAI-SAN! SAMURAI-SAN!
EH? IT'S THE HUNTER.

THE GUARDS SAW THAT DEVIL-WOMAN DIE IN THE EXPLOSION! THEY'RE ALL RUNNING AWAY! WE'RE SAFE!

WE'RE FREE! WE'RE FREE!
DID YOU HEAR THAT? WE'VE WON!
ARE YOU ALL RIGHT, TOMOE?

SHE CHOSE DEATH RATHER THAN CONCEDE TO ME, USAGI.

SHE WAS AN AMORAL DEMON, BUT SHE WAS STILL MY... SISTER.
23

TOMOE-SAN...?
GIVE HER A FEW MINUTES ALONE, MOTOKAZU.

YOU ACTED VERY BRAVELY. YOUR FATHER WOULD HAVE BEEN VERY PROUD OF YOU.
YOU WERE THERE WHEN HE WAS KILLED, WEREN'T YOU?

HE DIED AN HONORABLE DEATH.
I MISS HIM.
GOOD.

THE DEAD SHOULD BE MOURNED.

THE TREASURE of the MOTHER of MOUNTAINS

......!
BAA
GET DOWN!

GOOM!

OOM!

GOOM!

YAHH!

CRUMBLE!
CRUSH!
RUMBLE!

CRAK!

CRASH!
CRUMBLE!
CRUSH!

CRUNCH!
CRAK!

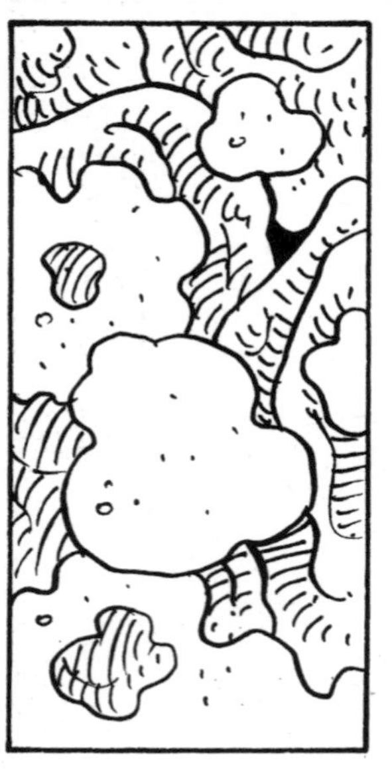

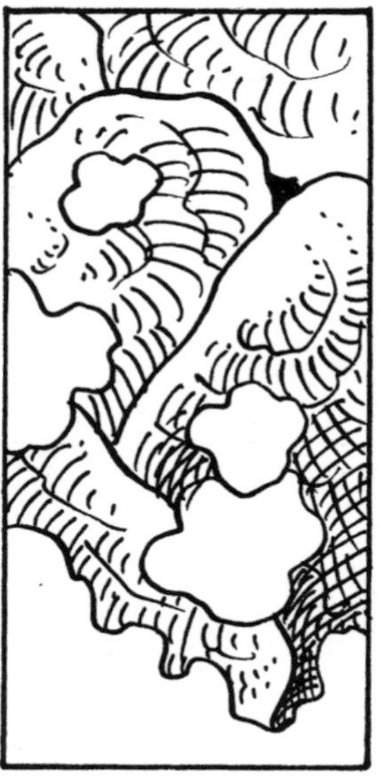

.....
UHH...
I'M ALIVE...
HOW LONG HAVE I BEEN BURIED HERE?
IT WILL TAKE MORE THAN AN EXPLOSION TO KILL ME, DEAR TOMOE.

MY FOOT IS TRAPPED... PROBABLY BROKEN.

KI!

UGH!

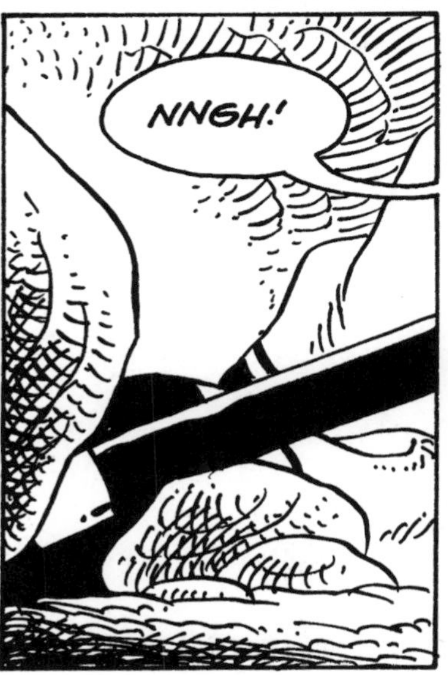
NNGH!

CRAK!
THUD!
5

IT'S NOT BROKEN. IT LOOKS LIKE LUCK IS WITH ME.

MAYBE NOT. THE ENTRANCE FEELS LIKE IT'S COMPLETELY BLOCKED.

BUT I'LL GET OUT, TOMOE. I'M NOT READY TO DIE...

...NOT WHILE YOU'RE STILL ALIVE.

I CAN'T SEE A THING.
I'M STUMBLING AROUND IN THE DARK.

UH--!

WHAT'S THIS?

SNIFF! SNIFF! OIL FOR THE LAMPS!
6

THERE SHOULD BE A BAG AROUND HERE AS WELL.
AH.

I'M IN LUCK. THE STRIKERS ARE STILL IN HERE.

SHRAK! SHRAK! SHRAK!

FLOOM!

THE GOLD!
THIS IS THE END OF THE MINE SHAFT.
I-I'M TRAPPED IN HERE!
7.

TO DIE WITH ALL MY GOLD... HOW IRONIC.
I ONLY REGRET THAT I DID NOT KILL TOMOE.
MY DESIRE TO MAKE HER SUFFER WAS TOO GREAT.
NEXT TIME I'LL SLAY HER OUTRIGHT.

NEXT TIME...

EH? THAT DRAFT I FELT EARLIER...
...I FEEL IT AGAIN.

BUT... THE VENTS HAVE BEEN DESTROYED.

IT'S COMING FROM THAT CRACK.
I CAN SQUEEZE IN THERE!

STRIPS OF CLOTH, SOAKED IN OIL, WILL MAKE A TORCH.
RRIPP!

8.

IT'S A TIGHT FIT-- AND GETTING TIGHTER.
UGH!
THERE IS NO WAY I CAN TURN BACK NOW!

I'M PROBABLY BURROWING DEEPER INTO MY COFFIN.

A CHAMBER!
AND I HEAR RUNNING WATER!
AN UNDERGROUND STREAM.

UH--!

OW!
THUD!

9.

THE STREAM IS NOT AS FULL AT THIS TIME OF YEAR...
...BUT IT COULD LEAD ME OUT OF HERE.

MY TORCH WON'T LAST MUCH LONGER.

SOME-TIME LATER...
THE STREAM DISAPPEARS UNDER THAT ROCK WALL!
WHO KNOWS HOW LONG IT RUNS UNDER THERE BEFORE IT COMES OUT...

WELL... I HAVE NO OTHER OPTION.

SPLASH!

SO--
SO
COLD...!

THE CURRENT IS DRAGGING ME ALONG.

AN AIR POCKET!

GASP! GASP! GASP!

11.

UH--!

SPLASH!

HAUK!

GASP! GASP!
12

¡COUGH!¡COUGH!
¡CHOKE!

PLOP!

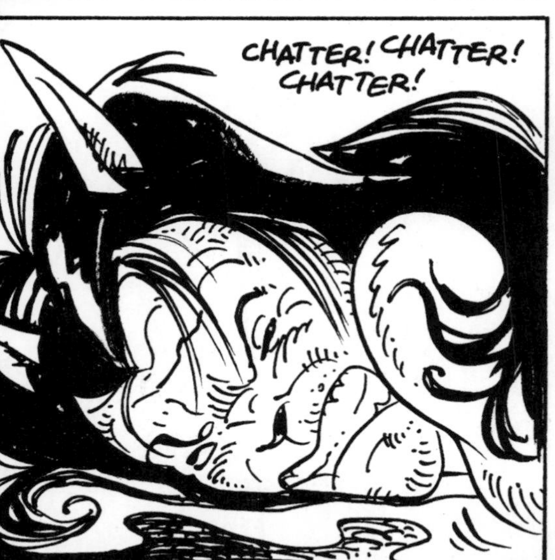
CHATTER! CHATTER! CHATTER!

EEP?
EEP?
EEP?
EEP?
13

EEP!
EEP!
EEP!
EEP!
EEP!
EEP!
EEP!
EEP!
EEP!
NGGH!
GRR!
HISS!
AHHHHH!
GRR!
HISS!
EEG!
14

GRR!
HISS!
GET AWAY FROM ME!
I AM NORIKO, THE BLOOD PRINCESS! I AM NOT MEAT FOR THE LIKES OF YOU SCAVENGERS!
GRR!
EEE!
15

FLOO--!
EEG!

GRRR!

EEE!
¡CHOMP!

THAT'S RIGHT--KEEP YOUR DISTANCE, YOU CARCASS-EATING VERMIN!
16

FILTHY BEASTS.

AND THEY TASTE TERRIBLE.

BUT IF THOSE *TOKAGE* ARE HERE, THERE MUST BE A WAY OUT!

WHERE IS IT?
WHERE IS THE WAY OUT OF THIS PIT?!
EEP!
EEK!
WHIMPER!

A--A *LIGHT?!*

UH...
UH...
UH...
UH...
UH...
UH...
EEP!

I CAN SMELL IT-- *FRESH AIR!*
IT SMELLS SO GOOD!
17

IT'S NIGHT.
THE STARS LED ME OUT.
I'M OUT...
...AND ALIVE.

I'M OUT, TOMOE! I'M ALIVE! YOU COULDN'T KILL ME!

DID YOU HEAR ME, DEAR SISTER?!
I'M--
--NOT--
--DEAD!

BUT YOU SOON WILL BE!

AHHH!

ARE YOU ALL RIGHT, TOMOE? I HEARD YOU CRY OUT!
JUST A DREAM... A BAD DREAM.
ABOUT NORIKO?
SHE CLAWED HER WAY OUT OF THE MINE-- EVEN THROUGH SOME KILLER *TOKAGE*!

SHE'S DEAD, TOMOE. IF THE EXPLOSION DID NOT KILL HER, THE CAVE-IN DID.
IT-- IT WAS SO REAL!

SHE TORMENTED YOU FOR A WEEK. IT'S NO WONDER SHE INVADES YOUR DREAMS.
19

SHE'S IN ENMA'S HELL. YOU'RE BEYOND HER REACH NOW.
YOU KNOW THE SAYING-- "YOUR ENEMY IS NOT DEAD UNTIL YOU SEE THE CORPSE."
IT WILL TAKE A MONTH TO UNCOVER THE MINE. EVEN THEN, HER BODY MIGHT NEVER BE FOUND.
REST ASSURED--IT WAS A DREAM AND NOTHING MORE.
USAGI...?
YES?
WOULD-- WOULD YOU STAY WITH ME FOR A WHILE?
20

LORD SANADA SENT WORD THAT NORIKO WAS DISCHARGED FROM HIS SERVICE MONTHS AGO.
HE DENIES MINING IN OUR LANDS AND ASSUMES NO RESPONSIBILITY FOR HER ACTIONS.

YOU DON'T BELIEVE HIM, DO YOU, *TONO**?
AS YOU YOURSELF TESTIFIED, NORIKO'S MEN WERE NOT WEARING CLAN CRESTS. WE CANNOT PROVE AN AFFILIATION TO LORD SANADA.
*LORD.

BUT WHO ELSE WOULD PROFIT FROM SUCH AN OPERATION?
YOU ACT OUT OF EMOTION, LADY TOMOE. I AM SURE LORD NORIYUKI WILL AGREE WITH ME THAT THIS MATTER IS CLOSED.

I AM AFRAID THAT LORD HORIKAWA IS RIGHT. WE CANNOT ACCUSE WITHOUT PROOF.
21

NOW WE MUST DEAL WITH THE MATTER OF A TRAITOR WITHIN OUR CLAN.

GULP!

MOTOKAZU, COME FORWARD.
YES, TONO.

YOU, A PAGE, HAVE BEEN CHARGED WITH DESERTION, MOTOKAZU.
DO YOU HAVE A STATEMENT IN YOUR DEFENSE?

NO, LORD NORIYUKI. I INTENTIONALLY LEFT MY POST AND WENT OFF ON MY OWN. I WILL ACCEPT WHATEVER PUNISHMENT YOU DEEM FIT.

WITH ALL RESPECT, TONO, HE CAME TO OUR RESCUE. IF NOT FOR MOTOKAZU, NEITHER USAGI NOR I WOULD NOW BE ALIVE.

NOT TO MENTION THAT BECAUSE OF YOUNG MOTOKAZU, THE GEISHU CLAN NOW KNOWS OF THE GOLD IN THE MOTHER OF MOUNTAINS.

REGARDLESS, HE WAS AWARE THAT HIS ACTIONS WERE WRONG WHEN HE ACTED, TONO.
22

I CANNOT FORGIVE YOUR ACTIONS, MOTOKAZU. SEIBO-*SENSEI*, YOU WILL STRIKE HIS NAME OFF THE ROSTER OF PAGES.

BUT I CANNOT OVERLOOK THAT WHAT YOU DID WAS FOR THE GOOD OF THE CLAN. SEIBO-*SENSEI*, YOU WILL ADD MOTOKAZU'S NAME TO THE LIST OF GEISHU *SAMURAI*.

SAMURAI?!

DO YOU AGREE WITH MY DECISION, SEIBO-*SENSEI*?
I DO INDEED, *TONO*!

TOMOE?
A WISE JUDGMENT, MY LORD!

LORD HORIKAWA?
I CANNOT FAULT YOUR VERDICT, LORD NORIYUKI.

TH-THANK YOU, *TONO*. I WILL DO MY BEST TO UPHOLD THE HONOR OF THE GEISHU CLAN.
WITH THE HELP OF MY FELLOW *SAMURAI*, OF COURSE.
23

HOW ARE YOUR WOUNDS HEALING, USAGI?
THEY'RE COMING ALONG NICELY. MY JOINTS ARE A BIT STIFF, THOUGH.

ARE YOU SURE YOU'RE UP FOR THIS?
ARE YOU TRYING TO BACK OUT?

HA HA HA! I'M READY WHEN YOU ARE!

COME ON, THEN.

HIIIIYAHH!!!

THE END

TOMOE'S STORY

THE PROCESS BY WHICH reality becomes a legend is as shrouded in mystery as the origins of a legend itself. How does a war leader who shows some grit against the Romans become King Arthur in chain mail, sitting around a round table with a fairy-witch waiting for him in a lake? How does a boy from Tupelo, Mississippi, named Elvis become a spiritual icon on a black-velvet painting?

Stan Sakai's work in *Usagi Yojimbo* is infused with legends. The past comes back to haunt the characters, in both corporeal and fantastic forms. Kitsune uses her past relationship with Usagi to annoy Tomoe and distract her from Kitsune's thieving ways. The sinister painter Goyemon uses the legend of Minamoto no Yorimitsu to enact a plot against Lord Noriyuki. In "Fox Fire" another legendary figure comes to life to make things difficult for our heroes.

Stan's reverence for research is somewhat legendary. While the stories he tells unfold with perfect clarity and even simplicity, an unseen wealth of background and historical knowledge gives every tale a solid grounding and structure that tie the overarching story together.

The lady samurai Tomoe, whose origins and character we learn in this volume, is an example of both legend and research. For a series that features anthropomorphic rabbits and foxes as main characters, there's still a reality to *Usagi* that makes certain elements more "normal" than others. Giant snakes and demon foxes we can accept—but what about a female samurai who is a trusted adviser and bodyguard? Surely that is an invention—except that Stan's noble feline warrior is based on Tomoe Gozen, a female samurai of the twelfth century who fought in the Battle of Awazu and decapitated at least one foe.

Of the fate of the historical Tomoe Gozen, many tales are told. Some say she survived the battle, others that she became a nun, others that she was taken in marriage. As with most "real legends," the outcome may depend on the storyteller's view of what constitutes a happy ending.

The stories in this volume bring together history, adventure, mystery, and good old-fashioned derring-do. But there is a bit more, as well. *"Chanoyu"*—or "Tea Ceremony"—is not only a meticulous depiction of the complex ceremony, but wordlessly shows repressed emotions throughout the ritual, a testament to Stan's cartooning skills. But the story would not be so moving if he hadn't done such a marvelous job of laying the foundations of the characters over the years.

In the business of comics publishing circa 2007, the ongoing comic book series has become something of an awkward concession to a previous business model. To my mind, only a handful of ongoing comics live up to the potential of the serial form, and *Usagi* stands foremost among them. Without this ongoing serial format, Stan wouldn't have had the time and momentum to create a great story like *"Chanoyu."* With over twenty years of publishing and over twenty collections, there is much to savor in the recurring themes and variations, the pleasure of seeing old characters reunited, and the sorrow at seeing them part . . . for months or even years. Such a rich tapestry is only possible when executed with great storytelling and flawless cartooning skills. By now, Stan Sakai is becoming a bit of a legend himself.

HEIDI MACDONALD
NEW YORK, NY
MARCH 2008

TOMOE'S STORY
1.

EEP?

HIYAAAAAAAAAA

KYAH!
HAHH!

KLAK!
KLAK!
KLAK!
KLAK!

HAH!
HYAH!

3

FWTT!
HYAHH!
HA! DO YOU CONCEDE?
YES...
...DO YOU?
HA HA HA HA HA HA HA HA HA

HA HA, TOMOE. THAT WAS A GOOD MATCH.
YES. TOO BAD IT WAS A TIE, USAGI.
YOUR STYLE IS SO... **UNORTHODOX.**

YES. KATSUICHI-*SENSEI* REBELLED AGAINST THE EIGHT TRADITIONAL FORMS TO DEVELOP HIS OWN STYLE OF SWORDSMANSHIP.
I AM ONE OF JUST THREE TO WHOM HE TAUGHT THIS NEW STYLE... AND I AM FAR FROM THE BEST.

YOUR **FALLING-RAIN STYLE** IS FORMIDABLE, TOMOE. I CAN SEE WHY YOUR SKILL MAKES YOU ONE OF LORD NORIYUKI'S MOST VALUED RETAINERS.

MY FAMILY HAS BEEN LOYAL TO THE GEISHU LORDS FOR GENERATIONS, USAGI, BUT HOW I BECAME LORD NORIYUKI'S PERSONAL RETAINER IS A VERY LONG STORY.
WE HAVE TIME AS WE REST UP FOR ANOTHER MATCH.

"VERY WELL... IT WAS YEARS AGO WHEN MY FATHER, TATSUTARO, WAS MASTER OF THE FALLING-RAIN SCHOOL OF FENCING. IT WAS THE OFFICIAL SCHOOL OF THE GEISHU CLAN. NORIYUKI'S FATHER, LORD MATAICHI, WAS OUR *DAIMYO** AT THE TIME...
5.

*FEUDAL LORD

"I WAS YOUNG AND NAIVE, AND BELIEVED THAT I, NOT MY BROTHER TAJIMA, WOULD SUCCEED OUR FATHER AS HEAD OF THE SCHOOL."
I'LL PUT YOU IN YOUR PLACE, TOMOE!

YOU WILL HAVE TO MOVE FASTER THAN THAT, BROTHER!
SWITT!

KLAK!
OW!
HYAH!

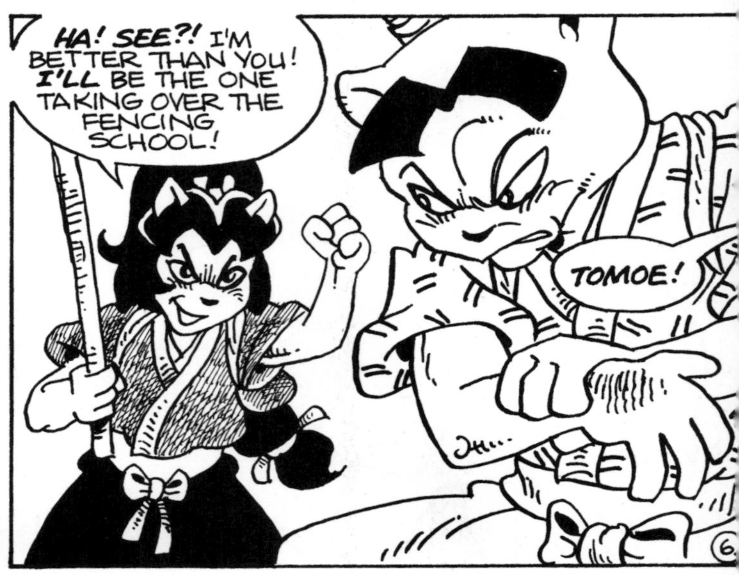
HA! SEE?! I'M BETTER THAN YOU! I'LL BE THE ONE TAKING OVER THE FENCING SCHOOL!
TOMOE!

IT IS UNSEEMLY TO GLOAT, TOMOE.
YES, FATHER.

TAJIMA IS SLATED TO FOLLOW ME AS INSTRUCTOR.
WHAT?
HEH, HEH, HEH.

THAT'S NOT FAIR! I'VE PROVEN I'M THE BETTER SWORDSMAN!
I DEMAND A REMATCH!

HUSH! IT DOES NOT MATTER WHO IS BETTER WITH THE SWORD.
TOMOE CAN NEVER HEAD OUR SCHOOL.

W-WHAT?
BUT... WHY?

YOU WILL BE A LADY-IN-WAITING IN OUR LORD'S COURT. IT WILL DO US GOOD TO HAVE YOU CLOSE TO LORD MATAICHI. IT IS YOUR DUTY TO YOUR FAMILY.

Y-YES, SIR.

SNIFF!

I WOULD LIKE TO BE ALONE, TAJIMA.
YES, FATHER.
7.

"YOU CANNOT IMAGINE HOW MY FATHER'S WORDS STUNG MY HEART.

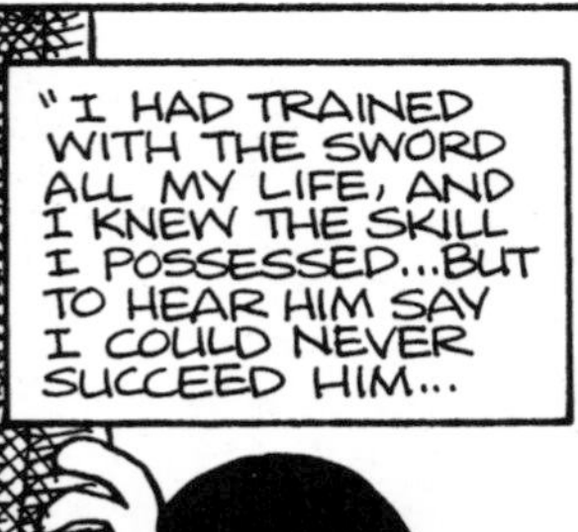

"I HAD TRAINED WITH THE SWORD ALL MY LIFE, AND I KNEW THE SKILL I POSSESSED...BUT TO HEAR HIM SAY I COULD NEVER SUCCEED HIM...

"THEN IT DAWNED ON ME **WHY!**"

YOU KNOW THE TRADITIONAL ROLE OF WOMEN IN OUR SOCIETY, TOMOE.
OUR SCHOOL WOULD BE A LAUGHING-STOCK IF A **FEMALE** WERE TO BECOME FENCING MASTER.

TAJIMA WILL MAKE A FINE TEACHER... BUT **YOUR** SKILLS ARE EXCEPTIONAL, DAUGHTER.
IT IS **MY** FAULT THAT YOU FEEL SUCH FRUSTRATION.

I SHOULD NEVER HAVE TAUGHT YOU YOUR SWORDSMANSHIP, BUT IT FILLED ME WITH PRIDE TO SEE HOW QUICKLY YOU ADVANCED.
BUT NOW I AM AFRAID IT WILL SOON BE TIME TO PUT YOUR BLADE BEHIND YOU.
FORGIVE ME.
8.

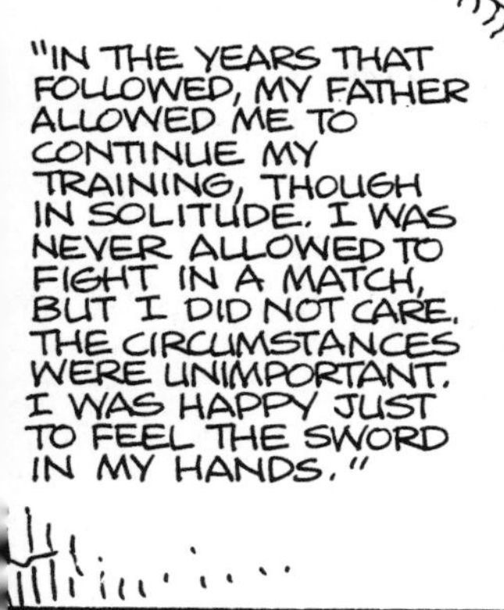

*LORD **MILITARY DICTATOR

THANK YOU FOR ACCEPTING MY DAUGHTER INTO YOUR SERVICE, LORD MATAICHI.
PLEASE TREAT HER WELL, AND WORK HER HARD.

YOUR DAUGHTER IS MOST WELCOME, TATSUTARO. I WILL FIND HER A FAVORABLE POSITION IN MY ENTOURAGE.
ER... SIR...
YES, COUNSELOR ODO?

PERHAPS SHE SHOULD BE ASSIGNED TO THE WOMEN'S WING INSTEAD.
I AM SURE YOUR WIFE, THE LADY ETSUKO, WOULD WELCOME THE DAUGHTER OF TATSUTARO.

A WONDERFUL IDEA, COUNSELOR ODO. TOMOE, YOU WILL BE A GREAT HELP IN RAISING OUR SON, NORIYUKI.
HEH, HEH, HEH.

ER... YES, SIR.
THANK YOU.
"SO DID COUNSELOR ODO FOIL MY FATHER'S PLAN TO KEEP ME CLOSE TO LORD MATAICHI.
10.

"LATER THAT DAY, I MET MISTRESS KAZUKO--THE HEAD OF THE LADIES' WING."
WELCOME, TOMOE. YOUR FAMILY IS HELD IN THE HIGHEST ESTEEM. I AM SURE YOU WILL WORK OUT WELL.
THANK YOU, LADY KAZUKO. I WILL DO MY BEST.

"BUT THINGS DID NOT GO WELL AT ALL."
HURRY. LADY ETSUKO IS WAITING FOR HER SUPPER.

WOOPS!
WHA--?!
TRIP!

TOMOE...
Y-YES, MA'AM?

GET OFF ME!
"I WAS NOT USED TO TRADITIONAL WOMEN'S ROLES.
11.

"I CONTINUED TO PRACTICE THE SWORD DAILY, UNTIL..."
TOMOE! WHAT ARE YOU DOING?! IT IS UNSEEMLY FOR A WOMAN TO WIELD A SWORD LIKE THAT!
GULP! LADY ETSUKO! LADY KAZUKO!
ER... I WAS TRAINED WITH THE SWORD, AND I--
NONSENSE! YOU WILL PUT YOUR BLADE AWAY IMMEDIATELY-- BEFORE YOU HURT SOMEONE!
REMEMBER THE SAYING: "THE SWORD IS THE SOUL OF THE SAMURAI, BUT A WOMAN'S SOUL LIES IN HER MIRROR."
BUT...
yes, ma'am.
PERHAPS THE DAUGHTER OF OUR SWORDMASTER COULD BE A GUARD IN THE LADIES' WING.
WELL...
AS YOU WISH, LADY ETSUKO.
"SO AT LEAST I CARRIED A SPEAR.
12.

"ONE NIGHT..."

COUNSELOR ODO! IS THERE ANYTHING WRONG?
I'M JUST CHECKING ON THE SECRET POSTERN, GUARD. IS EVERYTHING OKAY?

YES, SIR! I-- URK!

CREEEK!

I-I AM COUNSELOR ODO!

WHERE IS THE GEISHU LORD?
HE IS IN HIS CHAMBERS. HIS WIFE AND SON ARE IN THE WOMEN'S WING.
LORD HIKIJI WILL REWARD YOUR LOYALTY!
13

INTRUDERS!
INTRUDERS!
YARR!
URK!
GHAK!
EGHAA!
THUNK!
URK!
14

!
INTRUDERS IN THE CASTLE! INTRUDERS IN THE CASTLE!
IT IS OUR DUTY TO PROTECT LADY ETSUKO AND THE YOUNG HEIR!

WHAT?
SHINOBI!

ARRGH!
GYAK!
URK!

YARK!

LADY ETSUKO!
YOUNG LORD!
15.

THIS WING IS SWARMING WITH SHINOBI! I JUST PRAY THEY HAVE NOT PENETRATED LADY ETSUKO'S PRIVATE CHAMBER!
ARR!
UHH!
GURK!
SLAM!
WHIMPER!

HYAHHH!
UMPH!
ARGH!
.....
TOMOE!

STAY BEHIND ME, MY LADY!
17.

WHTT!
WHTT!
WHTT!
WHTT!

TING!
TANG!
TING!
TANG!

HI!!!!!!!--

YAAAAAAAAAAAAAAHHHH
URK!
UHH--!
OOGH!
FLOO!

18.

HUFF! HUFF! HUFF!
T-- TOMOE...?
ARE YOU ALL RIGHT, MY LADY?

Y-YES, TOMOE.
YOU SAVED OUR LIVES... BUT YOU'RE HURT!

A FEW CUTS... BUT NOTHING SERIOUS.
LADY ETSUKO!

THANK THE GODS YOU'RE SAFE-- AS IS LORD MATAICHI!

TOMOE'S SKILL SAVED US! AS OF TODAY, SHE WILL LAY ASIDE HER REGULAR DUTIES.
I APPOINT HER PROTECTOR OF THE HEIR!
THAT IS UNPRECEDENTED, BUT IT SHALL BE AS YOU WISH.
19.

"...AND I HAVE BEEN WITH LORD NORIYUKI EVER SINCE."
AS YOU KNOW, LORD MATAICHI DIED YEARS AGO, AND NOW LORD NORIYUKI IS THE HEAD OF THE GEISHU CLAN.
MUNCH! MUNCH!
WHAT OF COUNSELOR ODO?
HIS CONSPIRACIES WERE EVENTUALLY UNCOVERED, AND HE WAS ORDERED TO PERFORM SEPPUKU*
AHH... THAT WAS DELICIOUS.
WELL... ARE YOU READY FOR A REMATCH?
SURE... AND I WON'T BE SO EASY ON YOU THIS TIME.
HA HA!
AAAAAAAAAAAA
EEP!
* RITUAL SUICIDE
THE END

CREAK! CREAK! CREAK! CREAK!
CREEEAK!
CREEAK! CREEAAK!
CREAAK!
HALT!
I AM A PAINTER. PLEASE LET ME PASS. I HAVE A GIFT FOR LORD NORIYUKI.
SHOW ME WHAT IT IS, AND I'LL CONSIDER IT.
OOH! IT'S MAGNIFICENT! LORD NORIYUKI WILL WANT TO SEE YOU IMMEDIATELY!
1.

I AM SETTING UP A SHOP IN YOUR CAPITAL, AND I AM HERE TO PAY MY RESPECTS TO THE GREAT GEISHU LORD AND TO PRESENT THESE GIFTS!
THE DOORS
2.

LORD NORIYUKI, THANK YOU FOR GRANTING ME AN AUDIENCE.
I AM **GOYEMON,** AN ARTIST NEWLY ARRIVED IN THIS PROVINCE.
VERY WELL, SHOW THEM TO ME.

IF I REMEMBER CORRECTLY, YORIMITSU HAD TAKEN ILL AND IT WAS DISCOVERED THAT HE WAS SLOWLY BEING POISONED BY A GOBLIN-SPIDER DISGUISED AS A SERVANT.

AH, YOU KNOW YOUR HISTORY, LORD NORIYUKI.
THE DOORS ARE BEAUTIFUL! THE DETAILING IS EXQUISITE!
I WILL USE THEM FOR MY OWN CHAMBERS!
YOU DO ME AN HONOR, MY LORD.
YOU MUST LET ME THANK YOU. I WILL GIVE YOU A ROBE OF SILK AND AN ESCORT BACK TO YOUR SHOP.
SUCH HONORS, MY LORD! THIS WILL GIVE MY HUMBLE SHOP GREAT PRESTIGE!
NONSENSE! I GIVE ONLY WHAT IS DUE! WE CAN NEVER HAVE TOO MANY TALENTED PEOPLE SUCH AS YOURSELF HERE IN OUR PROVINCE!
HEH HEH. I AM BUT A LOWLY ARTIST, GRACIOUS LORD.
THE DOORS ARE BEAUTIFUL, TOMOE, BUT GRUESOME. THEY LEAVE ME UNEASY.
I FEEL THE SAME WAY, USAGI, BUT WHAT HARM CAN COME OF THEM?
5

YAAAHH!

SHUUUUU
TONO*! WHAT IS IT?
*LORD
I--I...

JUST A DREAM, I GUESS... A NIGHTMARE!
YOU'VE GOT SCRATCHES ON YOUR NECK!
HUH?

SEARCH THE ROOM!
I-I MUST HAVE CLAWED MYSELF DURING THE NIGHTMARE.
IT LOOKS MORE LIKE SOMETHING BIT YOU!

THE CHAMBER IS *EMPTY,* SIR.
VERY WELL, BUT POST GUARDS OUTSIDE THE DOORS.
WILL YOU BE ALL RIGHT, TONO?
YES. IT WAS NOTHING... BUT I'M SO *TIRED.* I GUESS NIGHTMARES TEND TO DRAIN YOU.
DON'T WORRY. I'LL BE *FINE*.

WELL, IF YOU SAY SO--
GOOD NIGHT, LORD NORIYUKI.

I'LL LEAVE THE DOOR AJAR. REPORT TO ME IF ANYTHING *UNUSUAL* OCCURS.
YES, MA'AM.

I'M WORRIED, USAGI. LORD NORIYUKI HAS NEVER BEEN TROUBLED BY DREAMS BEFORE.
PERHAPS SOMETHING IS WEIGHING ON HIS MIND THAT WE DON'T KNOW ABOUT.

NO, I FEAR IT'S *MORE* THAN THAT.
7.

GOOD MORNING, MY LORD-- YOUR BREAKFAST HAS ARRIVED.
MY LORD, I --
MY LORD!
CRASH!
YEEEEEEEE!

SHUU
USAGI! WAKE UP!
EH, TOMOE. WHAT IS IT?
IT'S HIS LORDSHIP--

TONO!

DOCTOR! WHAT'S WRONG WITH THE LORD?!
LADY TOMOE... I'M GLAD YOU'RE HERE.

LORD NORIYUKI IS IN A COMA, BUT I CAN'T FIND A THING WRONG WITH HIM! I'VE NEVER SEEN ANYTHING LIKE THIS!
9

WHAT OF THE SCRATCHES?
WHAT SCRATCHES?
THEY'RE GONE!

GUARD, DID YOU NOTE ANYTHING STRANGE LAST NIGHT?
NO, SIR! ALL WAS QUIET AFTER THE LORD CRIED OUT FROM HIS NIGHTMARE.

THERE'S SOMETHING UNEARTHLY GOING ON HERE, TOMOE.
I AGREE, USAGI.

DOCTOR, WE'VE GOT TO MOVE THE LORD TO ANOTHER ROOM!
IMPOSSIBLE! IN THE CONDITION HE'S IN, TO MOVE HIM MAY BRING ON HIS DEATH!

THEN HE MUST BE GUARDED AT ALL TIMES. I'LL STAY BY HIS SIDE TODAY, AND YOU CAN WATCH HIM BY NIGHT.

THANK YOU, USAGI. YOU AREN'T A MEMBER OF THE GEISHU CLAN, SO WE'RE GRATEFUL FOR YOUR FRIENDSHIP!

RUB
RUB

STRETCH!

HMM... I NEVER REALLY GOT A CHANCE TO TAKE A CLOSE LOOK AT THESE DOORS. THEY LOOK SO REAL--ALMOST AS IF THEY COULD--

SHUUUUU
!
11.

HI, USAGI. I'M HERE TO RELIEVE YOU.
WHEW!
ER... COME ON IN.

WHINE! WHINE! BARK! BARK! BARK!
?

YIPE!

WHAT BROUGHT THAT ABOUT?
KORO SEEMS ABSOLUTELY TERRIFIED!

CALM DOWN, KORO-- THERE'S NOTHING TO BE AFRAID OF!
USAGI HAS BEEN HERE ALL DAY.
BARK! BARK! BARK!

GRR...

WHIMPER...

GRR...

HOURS LATER...
IT'S ABOUT MIDNIGHT-- THE SAME TIME THAT LORD NORIYUKI CRIED OUT LAST NIGHT.
?
KRK KRK KRK
GUARDS! GUARDS!
BARK! BARK!
13

WHAT'S THE COMMOTION?
IT'S LADY TOMOE, SIR!
AND THE-- UHH--DOORS WON'T OPEN!
BREAK THEM DOWN!

THOK! THOK!
THUD!
UHH... THEY WON'T BUDGE, SIR!

TOMOE! WE CAN'T GET IN! WHAT'S HAPPENING?!
BAM! BAM!
THUD! THUD!

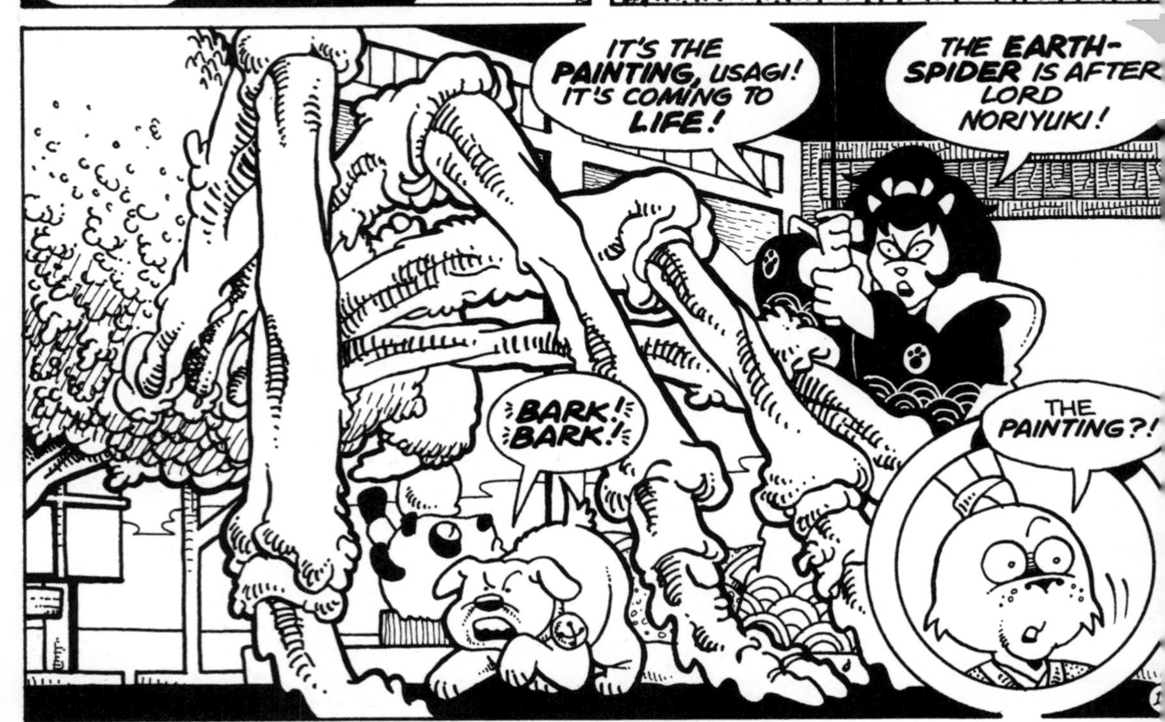
IT'S THE PAINTING, USAGI! IT'S COMING TO LIFE!
THE EARTH-SPIDER IS AFTER LORD NORIYUKI!
BARK! BARK!
THE PAINTING?!

WHERE IS THE ARTIST GOYEMON?
I KNOW WHERE HIS SHOP IS, SIR!
I WAS PART OF THE ESCORT SENT BY LORD NORIYUKI!
SHOW ME WHERE IT IS!
YES, SIR. IT'S NOT FAR.
FOUR OF YOU-- COME WITH ME!
THE REST--GET IN THAT ROOM!
AND HURRY! YOUR LORD'S LIFE IS AT STAKE!
LADY TOMOE! THERE'S NO WAY IN!
KEEP TRYING!
NORIYUKI! NORIYUKI! WAKE UP!
15.

SOON...

THERE IT IS, SIR!

SURROUND THE HOUSE IN CASE HE TRIES TO GET AWAY!
YES, SIR!

ARTIST!
SLAM!

SO...YOU'VE FOUND ME OUT, HAVE YOU, SAMURAI?
WELL, I HALF EXPECTED IT WHEN LORD NORIYUKI WAS NOT KILLED LAST NIGHT!
I SUSPECT THE DOORS WERE NOT COMPLETELY CLOSED...

...BUT HE IS NOT QUITE SO LUCKY TONIGHT!

I KNOW THAT INK SET*!
IT IS EVIL!

HEH, HEH, HEH. IT ONLY USES THE EVIL WITHIN ITS OWNER, SAMURAI.

WHAT DO YOU MEAN?
HOW DID YOU GET THAT INK SET?

HEH, HEH. I KILLED FOR IT!

RELEASE NORIYUKI FROM YOUR EVIL, GOYEMON!

I HAVE OTHER PAINTINGS, SAMURAI...
REMEMBER UWABAMI, THE GIANT SERPENT WHO COULD SWALLOW WHOLE A WARRIOR ON HORSEBACK?
17.

YAAAH!
CRASH
TOWNSPEOPLE-- EVACUATE TO SAFETY!
YAHHH!
SAMURAI-- ATTACK THE SERPENT!
WHAT?!
WE'RE THE CITY GUARDS!
THANK HEAVENS YOU'RE HERE!
HOW CAN WE SLAY SOMETHING LIKE THAT?

THE ARTIST IS BEHIND ALL THIS!
I'VE GOT TO STOP HIM BEFORE HE GETS AWAY AND CAUSES MORE HAVOC!
©

GOYEMON...

HEH, HEH. YOU'RE BACK, ARE YOU, SAMURAI? WELL, I HAVE ONE MORE PAINTING TO SHOW YOU!

A TENGU. THE MOUNTAIN GOBLIN WHOSE SKILL WITH THE SWORD IS UNSURPASSED!

19.

ELSEWHERE...
NORIYUKI! NORIYUKI!
WAN! WAN! WAN!
HIYAAA!
CHOP!
CHOP!
UHH!
THUD!
THWAK!

WAN! WAN! WAN!

SPLURP!
21.

HIIIIAAAAAAAAAAA

SKLOOSH

HA! NO ONE CAN DEFEAT A TENGU!
HIIIIIIIIYAAAAAAAAAAAAAAAAAAA
KLANG!
UH!
WUMP!
WHEEZE! WHEEZE! GASP!
23.

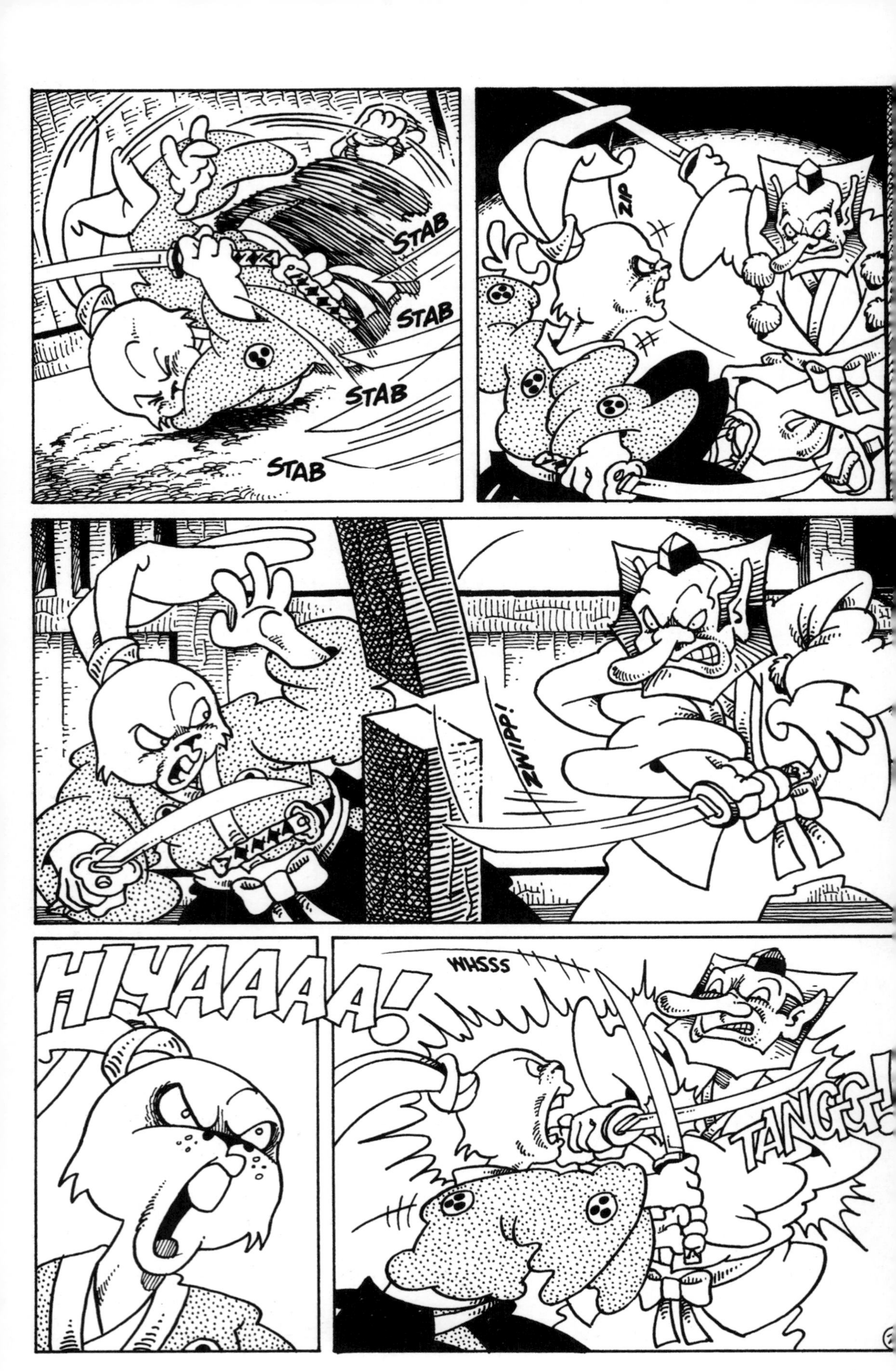
STAB
STAB
STAB
STAB
ZIP
ZWIPP!
HIYAAAA!
WHSSS
TANGG!

NOW YOU'VE GOT HIM! KILL HIM! KILL THE SAMURAI!
NNNNGGGG!
DIE!
YARG!
RYAA!
SHOONK!
25.

FYOOM!
?
WHAT'S HAPPENING?
THE SERPENT'S DISAPPEARING!!

THE STICKY WEBS ARE MELTING OFF!
LADY TOMOE!
HUH...? T-TOMOE... WHAT'S GOING ON...?
26

THE NEXT DAY...
...AND THE TENGU AND THE SERPENT VANISHED.
THANK YOU, USAGI.
I REMEMBER NOTHING OF THE PAST TWO DAYS.

WHAT OF THE PAINTINGS?

THEY FADED INTO NOTHINGNESS WITH THE DEATH OF THE DEMON ARTIST GOYEMON.
AND THE DOORS HAVE BEEN REMOVED AND BURNED.

A STRANGE ADVENTURE INDEED!
BUT THERE IS ONE THING THAT BOTHERS ME, LORD NORIYUKI.
WHAT'S THAT?

THE INK SET HAS NOT BEEN FOUND. WE WERE ALL PREOCCUPIED WITH THE DESTRUCTION CAUSED BY GOYEMON, AND IT MAY HAVE BEEN STOLEN.

DO YOU THINK THAT IS SOMETHING TO BE CONCERNED ABOUT?
YES, I DO. THE ARTIST SAID IT ONLY USES THE EVIL WITHIN ITS OWNER...
27.

"...I WONDER WHAT HE MEANT BY THAT."

FOX FIRE

YIP!
YIP!
YIP!
?

KITSUNE!*
IT LOOKS ABSOLUTELY TERRIFIED!
*FOX

HEY! WHERE ARE YOU GOING?!
!

GET OUT OF THERE, YOU STUPID--
OUCH! STOP SCRATCHING ME!
HEE HEE HEE!

EXCUSE US, SAMURAI! HAVE YOU SEEN A FOX RUN BY?
OUCH!
HA HA HA!

A FOX? ER... WHY?
OUCH!
HA HA HA!

WE'VE BEEN AFTER THAT VIXEN FOR QUITE A WHILE! FOX LIVER IS A POWERFUL MEDICINE. WE SHOULD BE ABLE TO GET A LOT FOR IT!

ER...WELL, IT RAN ON DOWN THE HILL.
OUCH!
GIGGLE GIGGLE SNORT!

HA HA! IT JUMPED IN YOUR CLOTHES!
HA HA, HA HA! THAT'S THE FUNNIEST THING--!
OUR THANKS, SAMURAI!

OFF YOU GO, GIRL!
I'VE NEVER LAUGHED SO MUCH!
OH, MY STOMACH HURTS!

DO YOU THINK I WAS WISE TO DECEIVE THOSE HUNTERS?
YOU COULDN'T VERY WELL JUST HAND THE FOX OVER TO THEM, COULD YOU?
NOT AFTER ALL THE ENTERTAINMENT IT GAVE ME!
3.

YOU KNOW THE LEGENDS SURROUNDING FOXES. THEY'RE GUARDIANS OF THE RICE CROPS AND MESSENGERS OF *INARI,* THE GOD OF HARVESTS--AND THEY'RE ALSO NOTORIOUS *TRICKSTERS!*

THEY SAY WHEN A FOX REACHES A HUNDRED YEARS, ITS SPIRIT CAN POSSESS A PERSON, CAUSING INSANITY. IT CAN ALSO SHAPE CHANGE AT WILL.

AT THE AGE OF *ONE THOUSAND,* IT TURNS GOLDEN, GROWS *NINE TAILS,* AND GAINS GREAT WISDOM!

WELL, THEN, THAT MUST HAVE BEEN A *YOUNG* FOX, BECAUSE IT HAD ONLY *ONE* TAIL! *HA HA!*
RATS! IT'S STARTING TO *RAIN!*
IT *RUINS* MY HAIR!

SOON...
SHAAAAAAAAAAAAA
4

HELLO IN THERE!
WE ARE TWO SAMURAI SEEKING SHELTER FROM THE RAIN!
BAM! BAM! BAM!
ENTER, SAMURAI, AND BE MY GUESTS.

!
THANK YOU!

I AM MIYAMOTO USAGI, AND THIS IS TOMOE, A RETAINER OF LORD NORIYUKI.
I AM KUZUNOHA. PLEASE SHARE MY MEAL, USAGI-SAN.
5.

IT'S DELICIOUS! YOU CERTAINLY ARE A GOOD COOK, KUZUNOHA.
ULP!
YOU'RE MUCH TOO KIND, USAGI-SAN. IT IS BUT POOR FARE.

IT CERTAINLY IS! THIS RICE TASTES LIKE MUD!

WHAT ARE YOU DOING?
GETTING MORE WOOD FOR THE FIRE. IT'S MUCH TOO CHILLY IN HERE.

"CHILLY"? IT'S PERFECTLY COZY IN HERE!
NOW EAT YOUR FOOD. IT WILL WARM YOUR BONES!

USAGI IS USUALLY NOT SO TERSE.
HE'S BEHAVING STRANGELY!

YES, PLEASE ENJOY YOUR MEAL, LADY TOMOE.
...

EAT IT WHILE IT'S STILL HOT.
6

OHHH, MY BACK! IT FEELS LIKE I SLEPT ON A BED OF ROCKS AND TWIGS!
:YAWN!: I'VE NEVER SLEPT SO WELL IN MY LIFE!
BUT, THEN, I ATE A WONDERFUL DINNER--UNLIKE YOU!

LET'S GATHER OUR STUFF TOGETHER AND GET AN EARLY START, USAGI!
UGH!
YOU GO ON AHEAD. I THINK I'LL STAY HERE A FEW DAYS.

STAY?
BUT WHY?!

WE OWE KUZUNOHA SOMETHING FOR HER HOSPITALITY. I'M SURE SHE HAS SOME WORK THAT NEEDS TO BE DONE AROUND HERE.

IF YOU WANT TO SHOW YOUR APPRECIATION, WHY NOT JUST LEAVE HER A FEW COINS? WE DON'T HAVE THE TIME TO--
TO GIVE HER MONEY WOULD BE AN INSULT! YOU DON'T HAVE TO STAY, BUT I FEEL AN OBLIGATION.
7.

WELL, I GUESS I CAN AFFORD TO STAY A WHILE TOO!
YOU CAN GO OR STAY. IT DOESN'T MAKE A DIFFERENCE TO ME.

GOOD MORNING, USAGI-SAN!
AH, KUZUNOHA!
I'M GOING TO FETCH SOME WATER. WOULD YOU LIKE TO JOIN ME?
OF COURSE!

WHAT IS GOING ON WITH THOSE TWO?
USAGI IS NOT ACTING LIKE HIMSELF THERE'S SOMETHING WEIRD ABOUT KUZUNOHA!
I'D BETTER FOLLOW THEM!

LATER...
THEY'RE AT THE RIVER, BUT THEY STILL HAVEN'T GOTTEN THE WATER.

WHA--!

!

REFLECTIONS AND SHADOWS SHOW THE TRUE NATURE OF A SUPERNATURAL CREATURE. KUZUNOHA IS A FOX!

SHE MUST HAVE USAGI UNDER A SPELL!
USAGI! USAGI!
SPLASH!
SPLASH!

WHERE ARE THEY?!

A FOX! IT LOOKS LIKE THE ONE USAGI RESCUED!

WAIT! COME BACK HERE!

WHAT HAVE YOU DONE WITH USAGI?!
9.

LATER...
GADS! WHAT AN IDIOT I AM! LOST IN THE WOODS-- WANDERING AROUND FOR HOURS!
VIXEN!
GET AWAY FROM HER, USAGI! SHE'S A FOX! YOU'RE UNDER HER ENCHANTMENT!
TOMOE?! WHAT ARE YOU TALKING ABOUT?
ARE YOU OUT OF YOUR MIND?
I'LL MAKE YOU REVEAL YOUR TRUE FORM!
TOMOE! SHEATHE YOUR SWORD!
USAGI-- SHE'S FRIGHTENING ME! MAKE HER GO AWAY!
MOVE ASIDE, USAGI! CAN'T YOU SEE HER FOR WHAT SHE IS?!
GET OUT, TOMOE! YOU ARE NO LONGER WELCOME HERE!
10

BUT, USAGI...
OUT! I'LL FIGHT TO PROTECT HER, TOMOE!

I MEAN IT!

I'LL LEAVE--BUT ONLY BECAUSE I KNOW YOU'RE NOT YOURSELF, USAGI!
DON'T DO ME ANY FAVORS.
JUST GET OUT!

SLAM!

OH, USAGI! I WAS SO SCARED!

THERE, THERE, KUZUNOHA, SHE'S GONE NOW.

YES, SHE'S GONE!
11.

...

IT'S STARTING TO RAIN AGAIN! RATS! THAT'S ALL I NEED NOW!

?

I'D BETTER FOLLOW THEM!
IT'S A GOOD THING I STAYED IN CASE USAGI NEEDED MY HELP!

USAGI!
USAGI!

WHERE'S KUZUNOHA? SHE COULDN'T HAVE JUST DISAPPEARED--OR COULD SHE?!

FOX FIRES! SHE WAS TAKING USAGI TO A GATHERING OF FOXES!

UHH--!
FLOOM!

KUZUNOHA...

YOU SHOULD HAVE LEFT WHEN YOU HAD THE CHANCE, SAMURAI!
ROWRR

FLOOO

HIIIYAAAA
13

AARRRGH!

SNARL!
SO--YOU CAN BE HURT!
I'LL RIP OUT YOUR LIVER!

!

GROOOOWL

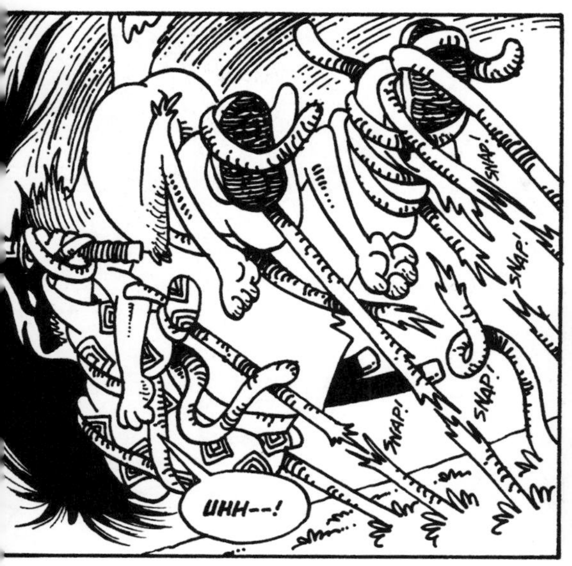
SNAP!
SNAP!
SNAP!
SNAP!
SNAP!
UHH--!

HEH! HEH! HEH! HEH!

YARG!

GNASH! GRRRR! GROWL!
CHOMP!

15.

USAGI!
HE'S STILL UNDER HER SPELL!

USAGI!
USAGI?!

SNAP OUT OF IT!
UHH!
SLAP!

...

TOMOE?! WHAT'S GOING ON?
USAGI! YOU'RE YOURSELF AGAIN!

WHAT DO YOU MEAN? I--
YELP!

SO, LITTLE SISTER, YOU WOULD TURN AGAINST YOUR OWN!
WHIMPER...
16

SO, TOMOE WAS RIGHT, KUZUNOHA.

USAGI!

MONSTER...

DON'T LET HER ESCAPE!
GRRR...

COME BACK HERE, MONSTER!
USAGI! NO!

WE CAN'T CATCH UP TO HER, BUT YOU'VE SEEN THROUGH HER ENCHANTMENT! YOU'RE BEYOND HER POWER NOW!
WHAT ABOUT THE OTHER FOX?

IT'S THE ONE I RESCUED FROM THE HUNTERS!
POOR THING HAS BEEN MAULED!
I THOUGHT SHE WAS THE ONE WHO HAD BEWITCHED YOU!
17.

ELSEWHERE...
I'LL GET MY REVENGE!

THOSE FOOLS!

I'LL GET MY FELLOWS, AND WE'LL RETURN TO SLAY THEM-- SLOWLY!
AND LEAVE THEIR CARCASSES FOR THE CROWS!

AARRRRRRR
THUK!

SPLAT!

HA! DID YOU SEE THAT? I GOT HER!
WE SHOULD GET A GOOD PRICE FOR THAT ONE!
18.

MEANWHILE...
WE'VE GOT TO GET HER OUT OF THE RAIN!
KUZUNOHA'S HUT! WE'LL TAKE HER THERE! AT LEAST IT'S DRY AND WARM!

IS THAT THE HUT? IT'S LITTLE MORE THAN A BROKEN DOWN SHACK!
TO HAVE MAINTAINED AN ILLUSION OF A PEASANT'S CHARMING HOME--KUZUNOHA'S POWERS ARE FORMIDABLE INDEED!

"BUT WE HAD NO CHOICE AND WE STAYED THERE FOR A FEW DAYS, TENDING TO OUR RESCUER UNTIL SHE WAS WELL ENOUGH TO TRAVEL...

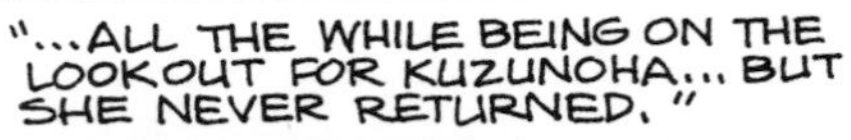
"...ALL THE WHILE BEING ON THE LOOKOUT FOR KUZUNOHA... BUT SHE NEVER RETURNED."

19.

AN AMAZING ADVENTURE!
WHY DO YOU THINK THAT FOX CAME TO YOUR AID?
WHO CAN FATHOM THE MIND OF SUCH A CREATURE, LORD NORIYUKI?
PERHAPS SHE WAS GRATEFUL TO US FOR HAVING SAVED HER LIFE.

HOW IS SHE?
HER INJURIES WERE NOT AS BAD AS WE FIRST HAD THOUGHT.
SHE HAS FULLY RECOVERED.

AND WHERE'S USAGI NOW?

"HE SAID HE HAD TO SAY GOOD-BYE TO A FRIEND."

END

THUK!
HO-HUM...

YAWN!

WHAT A WASTE OF TIME THIS IS.

AHEM.
ULP!
1

UH...UH... MASAMUNE-SAN!
YOU ARE A DISGRACE AS A GUARD.
YOU MUST OVERCOME YOUR WEARINESS AND STAY ALERT!
BUT WE ARE IN THE GEISHU CASTLE, ON A PEACEFUL MISSION. SURELY THERE IS NO DANGER HERE.
YOU PROTECT THE KOJIMA TRADE DELEGATION. YOU MUST REMAIN VIGILANT, ESPECIALLY WHEN WE ARE ON ANOTHER CLAN'S SOIL.
YES, SIR! I UNDERSTAND! THANK YOU, SIR!

YOU WILL BE PUT ON REPORT. NEXT TIME I WILL NOT BE SO LENIENT.
YES, SIR! THANK YOU, SIR!

HA! IT'S SO SIMPLE TO FOOL AN IDIOT LIKE THAT MASAMUNE. BESIDES, I DON'T SEE WHAT THE BIG DEAL IS.
PLOK!

WE'RE IN THE MIDDLE OF FRIENDLY TERRITORY. THERE IS NO CHANCE OF A PROBLEM HERE.
SNAP!
EH--?

MASAMUNE IS COMING BACK.
I'D BETTER SHOW HIM I'M--HEH HEH--EVER VIGILANT.

HALT! WHO'S THERE?

!

SLASH!
3

The Ghost in the WELL
Part 1

SUCH A PLEASANT EVENING.

I REALLY DO ENJOY BEING IN THE GEISHU PROVINCE.

I GUESS NEXT TO MY OWN VILLAGE, I FEEL MOST AT HOME HERE.

IT'S SUCH A NICE, PEACEFUL NIGHT, PERFECT FOR A STROLL.

TOO BAD TOMOE HAS BEEN OCCUPIED WITH THOSE TRADE NEGOTIATIONS. I WOULD HAVE ENJOYED HER COMPANY TONIGHT.
5.

IT LOOKS LIKE I'M NOT THE ONLY ONE ENJOYING THE PEACE AND QUIET TONIGHT.
WHOEVER HE IS, HE'S SURE IN A HURRY.
WHAT'S GOING ON?
WHERE DID HE GO?
OOO
SLASH!
SLASH!
6.

SHAK!
SPLASH!

WHAT WAS THAT?

THERE'S NO ONE THERE!

I WISH I HAD MY SWORDS.

WHOEVER IT WAS, HE WENT THIS WAY.
HE'S NOT HIDING IN THE TREES OR BUSHES.
7.

HE COULD NOT HAVE CLIMBED UP THE WALL SO QUICKLY.
SO WHERE IS HE?

MAYBE HE'S HIDING IN THE WELL.

STRANGE. IT'S SEALED SHUT.

THE BOARDS ARE NAILED FROM THE OUTSIDE, SO HE COULD NOT HAVE GONE IN HERE.

WHERE COULD HE HAVE DISAPPEARED TO?
8.

WHO--?

TOMOE.
I WAS LOOKING FOR YOU.
WHY ARE YOU SO WET? DID YOU FALL IN THE POND?

I SAW SOMEONE RUNNING THROUGH THE GARDEN. I FOLLOWED, BUT I LOST HIM AT THIS SEALED WELL.
O-OKIKU'S WELL.

WHAT'S THE MATTER? WHO IS OKIKU?
I'LL TELL YOU AS WE GET YOU SOME DRY CLOTHING.

TEN YEARS AGO, OKIKU WAS A MAID WHO FELL IN LOVE WITH A MID-LEVEL RETAINER NAMED AOYAMA.

THEY HAD A RELATIONSHIP, BUT HE DID NOT REALLY RETURN HER AFFECTION.

OKIKU INSISTED ON SEEING HIM ONE LAST TIME. SHE BEGGED AOYAMA TO MEET HER IN THIS GARDEN... AT THE WELL.
9.

WHEN AOYAMA ARRIVED, OKIKU THREW HERSELF INTO THE WELL. HE TRIED TO SAVE HER, BUT IT WAS FUTILE.

OKIKU'S BODY WAS NEVER RECOVERED.

SOON AFTER, PEOPLE BEGAN TO REPORT GHOSTLY SIGHTINGS OF SOMEONE CRYING AT THE WELL.

THE WELL WAS DEEMED CURSED-- AND SEALED SHUT.

WHAT OF AOYAMA?
THE REPORTS OF THE APPARITION DROVE HIM INSANE. THE MARRIAGE WAS CALLED OFF, AND HE HUNG HIMSELF.

AN UNFORTUNATE END FOR A SAMURAI.
YES.
10

EXCEPT FOR HER OBSESSION WITH AOYAMA, OKIKU WAS A DEVOTED GEISHU VASSAL.
POOR OKIKU.
SOMETHING KEEPS HER SPIRIT HERE, BUT I HAVE NEVER HEARD OF IT LEAVING THE WELL.
HAVE YOU EVER SEEN THE GHOST?
ONCE, A FEW YEARS AGO. I TELL MYSELF THAT I IMAGINED IT, BUT I KNOW IT WAS HER.
WAS IT A GHOST YOU FOLLOWED?
I DON'T KNOW.
IT WAS ONLY A SHADOW I SAW.
BUT WHY WOULD OKIKU'S SPIRIT REMAIN TO HAUNT THE GEISHU CASTLE?
THAT IS A MYSTERY.
AH! I LOVE WEARING CLEAN CLOTHES.
AS A WANDERER, I SOMETIMES GO FOR WEEKS WITHOUT CHANGING.
YEAH. I NOTICED THAT WHEN I SAW YOU A FEW WEEKS AGO. HA HA!
HA HA!
ALARM! ALARM!
11.

THAT CAME FROM THE COMPOUND USED BY THE KOJIMA DELEGATES!

I AM TOMOE AME! VASSAL OF THE GEISHU CLAN!
WHAT IS THE CAUSE FOR ALARM?
HALT! NO GEISHU IS ALLOWED WITHIN THESE WALLS UNLESS MASAMUNE-SAN AUTHORIZES IT!

THEN SUMMON HIM AT ONCE!
CERTAINLY, LADY TOMOE!
MASAMUNE-SAN!

WHAT IS THE PROBLEM, MASAMUNE-SAN?
ALLOW LADY TOMOE ENTRANCE.
YES, SIR.

BUT WHO ARE YOU?

I AM MIYAMOTO USAGI.
YOU ARE NOT OF THE GEISHU CLAN.
12

USAGI IS A FRIEND OF THE GEISHU CLAN AND HAS HELPED US MANY TIMES.
I WOULD WELCOME HIS INSIGHT IN THIS AFFAIR--
--WHATEVER THIS IS.
IF LADY TOMOE VOUCHES FOR YOU, YOU MAY ENTER AS WELL.
THANK YOU.

I AM MASAMUNE SABURO, A *HATAMOTO** OF THE KOJIMA CLAN.
*AN UPPER-ECHELON SAMURAI
ONE OF OUR GUARDS HAS BEEN MURDERED. I DISCOVERED THE BODY DURING MY ROUNDS.
13

LOOK AT HIS NECK!
RIPPED OPEN, AS IF BY GIANT CLAWS.
WHAT KIND OF WEAPON COULD HAVE MADE THESE MARKS?
BESIDES MY OWN FOOTPRINTS AND THOSE OF THIS GUARD'S, THERE WERE NO TRACKS IN THE GRASS. THE ASSASSIN MUST HAVE KILLED FROM A DISTANCE.
I THINK I SAW THE MURDERER EARLIER TONIGHT.
OH?
WHAT DID HE LOOK LIKE?
ER... I DON'T KNOW.
WHERE DID HE GO?
I DON'T KNOW.
IS THIS THE KIND OF HELP YOU HAVE RENDERED THE GEISHU CLAN IN THE PAST?
I AM NOT IMPRESSED.
14

WHAT IS GOING ON HERE? WHY IS THERE SUCH A COMMOTION IN THE MIDDLE OF THE NIGHT?
I APOLOGIZE, DELEGATE DAIDA, BUT ONE OF OUR GUARDS HAS BEEN KILLED.

A MURDER?! WHAT KIND OF SECURITY DO WE HAVE WHEN MY GUARDS CAN BE KILLED?

THE GEISHU CLAN WILL TAKE FULL RESPONSIBILITY FOR THE DEATH, DAIDA-SAMA!

WHY, I MIGHT BE WANTONLY MURDERED IN MY SLEEP! DOUBLE THE GUARDS AROUND MY ROOM IMMEDIATELY!

THE MURDERER... DID YOU CATCH THE MURDERER?!
NO.

BUT USAGI HERE DID SEE SOMETHING SUSPICIOUS.
15.

WH-WHAT DID YOU SEE?
JUST A SHORT WHILE AGO, I SAW A FIGURE RUN THROUGH THE GARDEN.

WHERE DID HE GO?
UH... IT SEEMS HE DISAPPEARED INTO A HAUNTED WELL.
I THINK.

HAU-HAU-HAUNTED?! YOU MEAN A GHOST?!

I-I'LL BE IN MY QUARTERS! TRIPLE MY GUARDS!
YES, DAIDA-SAMA!

ARE YOU MOCKING US? I HAVE NO TIME FOR YOUR JOKES, USAGI-SAN.
UH...
16

WE APOLOGIZE FOR THE DEATH OF YOUR VASSAL, LORD DAIDA.

THANK YOU, LORD NORIYUKI. HE WAS BUT A LOWER LEVEL GUARD--AN INCOMPETENT ONE, AT THAT.

BUT HE WAS KILLED WITHIN THE GEISHU CASTLE, SO WE MUST BEAR RESPONSIBILITY FOR YOUR LOSS.

THANK YOU, LORD NORIYUKI.
WE WILL CONTINUE TO INVESTIGATE THE DEATH. I ASSURE YOU THE CULPRIT WILL BE FOUND.

I HOPE THIS INCIDENT WILL NOT ADVERSELY AFFECT OUR TRADE NEGOTIATIONS, LORD DAIDA.

AN AGREEMENT WILL BENEFIT THE KOJIMA AS WELL AS THE GEISHU CLANS. I WOULD RESPECTFULLY REQUEST, HOWEVER, THAT TODAY'S NEGOTIATIONS CONCLUDE BEFORE NIGHTFALL.
17.

NOW, LET US CONTINUE WITH OUR NEGOTIATIONS, LORD NORIYUKI.
EH?
YES, THAT CLAUSE IS ACCEPTABLE, NORIYUKI-SAMA.
WHY WAS SABURO STARING AT ME SO INTENTLY?
ENOUGH OF THIS. I SHOULD BE PAYING ATTENTION TO THE TRADE TALKS.
18

I KNOW THERE WAS SOMEONE IN THE GARDEN LAST NIGHT.
THE GEISHU INVESTIGATORS MUST HAVE FINISHED THEIR SEARCH OF THE AREA BY NOW.

NOW I'LL SEE WHAT I CAN FIND.

SUCH POWER. WHAT COULD HAVE DONE THIS TO A TREE?

I'M SURE THERE WAS NO ONE NEARBY TO DO THIS.

WHAT COULD HAVE DESTROYED A TREE-- FROM A DISTANCE?

WHATEVER IT WAS, IT WAS POWERFUL ENOUGH TO CUT INTO GRANITE.

THE WEAPON THAT MADE THESE GOUGES COULD HAVE TORN OUT THE GUARD'S THROAT.
19.

MAYBE IT WAS OKIKU'S GHOST.
BUT WHY WOULD SHE WANT TO KILL THE KOJIMA GUARD -- TO STOP THE TRADE NEGOTIATIONS? THE TREATY WOULD BRING TWO CLANS CLOSER -- AND BENEFIT THE GEISHU PROVINCE.
I WISH INSPECTOR ISHIDA WERE HERE.
HE COULD SOLVE THIS MYSTERY IN NO TIME.
I THOUGHT I WOULD FIND YOU HERE.
AH, TOMOE. HOW ARE THE NEGOTIATIONS GOING?
VERY WELL. WE SHOULD HAVE A FAIR AGREEMENT IN A WEEK--PROVIDING THERE ARE NO MORE GHOSTLY MURDERS.
20

ARE YOU CLOSER TO FINDING THE KILLER?
NO. BUT TO ENSURE THERE ARE NO MORE DEATHS, WE TRIPLED THE GUARDS.

SINCE THE MURDER OCCURRED IN THE KOJIMA COMPOUND, SABURO IS CLOSELY INVOLVED IN THE INVESTIGATION.

I BELIEVE SABURO THINKS I'M CRAZY... OR AT LEAST A TROUBLEMAKER. I DON'T TRUST HIM. THERE'S MORE TO HIM THAN IT SEEMS.

I KNOW WHAT YOU MEAN. I DON'T THINK HE IS HERE JUST AS A MEMBER OF THE KOJIMA TRADE DELEGATION.
TOMOE!

LORD HORIKAWA!
I'M SURPRISED AT YOU! YOU KNOW IT IS INAPPROPRIATE TO DISCUSS OUR CLAN AFFAIRS WITH AN OUTSIDER!
21.

USAGI IS NOT AN OUTSIDER!
HE IS NOT OF THE GEISHU CLAN.

DOES HE WEAR THE GEISHU *MON**?
*CLAN CREST

YOU KNOW HE DOESN'T.

THEN HE IS AN OUTSIDER. A MENDICANT *RONIN*.

DID YOU COME HERE JUST TO INSULT MY FRIEND?
NOT AT ALL, LADY TOMOE. LORD NORIYUKI HAS SUMMONED YOU.
HE AWAITS YOU IN HIS STUDY.
22

I APOLOGIZE FOR HAVING TO LEAVE YOU SO ABRUPTLY, USAGI.

HARUMPH! GOOD EVENING...
...RONIN.

I'M GETTING THE FEELING I'M NOT AS WELCOME HERE AS I FIRST THOUGHT.
23

MAYBE WE SHOULD POSTPONE THE NEGOTIATIONS, AFTER ALL. ARE YOU SURE IT IS SAFE FOR ME HERE?
YES, DELEGATE DAIDA. THE GUARDS HAVE BEEN TRIPLED.
NOT EVEN A GHOST CAN GET THROUGH OUR SECURITY.

the Ghost in the Well part 2
THE TRADE NEGOTIATIONS ARE GOING WELL.
LORD NORIYUKI MAY BE YOUNG, BUT HE HAS INSIGHT AND A VISION FOR THE FUTURE OF THE GEISHU CLAN.
1.

IT WILL NOT BE LONG BEFORE THE KOJIMA AND GEISHU CLANS WORK OUT A FAIR AGREEMENT.
AND OUR LORD WILL THANK ME FOR IT.

GURK!
SLASH!
LOOK OUT!
WHAT?

SKRAK!

YAHH!

ALARM! ALARM!

SKRATK!

ASSASSINS ARE ABOUT! PROTECT LORD DAIDA!
SHACT!

ARGH!
GYAHH!

WHAT'S ATTACKING US?!
GYAHH!
HURRY, LORD DAIDA--GET INSIDE!
HUFF! HUFF! GASP!
INSIDE--! GET INSIDE!
GYAH!
SHRACT!
SHRACT!
SHRACT!
YAHH!
ARE YOU ALL RIGHT?
NO! I SKINNED MY KNEES!
STAY IN THERE!
DON'T LEAVE ME ALONE!
4.

STAY WITH LORD DAIDA!
PROTECT HIM WITH YOUR LIVES!
YES, MASAMUNE-SAN!

THERE THEY ARE--
ESCAPING OUTSIDE OUR COMPOUND!

CLOSE THE GATE! LET NO ONE ENTER OR LEAVE!
YES, SIR!
5

I'M DETERMINED TO GET TO THE BOTTOM OF THIS.
SABURO ALREADY THINKS I'M AN INCOMPETENT FOOL.
THE ANSWER TO THE MYSTERY LIES WITHIN THIS GARDEN...
...AND OKIKU'S WELL.
EH--?
6.

A GINKGO LEAF--?

--PARTIALLY UNDER ONE OF THE BOARDS!

HOW CAN THIS BE, IF THE BOARDS ARE NAILED SHUT--?

SO THIS IS HOW THAT ASSASSIN ESCAPED.

THE NAILS DO NOT GO ALL THE WAY THROUGH THESE BOARDS. THE TIPS HAVE BEEN CUT OFF.

THE OTHER BOARDS ARE NAILED SHUT, THOUGH.

THIS HAS A HINGE THAT LOCKS IT TO THE OTHER BOARDS FROM THE INSIDE.

AND HERE'S A ROPE DESCENDING INTO THE WELL.

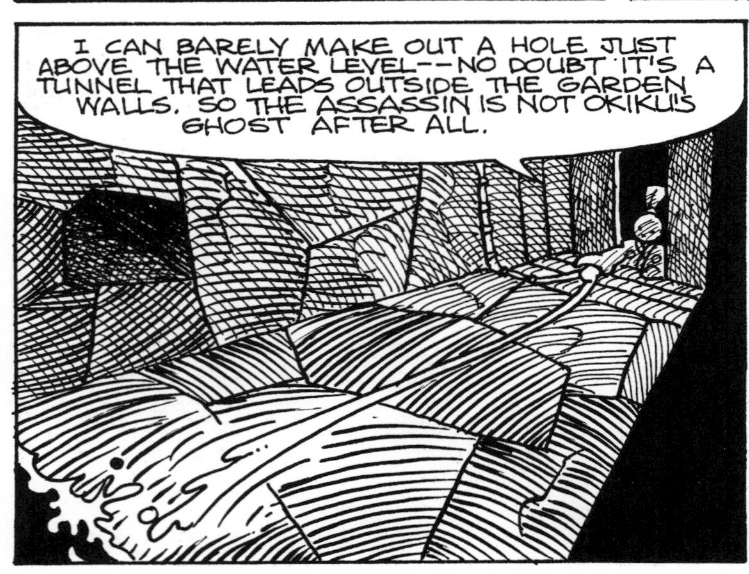
I CAN BARELY MAKE OUT A HOLE JUST ABOVE THE WATER LEVEL--NO DOUBT IT'S A TUNNEL THAT LEADS OUTSIDE THE GARDEN WALLS. SO THE ASSASSIN IS NOT OKIKU'S GHOST AFTER ALL.

ALARM! ALARM!
AGAIN?
8

THAT CAME FROM THE KOJIMA DELEGATION'S COMPOUND!

WHO ARE THOSE GUYS?
I'D BETTER FOLLOW THEM.

WAIT--!
SOMEONE'S COMING!

HOLD IT!
USAGI! I KNEW YOU WERE INVOLVED IN THIS!
9.

NO--! WAIT, SABURO!
TANG!

TANG!
TANG!
TANG!
TANG!
STOP! YOU'RE MAKING A MISTAKE!

YOU WON'T SWAY ME WITH YOUR LIES!
I'VE TRIED TO BE SENSIBLE, BUT THERE IS NO GETTING THROUGH TO YOU!
I'VE DISTRUSTED YOU FROM THE START, USAGI!

TANG!

SO, YOU DO HAVE SOME SKILL WITH THE SWORD.
10

USAGI-- SABURO--WHAT'S GOING ON?
YOUR FRIEND HAS GONE CRAZY, TOMOE!
NONSENSE! BOTH OF YOU-- SHEATHE YOUR SWORDS!

THERE WAS ANOTHER ATTEMPT ON DIPLOMAT DAIDA'S LIFE! I WAS FOLLOWING THE ASSASSINS WHEN USAGI AMBUSHED ME.

I DID NOT ATTACK YOU, YOU IDIOT. I WAS RUNNING TOWARDS YOUR ALARM WHEN I SAW THREE FIGURES RUNNING TOWARDS THE GARDEN.

THE GARDEN? THEN THEY WILL BE TRAPPED WITHIN ITS WALLS.
NO. OKIKU'S WELL IS NOT SEALED, AND THERE IS A SECRET TUNNEL.

WHAT?!
COME ON.
11.

SOON...
NEKO NINJA! NOW IT BECOMES CLEARER!

WHRRR--!
WHRRR--!
WHRRR--!

FLING!

LOOK OUT!
FWTT!
KRAK!
IT'S SOME SORT OF SICKLE AND CHAIN!
12

CRAK!!

TANG!

13.

THEY'RE SPREADING OUT--TRYING TO ENCIRCLE US!

HIYAHHHHH

YAHHHHHH

TANG!
HA!

TWILL! TWILL!

YOUR SWORD IS USELESS, *SAMURAI*, BUT MY CLAW CAN BE USED AS A HAND-WEAPON.
UGH--!

CHAK!
SHAKT!
I CAN'T GET CLOSE ENOUGH TO USE MY BLADES.
15

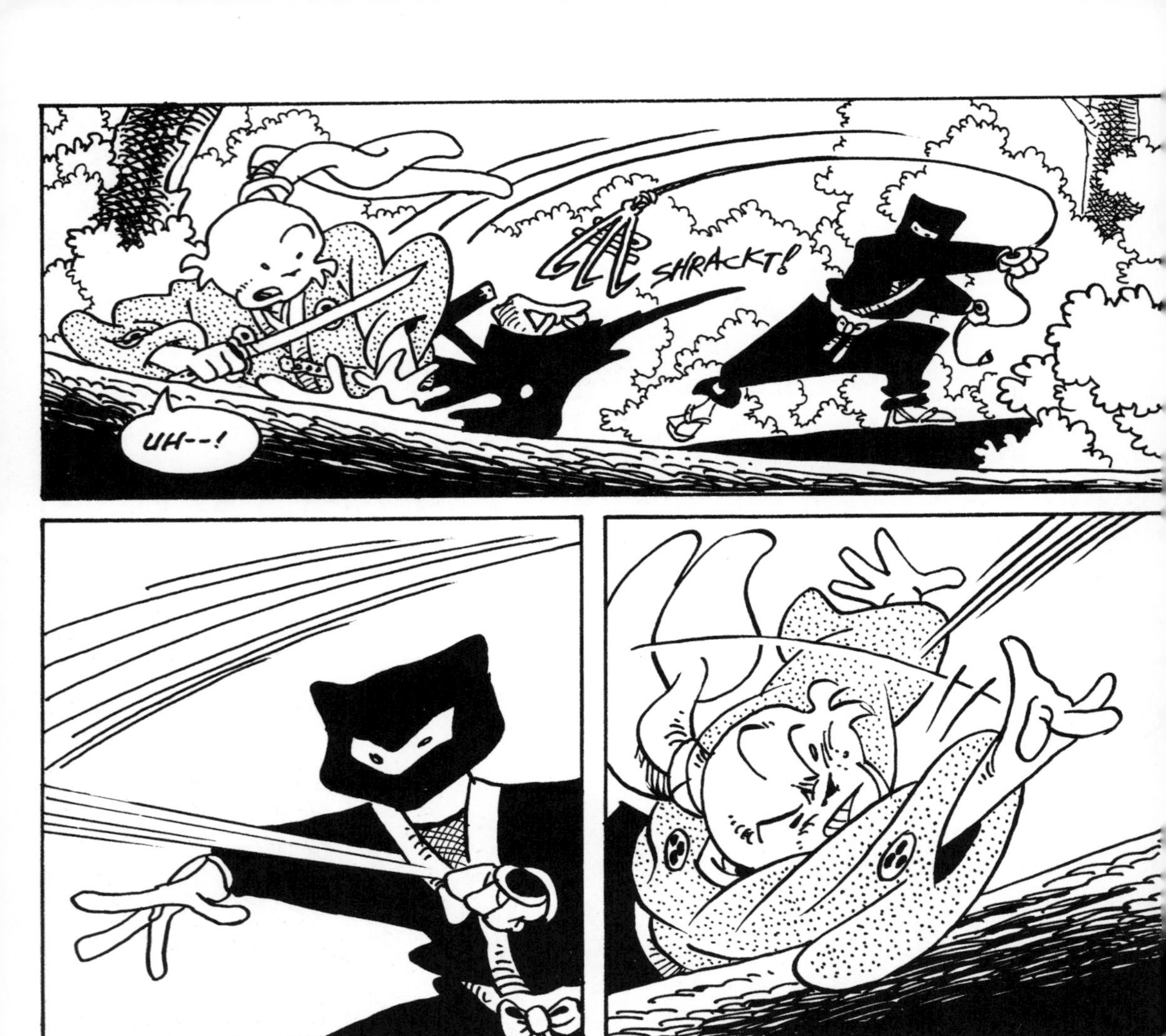
SHRACKT!
UH--!

SHAKT!
UH--!

....
SHUK!

16

STRUGGLE ALL YOU WANT, SAMURAI! YOUR SWORD AND YOUR SWORD ARM ARE TANGLED.
MY BLADE IS USELESS AS LONG AS HE KEEPS THE CHAIN TAUT--

--BUT IF THERE WERE A SUDDEN SLACK...

ULP!

OOK!
17.

CHAK!

HIYAHHH!!

CHOP!

COME BACK HERE!

ZWIP!!
UGH!
MISSED!
18

TOMOE-- STOP! DON'T FOLLOW HIM INTO THE WELL!

I CAN'T LET HIM GET AWAY!
THERE MAY BE TRAPS--OR HE COULD BE LYING IN AMBUSH!

EYAHH!!
!
WHAT A BONE-CHILLING CRY!

WHAT HAPPENED?
HE MUST HAVE GOTTEN TANGLED UP WITH THE ROPE LADDER.

UGH! WHY IS HE SO HEAVY?
MAYBE HE'S SNAGGED ON SOMETHING.

!
GODS.
19.

I-IT'S THE REMAINS OF OKIKU! BUT THEY SEARCHED THE WELL FOR WEEKS AND NEVER FOUND HER!
SHE IS ENTANGLED WITH THE ROPE AS WELL!

ARE YOU SURE?
THE ROPE IS NOT AROUND HER BODY.

BUT HER HAND IS AROUND HIS THROAT. WAS IT MERE CHANCE THAT SHE WAS SNAGGED ON HIS BODY, OR DID HER SPIRIT STOP HIS ESCAPE?

UNINTENTIONAL OR NOT, EVEN AFTER THE END SHE ACTED AS WOULD A FAITHFUL GEISHU RETAINER!

THIS IS EVEN STRANGER.
20

HER SKULL WAS CLOVEN.

OKIKU WAS KILLED BY A SWORD-- SO IT WAS MURDER, NOT SUICIDE.
YEAH.

AOYAMA KILLED HER SO HE WOULD BE FREE TO MARRY ABOVE HIS STATION.

IT WAS HIS GUILT THAT DROVE HIM MAD, AND TO SUICIDE.

POOR OKIKU...

WE WILL PERFORM THE PROPER RITES.
HER SPIRIT WILL FINALLY BE AT PEACE.
21

THE NEKO NINJA ALMOST RUINED THE TRADE NEGOTIATIONS.
BUT WHY?

WHO WOULD PROFIT FROM THE NEGOTIATION TALKS BEING CANCELED?

WHO CONTROLS THE NEKO NINJA CLAN?

LORD HIKIJI.

SO THE LORD OF THE BLACK SUN IS STILL UP TO HIS INTRIGUES.
LADY TOMOE! ARE YOU ALL RIGHT?
22

THREE WEEKS LATER...

...IN THE KOJIMA PROVINCE.

KIIK!
KIIIK!
KIIIIK!

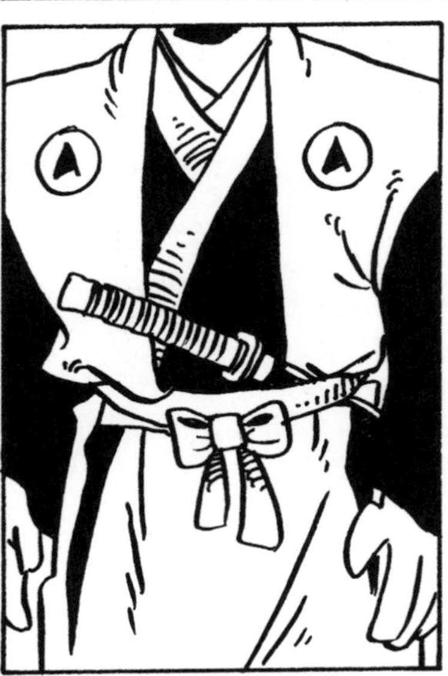

SIR!
REPORT, SABURO.
YES, SIR.

OUR TRADE AGREEMENT WITH THE GEISHU CLAN HAS BEEN APPROVED BY BOTH PARTIES.
IT IS A FAIR TREATY. BOTH SIDES WILL BENEFIT.
23.

AND WHAT OF YOUR OTHER MISSION IN THE GEISHU PROVINCE?
TO FORM AN ESTIMATION OF LADY TOMOE? SHE IS AN HONORABLE *SAMURAI* FROM A DISTINGUISHED FAMILY, AND HER BEAUTY IS UNSURPASSED.
SHE WILL MAKE AN EXCELLENT WIFE, LORD ITO.
GOOD. LORD HORIKAWA HAS CONSENTED TO ACT AS THE GO-BETWEEN. WE WILL BEGIN THE MARRIAGE NEGOTIATIONS IMMEDIATELY.
THE END

THE THIEF and the LOTUS SCROLL

THIEF! THIEF!
WHAT'S GOING ON?

LADY TOMOE--THE LOTUS SCROLL HAS BEEN STOLEN FROM THE MIDORI TEMPLE!

WE ARE SEARCHING EVERY AVENUE OF ESCAPE THE THIEF COULD HAVE TAKEN.
DO NOT LET US INTERFERE WITH YOUR SEARCH.
YES, MA'AM.

LET'S HOPE THEY RECOVER THE SCROLL.
OF COURSE.

GATHER 'ROUND! GATHER 'ROUND!
EH--?
WHAT IS IT?
2.

GATHER 'ROUND AND HEAR HOW LADY TOMOE SLEW THE EVIL SPIDER GOBLIN!
DO YOU KNOW HER, USAGI?
YEAH.

THE GOBLIN WAS AFTER THE GOOD LORD NORIYUKI...

...BUT THE BEAUTIFUL LADY TOMOE CAME TO THE RESCUE!
FLICK!

SHE LEAPT INTO THE AIR...
FLIP!

...AND SMOTE THE FOUL CREATURE IN TWO!
SKITCH!

THANK YOU FOR LISTENING. IF YOU ENJOYED MY PERFORMANCE, PLEASE SHOW YOUR APPRECIATION.

CHING!
TING!
CHING!
3

EXCUSE ME FOR A MOMENT, TOMOE.
SURE. I WANT TO TALK TO THE POLICE ANYWAY.

KITSUNE.
AH, USAGI-SAN! WHAT A PLEASANT SURPRISE!

I JUST HEARD THAT A VALUABLE SCROLL HAS BEEN STOLEN FROM A TEMPLE.
REALLY? HOW TERRIBLE! IMAGINE-- SUCH PEOPLE IN THE WORLD!

THE GEISHU CLAN ARE MY FRIENDS. IF YOU--
YOU SUSPECT **ME** OF THE THEFT?! OH, YOUR WORDS WOUND ME, USAGI!

WELL... BUT THIS CERTAINLY SOUNDS LIKE ONE OF YOUR CAPERS.

I ASSURE YOU ON OUR FRIENDSHIP THAT I HOLD SO DEAR, I DID NOT STEAL ANY SCROLL, USAGI.

I CAN ASK FOR NO MORE THAN THAT.
THANK YOU FOR YOUR TRUST, USAGI DEAR.
AND I FORGIVE YOUR SUSPICION OF ME EARLIER.

THEY COULD FIND NO TRACE OF THE THIEF. HE SEEMS TO HAVE DISAPPEARED COMPLETELY.

WHO IS YOUR FRIEND, USAGI?
I AM CALLED KITSUNE, MA'AM.

YOU DO ME HONOR WITH YOUR STORY, KITSUNE, BUT I FEAR YOU MAY HAVE EXAGGERATED A BIT.

OH, I DOUBT IT. WHO HAS NOT HEARD OF THE BEAUTIFUL AND COURAGEOUS LADY TOMOE? I, ON THE OTHER HAND, AM A HUMBLE STREET PERFORMER.

USAGI-SAN HAS INTERESTING FRIENDS.
UH...OUR PATHS HAVE CROSSED A FEW TIMES.

USAGI IS SO MODEST, AREN'T YOU, DEAR USAGI? WE'VE SHARED MANY ADVENTURES--AND OTHER THINGS--TOGETHER.

WHAT DO YOU MEAN, OTHER THINGS?

OH, YOU KNOW--JUST A MEAL OR TWO--AND NOTHING A WOMAN OF LADY TOMOE'S POSITION WOULD WANT TO HEAR.

IS THAT RIGHT? YOU WOULD BE SURPRISED AT WHAT A WOMAN IN MY POSITION HEARS.

WHY, LADY TOMOE! YOU DO MAKE ME BLUSH!
6.

I'LL LEAVE YOU TO GET REACQUAINTED, THEN.
GOOD-BYE.
GOOD-BYE, LADY TOMOE.

WHY DID YOU HAVE TO SAY THOSE THINGS?
WHATEVER DO YOU MEAN, USAGI DEAR?

AND DON'T CALL ME "DEAR"!
OF COURSE, USAGI DARLING.
CUT IT OUT!

TOMOE! WAIT FOR ME!

I KNEW THAT WOULD GET RID OF THEM.

IT'S SAFE TO COME OUT NOW, KIYOKO.
THAT WAS CLOSE. THEY ALMOST CAUGHT ME.

I DON'T THINK LADY TOMOE LIKES ME VERY MUCH.
HA HA! BUT YOU'RE SO LOVABLE!

THIS WAS YOUR FIRST SOLO JOB-- BUT WHY DID YOU DECIDE TO STEAL A SCROLL, KIYOKO?
I THOUGHT IT LOOKED PRETTY.

I GUESS THAT IS AS GOOD A REASON AS ANY OTHER.

IF IT IS AS BEAUTIFUL AS YOU SAY, NO DOUBT THERE ARE MANY WHO WOULD LIKE TO POSSESS IT.
8.

ALL IN ALL, A GOOD DAY'S WORK!

LET'S FIND A FENCE TO WHOM WE CAN SELL THE SCROLL.

I FEEL SORRY FOR USAGI, THOUGH.

AT LEAST I DID NOT HAVE TO LIE TO HIM. I MIGHT HAVE BENT THE TRUTH, THOUGH.

BUT A GIRL'S GOT TO DO WHAT SHE CAN TO GET BY...
...RIGHT, ONEE-SAN*?
HA HA HA! THAT'S RIGHT, IMOTO-CHAN**!
*OLDER SISTER
**YOUNGER SISTER
9.

NO.
NO.
NO.

I CAN'T TAKE THE SCROLL. IT'S TOO CONSPICUOUS.
BUT IT'S SO PRETTY.

I CAN'T HANDLE IT! *SLURP!*
IS THIS SOME RUSE TO GET MORE MONEY OUT OF US?

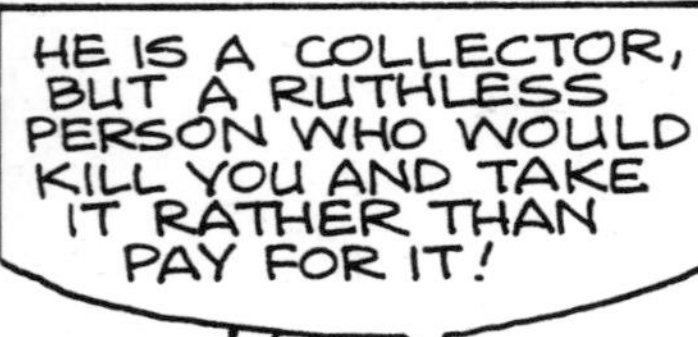
OF COURSE NOT. I'M AN **HONEST** FENCE!

ONLY ONE PERSON WOULD WANT IT-- BOSS SANNO.
THEN SELL IT TO HIM.

HE IS A COLLECTOR, BUT A RUTHLESS PERSON WHO WOULD KILL YOU AND TAKE IT RATHER THAN PAY FOR IT!

ONCE HE LEARNS THAT YOU HAVE THE SCROLL, YOUR LIVES WON'T BE WORTH A COUNTERFEIT *BU*. NOW TAKE IT AND GET OUT OF HERE!
10.

I WANT THAT SCROLL!

I TRIED TO BUY IT, BUT THE TEMPLE WOULD NOT SELL IT TO ME!
AND NOW IT'S STOLEN!
WILL YOU BUY IT FROM THE THIEVES?

IT WAS STOLEN IN **MY** TERRITORY! WHY SHOULD I BUY WHAT SHOULD HAVE BEEN MINE IN THE FIRST PLACE?

IT MAY BE BAD LUCK TO STEAL FROM A TEMPLE, BUT NOT FROM THIEVES!

QUESTION ALL THE PROCURERS OF STOLEN PROPERTY. SOMEONE MUST KNOW WHO THOSE THIEVES ARE!
GET ME THAT SCROLL!
11.

AND SO...
NO! NO! PLEASE! I DON'T KNOW WHO STOLE IT!

STOP! STOP! I WOULD TELL YOU IF I KNEW!

UH... UH... UH...
EEP!

BAM! BAM! BAM!

YES, YES. WHAT DO YOU WANT?
DO YOU HAVE SOMETHING TO SELL ME?

BEAT HIM!
WHAT DO YOU WANT?!

YAAHHHH

COME IN! COME IN! THE BEST FOOD IN TOWN!

MMM...

AH, THAT WAS DELICIOUS! I DON'T GET TOO MANY MEALS LIKE THAT ON THE ROAD!

THEN ENJOY IT WHILE YOU CAN.
IS IT STILL YOUR INTENTION TO DEPART TOMORROW?

YES.
THEN JOIN ME IN THE *CHANOYU** BEFORE YOU LEAVE.
* TEA CEREMONY

IT WOULD TRULY BE MY HONOR.
13

EXCUSE ME. DO YOU DESIRE ANYTHING ELSE?
NO, INNKEEPER. WE ARE DONE. THE FOOD WAS EXCELLENT!
HERE YOU ARE, INNKEEPER.
THANK YOU, LADY TOMOE.
PLEASE COME BACK ANY TIME!
THANK YOU, I WILL.
AH...SUCH A BEAUTIFUL EVENING!
LET'S TAKE A WALK THROUGH THE TOWN, AND WORK OFF THAT MEAL.
GOOD IDEA. I FEEL AS IF I'M GOING TO BURST.
14

THERE'S THAT FRIEND OF YOURS.
I'M SORRY, USAGI, BUT I DON'T PARTICULARLY LIKE HER VERY MUCH. LET'S WALK DOWN ANOTHER STREET.
SHE'S WITH KIYOKO! I HAD FORGOTTEN KITSUNE TRAVELS WITH HER.
IF THE THIEF WASN'T KITSUNE, IT COULD HAVE BEEN KIYOKO.
WHAT ARE YOU TALKING ABOUT?
COME ON. I THINK WE'RE ABOUT TO SOLVE A MYSTERY.
HUH?
KITSUNE IS NOT THE COMMON STREET PERFORMER SHE APPEARS.
OH?
THEN WHAT IS SHE?
15

TWO MINUTES EARLIER...
I FOUND THEM! I FOUND THEM!

THEY'RE THREE STREETS OVER!
ARE YOU SURE IT'S THEM?

THEY FIT THE DESCRIPTION THAT FENCE GAVE US... MAY HE REST IN PEACE...
...AND THE YOUNG ONE IS CARRYING A BAG THAT COULD CONTAIN THE SCROLL.

GOOD. REMEMBER--BOSS SANNO DOESN'T WANT ANY WITNESSES LEFT ALIVE.

A WOMAN AND A GIRL AGAINST ALL OF US? THERE WON'T BE ANY WITNESSES LEFT AT ALL.
THIS COULD MEAN A BIG BONUS FOR US!
16.

ONE MINUTE EARLIER.
SO WHAT DO WE DO WITH THE SCROLL, ONEE-SAN?
I DON'T KNOW. LET'S THINK THIS THROUGH.

WE CAN'T SELL IT. MAYBE WE CAN RETURN IT TO THE TEMPLE...
...IF THERE IS A SUITABLE REWARD.

WE CAN'T JUST WALK IN WITH IT, THOUGH. WE WOULD BE SUSPECTED OF THE THEFT.
BUT WE DID STEAL IT! HA HA HA!

WE'LL HAVE TO COME UP WITH SOME REASONABLE STORY.

HOW ABOUT IF WE SAY WE TOOK IT FROM SOME GANGSTER THUGS?

NONSENSE. BESIDES, WHERE ARE WE GOING TO FIND GANGSTER THUGS?
UH...
17.

!
HIYAAHH!

STAY BEHIND ME, KIYOKO!
SWIT!

WHT!
ZWIT!
FWIT!

URK!

BONK!
UH--!
18

RUN, KIYOKO! I'LL HOLD THEM OFF!
BUT...
GO!

STOP HER! SHE HAS THE SCROLL!
RUN, KIYOKO!
I'M AFTER HER!

YOU CAN'T GET AWAY, BRAT!

COME HERE!

GOT YOU!
EEE!

EEEE--!
.....
19.

USAGI--?!
UH--!
OOK!

URK!
UGH!

FLOOK!

OOOo--!

ULK!

GLOOK!

THAT IS THE LAST OF THEM!
ARE YOU TWO OKAY?
YEAH. THANKS TO YOU AND TOMOE-SAN.

I RECOGNIZE SOME OF THESE RUFFIANS. THEY ARE GANGSTER THUGS IN THE EMPLOY OF BOSS SANNO.

BUT WHY DID THEY ATTACK *YOU*?
UH...

UH...USAGI-*SAN* TOLD US THAT A TEMPLE SCROLL HAD BEEN STOLEN. WE DISCOVERED THAT THESE GANGSTER THUGS WERE BEHIND THE ROBBERY. WE RECOVERED IT. SEE-- HERE IT IS!
ISN'T THAT RIGHT, *ONEE-SAN*?

YES, YES. NO DOUBT THEY WANTED TO TAKE IT BACK FOR THEIR BOSS.
IT'S A GOOD THING YOU TWO CAME ALONG WHEN YOU DID!

I REMEMBER HEARING THAT BOSS SANNO WANTED THE LOTUS SCROLL...
...BUT I DID NOT THINK HE WOULD DARE STEAL IT FROM THE TEMPLE.
21

WHAT YOU SAY YOU DID IS COMMENDABLE, BUT YOU SHOULD HAVE ALERTED THE AUTHORITIES. IT WAS DANGEROUS TO HAVE ACTED ON YOUR OWN.
IF USAGI AND I HAD NOT BEEN WALKING BY--
OH, BUT YOU WERE, AND THE SCROLL IS SAFE.

UH... PERHAPS THERE IS A REWARD?
OH, I'M SURE THERE IS.

BUT I'M SURE THEY WOULD WANT TO DONATE ANY REWARD RIGHT BACK TO THE TEMPLE.
!

ISN'T THAT RIGHT, KITSUNE?

WH-WHY WOULD WE DO THAT?

YOU ARE SO CIVIC-MINDED, YOU WOULD NEVER THINK OF PROFITING FROM ANY CRIME.
22.

AND BY DECLINING ANY REWARD, THE MATTER WILL BE ENDED. I'M SURE THEN THAT THERE WILL BE NO NEED FOR AN INTENSIVE INVESTIGATION INTO THE SCROLL'S THEFT.

SINCE YOU PUT IT **THAT** WAY, USAGI **DEAR**...
...WE WILL GLADLY FOREGO ANY REWARD FOR THE SCROLL'S RETURN.

BUT... ONEE-SAN!
NO, KIYOKO. THE GEISHU ARE USAGI'S FRIENDS. IT IS THE LEAST WE CAN DO.

THAT IS VERY GENEROUS OF YOU, KITSUNE.
AS USAGI SAID, WE ARE VERY CIVIC-MINDED.

WELL, WE SHOULD BE GOING NOW. PLEASE SEE THAT THE SCROLL IS PROPERLY RETURNED.
DON'T WORRY, WE WILL.
23

WE MUST EARN SOME TRAVELING MONEY TO CONTINUE ON OUR WAY.
JUST ONE MOMENT, PLEASE.

I MISJUDGED YOU, KITSUNE-SAN. I APOLOGIZE. I'M SURE I CAN AFFORD A FEW COINS, ESPECIALLY AFTER YOUR MAGNANIMITY.

THAT'S FUNNY.
I CAN'T FIND MY PURSE.

THAT'S OKAY.
YOU CAN PAY US NEXT TIME.
HOW EMBARRASSING! I MUST HAVE LEFT IT AT THE INN!
GOOD-BYE, YOU TWO!
ON SECOND THOUGHT, I'M SURE WE HAVE ENOUGH MONEY TO LAST US QUITE A WHILE!

THE END

Chanoyu*

KIIIIII--!

4.

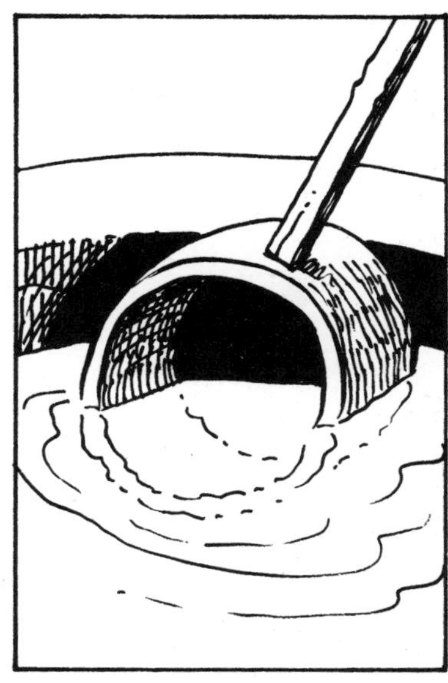

SPLASH!
SPLASH!

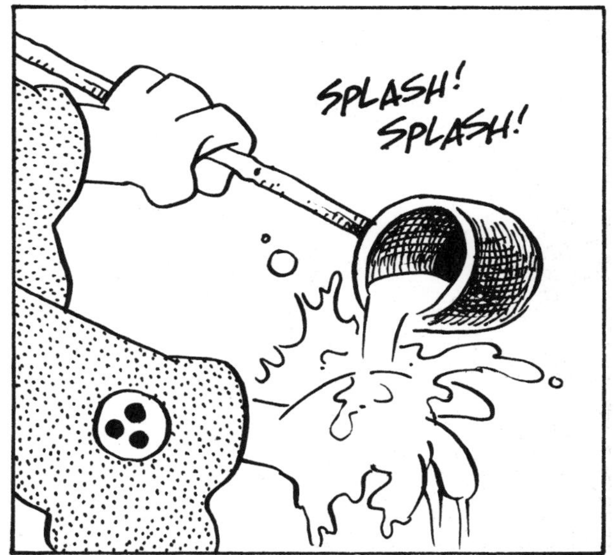
SPLASH!
SPLASH!

SIP!
SWISH!
SWISH!

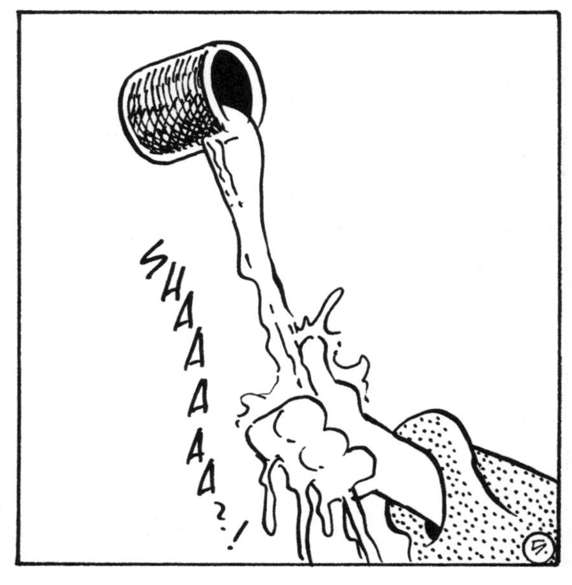
SHAAAAAA?!

SHUUU-!

ENTER WITH THE WATER CONTAINER.

8.

PLEASE PARTAKE OF A FEW SWEETS, USAGI-SAN.

なり

A PINE SPRIG-- A SYMBOL OF LONGEVITY--AND THE CAMELLIA--PURITY. A WONDERFUL SENTIMENT.

KITARU NARI-- WELCOME.
来る

AS YOU ARE ALWAYS WELCOME INTO OUR LIVES, USAGI-SAN.

YOU HONOR ME WITH YOUR HOSPITALITY-- AND YOUR FRIENDSHIP.
10

IT HAS STRONG BRUSH STROKES, BUT IS FEMININE AT THE SAME TIME.
YOURS, TOMOE-SAN?
IT IS BUT A CLUMSY ATTEMPT WITH INK AND BRUSH.
IT IS EXQUISITE. YOU HAVE TALENTS I HAD NOT BEFORE SUSPECTED.
EVEN BETWEEN GOOD FRIENDS, THERE ARE THINGS THAT ARE HIDDEN.
THAT IS THE NATURE OF FRIENDSHIP, BUT MORE IS REVEALED OVER TIME.
YES.
I WILL BEGIN THE TEA.
11.

PICK UP THE LADLE.

SET IT DOWN, AND BOW TO THE GUEST.

REMOVE THE SILK CLOTH FROM YOUR BELT.

WIPE THE TEA CONTAINER.

WIPE THE TEA SCOOP.
12

POUR A HALF SCOOP OF HOT WATER--

--INTO THE TEA CUP--

--AND WARM AND SOFTEN THE BAMBOO WHISK.

THEN EMPTY THE WATER INTO THE WASTE WATER CONTAINER.

WIPE THE RIM OF THE TEA BOWL THREE AND A HALF TIMES.

PLACE TWO SCOOPS OF POWDERED TEA INTO THE BOWL.

REPLACE THE TEA CONTAINER IN FRONT OF THE WATER JAR, WITH THE SCOOP ON THE LID.

REMOVE THE LID OF THE WATER JAR WITH YOUR RIGHT HAND, AND LEAN IT AGAINST THE SIDE OF THE JAR.
13

DRAW A SCOOP OF COLD WATER AND POUR IT INTO THE KETTLE.

TAKE A SCOOP OF HOT WATER FROM THE KETTLE AND POUR TWO-THIRDS OF IT INTO THE TEA BOWL. POUR THE REMAINDER BACK INTO THE KETTLE.

PLACE THE LADLE ON THE KETTLE.

WHISK.
SHA- SHA- SHA-

SHA- SHA- SHA- SHA- SHA-

PLACE THE WHISK IN FRONT OF THE WATER CONTAINER.

TURN THE BOWL CLOCKWISE, SO ITS FRONT WILL FACE THE GUEST WHEN SERVED.

14.

I WILL PARTAKE OF YOUR TEA.

TURN THE BOWL CLOCKWISE--

--SO THAT ITS FRONT FACES YOUR HOST.

SIP
15.

YOUR TEA HAS JUST THE RIGHT AMOUNT OF BITTERNESS. IT REMINDS ME OF THE WINDS BLOWING THROUGH THE AUTUMN GRASS.

THE BITTERNESS OF LIFE, TO MATCH ITS SWEETNESS.

SLURP!

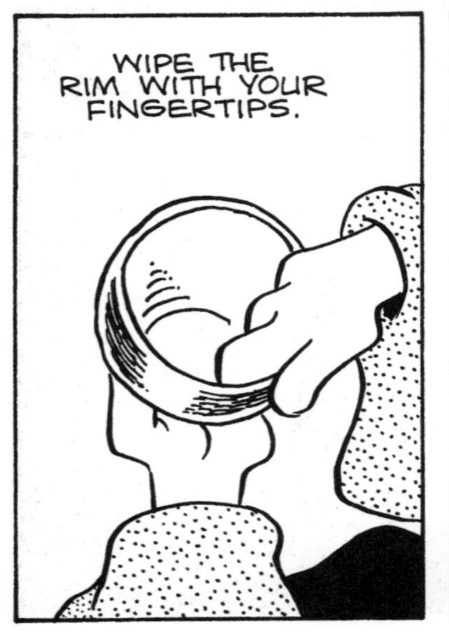
WIPE THE RIM WITH YOUR FINGERTIPS.

TURN THE BOWL COUNTERCLOCKWISE SO THAT IT AGAIN FACES YOU.

SET IT DOWN.
16.

PICK UP THE BOWL.

ADMIRE ITS ART AND CRAFTSMAN-SHIP.

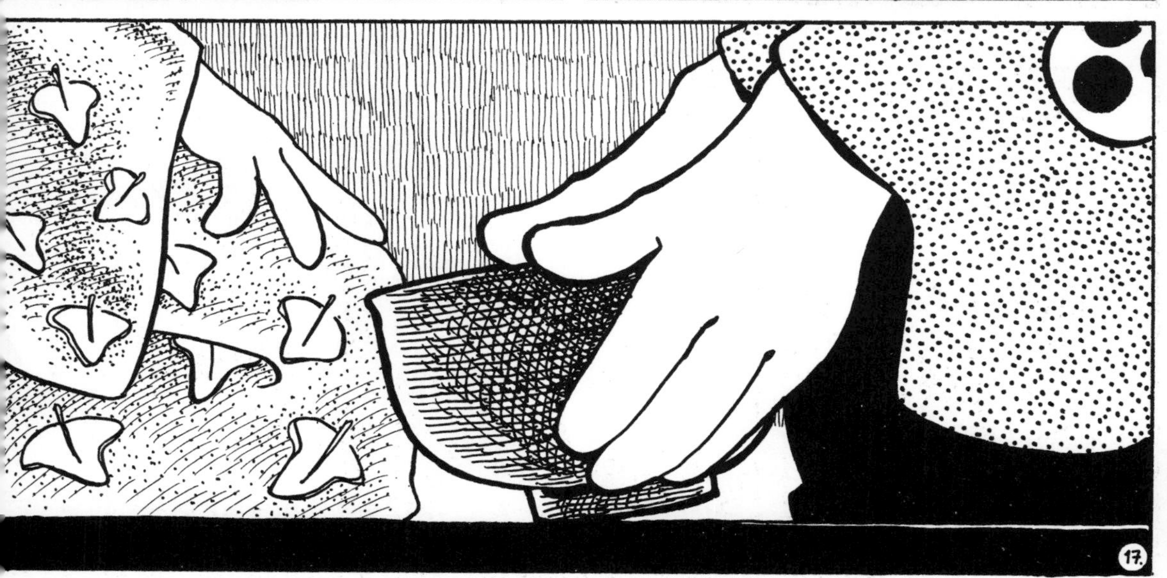
17.

SPLISH!
SPLISH!
SPLISH!

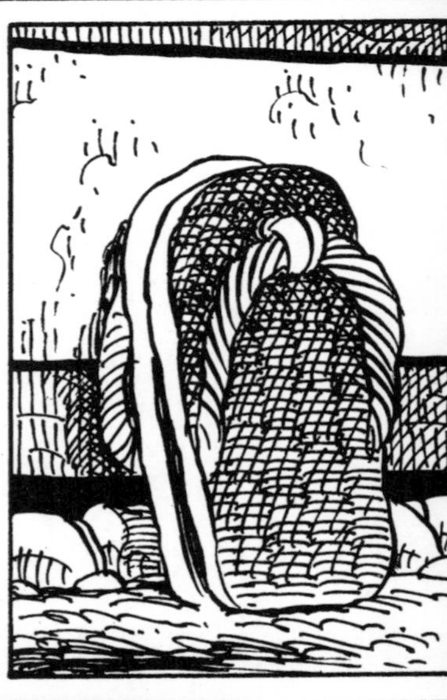

THE TEA CEREMONY WAS IMPECCABLE. THANK YOU FOR THE EXPERIENCE.

YOU ARE TOO KIND.

19

23.

GOOD-BYE, TOMOE.
CAW! CAW!
THE END

REMNANTS of the DEAD

HA HA! YOU MISSED ON PURPOSE!
WHY WOULD I DO THAT?
YOU'VE STILL GOT TO TAKE THE PENALTY, USAGI-SAN.
ALL RIGHT. GO AHEAD, HANAKO.
HOLD STILL.
HA! HA!
HA HA! YOU SURE LOOK FUNNY!
HA! HA!
HA HA HA! HAVING FUN?

AH, WELCOME HOME, ENDO-SAN!
DADDY!
I'M BACK FROM MY DAILY TEMPLE VISIT.
PRIEST JEZO SENDS HIS REGARDS, HANAKO.

PLEASE DO NOT FEEL OBLIGATED TO ENTERTAIN MY DAUGHTER, USAGI-SAN.

HE DOESN'T MIND. ISN'T THAT RIGHT, USAGI-SAN?
OF COURSE I DON'T MIND.

THANK YOU, BUT I SHOULD NOT NEGLECT OUR GUEST.

PLEASE JOIN ME IN SOME TEA, USAGI-SAN. RUN ALONG AND PLAY, HANAKO.
AWW... I WANTED TO PLAY ANOTHER GAME OF HANA-TSUKI!
LATER, HANAKO.
3

THANK YOU FOR YOUR HOSPITALITY, MERCHANT ENDO.
THINK NOTHING OF IT, MY FRIEND.

I DO MUCH BUSINESS WITH LORD NORIYUKI'S WHITE HERON CASTLE. IT IS THE LEAST I CAN DO FOR A FRIEND OF LADY TOMOE.

BESIDES, HANAKO LIKES YOU. SHE DOES NOT HAVE MANY PLAYMATES AROUND HERE.
SHE IS VERY SPECIAL.
HA HA! SHE COULD PLAY *HANATSUKI* ALL DAY.

SIP! THIS IS EXCELLENT TEA.

THANK YOU. IT IS ONE OF THE ITEMS I PROVIDE THE CASTLE. I HAVE AN EVEN BETTER GRADE OF TEA THAT IS OFTEN USED IN THE *CHANOYU**.
IT IS A PITY YOU DID NOT GET TO EXPERIENCE IT.
SIP!
*TEA CEREMONY
4

LORD NORIYUKI IS VERY SELECTIVE WITH WHOM HE CONDUCTS TRADE.
YES. IT GIVES MY HUMBLE ESTABLISHMENT GREAT PRESTIGE.
THE GODS LOOK FAVORABLY DOWN UPON ME. THAT IS WHY I GO TO THE TEMPLE DAILY.

BUT I AM TOLD THERE ARE SOME WHO ENVY MY POSITION.
I HAVE EVEN BEEN ADVISED TO HIRE SOME YOJIMBO*.
*BODY-GUARDS

CERTAINLY, YOUR RIVALS WOULD NOT ATTEMPT ANYTHING DRASTIC.

OF COURSE NOT. THE GUARDS WOULD BE ONLY FOR SHOW. IT IS THE GODS THAT PROTECT ME TO REWARD MY DEVOTION.

BUT--ENOUGH BUSINESS TALK. LET US ENJOY THIS TEA AND YOUR VISIT HERE.
7

ELSEWHERE, HOURS LATER...

SO, YOU UNDERSTAND WHAT MUST BE DONE?

HEH! KILL A MERCHANT? IT'S A SIMPLE JOB.

ALMOST BENEATH OUR SKILLS...

...IF IT WERE NOT FOR ALL THE MONEY YOU'RE PAYING US.

WHO IS THE *OKORI** ANYWAY, SAIKO?
THAT IS NOT YOUR CONCERN. IF YOU WANT TO JOIN KOROSHI, THE LEAGUE OF ASSASSINS, YOU MUST LEARN TO TAKE ORDERS.
*CLIENT
6.

CERTAINLY, WE DON'T SPEND ALL OUR TIME KILLING.

DO WE?

OW!

YAHH!
HEY!

YES, WE DO! UNDERSTAND?!
Y-YES, MA'AM!

GOOD. NOW GET UP. WE HAVE WORK TO DO!
GULP!
7.

THERE AREN'T EVEN ANY GUARDS, AND THE HOUSEHOLD SERVANTS WILL BE NO OBSTACLE.

I DON'T EVEN NEED THOSE THREE IDIOTS--

--BUT THE *MOTOJIME** INSISTS I NEED TO REPLACE MY DEAD PARTNERS.
*HANDLER
8

NO GUARDS. NO SECURITY. NOTHING! HE'S A FOOL.

HURRY. GET IN.
QUIETLY.

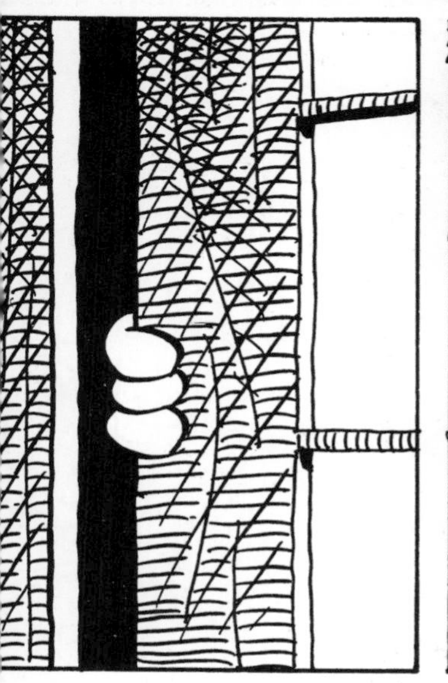

9.

THE COAST IS CLEAR. THE MERCHANT'S ROOM IS AT THE END OF THE HALL.

KIIII--!

SORRY--!

HMM...?

USAGI-SAN?
DO YOU WANT TO PLAY *HANATSUKI*?
?
11.

WHO ARE YOU?
WHAT ARE YOU DOING HERE?
DO YOU WANT TO PLAY *HANATSUKI*?
!
!
!
!
!
GET HER!
YEAH, KID. LET'S PLAY *HANATSUKI*. JUST STAY THERE, AND DON'T MOVE.
ULP!
ZWIP!
12

GET BACK IN YOUR ROOM, HANAKO.
UH...
HE'S ONLY ONE GUY-- KILL HIM!
WHO ARE YOU-- BURGLARS?
OR ASSASSINS AFTER MERCHANT ENDO?
KILL HIM-- QUICKLY!
GURK!
13

WHAT'S GOING ON HERE?
HANAKO-- WHERE ARE YOU?

DADDY!

HANAKO--STAY BACK!
NO! HANAKO-- STAY AWAY!
OOK!
DON'T HURT MY DADDY!

GURK!
DADDY!
14

*UY BOOK 19: FATHERS AND SONS

LET HER GO.
ONE STEP CLOSER, AND SHE DIES!

KRK!

YOU TOO, MERCHANT--
--STAY BACK!
USAGI-SAN!

SHUT UP, KID!
LET ME WALK OUT OF HERE, SAMURAI, OR THE GIRL DIES!

RELEASE HER, AND YOU CAN LEAVE THROUGH THE FRONT GATE!
YOU HAVE MY WORD ON IT!

HARM HER, AND YOU WILL WISH YOU HAD DIED WITH YOUR FATHER.
16.

BACK UP! I'LL SLIT HER THROAT BEFORE YOU CAN TAKE TWO STEPS TOWARD ME!
OKAY, OKAY. I'M GOING.
GET OUTSIDE, BUT STAY WHERE I CAN SEE YOU!
DON'T WORRY, HANAKO. YOU'LL BE SAFE!
WHAT'S THE COMMOTION?
WHAT'S GOING ON? IS THE MASTER ALL RIGHT?
STAY BACK, AND DON'T INTERFERE!
WHIMPER!
YOU'VE BEEN SMART SO FAR, SAMURAI!
KEEP IT THAT WAY, AND SHE WON'T GET HURT.
I KNOW YOUR SKILL WITH THE SWORD. ONE WRONG MOVE, AND SHE DIES!
17

STAY WITHIN THE WALLS. ONE STEP BEYOND THE GATE, AND I KILL HER.
DON'T WORRY. WE'LL DO AS YOU SAY!

OKAY, YOU'RE OUT. NOW LET HER GO. SHE WOULD ONLY HAMPER YOUR ESCAPE.
TAKE HER!
OH--!

HANAKO!
SHE'S ALL RIGHT-- JUST SCARED AND SHAKEN!
DADDY!
I REMEMBER HOW FAST SHE RAN WHEN SHE ESCAPED THE FIRST TIME!
18.

AT LEAST I GOT AWAY. WE CAN KILL THE MERCHANT SOME OTHER TIME.
EH--?
THE SAMURAI--!
BE CAREFUL, SAIKO. YOU COULD HURT SOMEONE.
WHAT--?
19

MOTOJIME-SAN! A LONG-EARED SAMURAI THWARTED OUR ASSASSINATION!
WE FAILED!

A LONG-EARED SAMURAI, YOU SAY...?
HE KILLED THE OTHERS, AND THE MERCHANT STILL LIVES!

AND NOW HE IS AFTER YOU?
YES.

I KNOW THIS SAMURAI. HE IS FORMIDABLE.
Y-YES.

TOO FORMIDABLE FOR THE LIKES OF YOU.
WHAT?

SOON, RONIN, SOON...

SAIKO!

DEAD.
THOUGH I CAN'T SAY I FEEL SORRY FOR HER.

BUT WHO KILLED HER?
21.

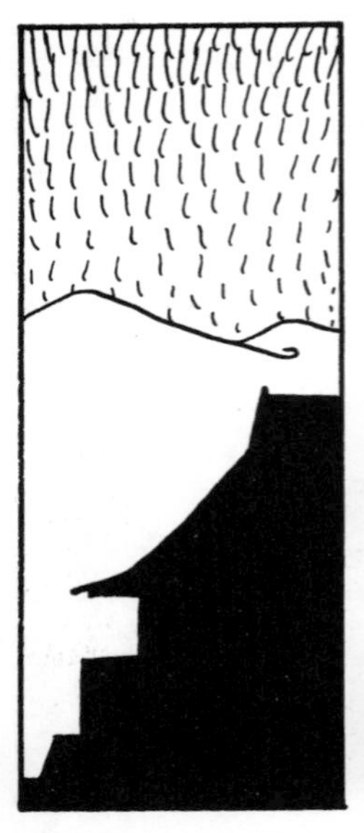

GOOD MORNING, HANAKO.
I WAS WAITING FOR YOU TO GET UP, SO I COULD SAY GOOD-BYE.
MUST YOU LEAVE SO SOON, USAGI-SAN?
I GET RESTLESS WHEN I STAY IN ONE PLACE TOO LONG.

WHERE IS FATHER? HE WAS NOT IN HIS ROOM.

HE WENT TO THE TEMPLE. BUT DON'T WORRY. LORD NORIYUKI SENT SOME OF HIS *SAMURAI* TO PROTECT HIM UNTIL GUARDS CAN BE HIRED.

I WILL MISS YOU, USAGI-SAN.
I WILL BE BACK THIS WAY AGAIN, HANAKO.

WE'LL PLAY *HANATSUKI* WHEN I RETURN, HANAKO.
THEN HURRY BACK, USAGI-SAN!
22

ALL YOU GUARDS ARE UNNECESSARY!
THE ASSASSINATION ATTEMPT LAST NIGHT FAILED. THAT SHOULD DISCOURAGE ANY FUTURE ATTEMPTS.
AS I TOLD USAGI-SAN, THE GODS WATCH OVER ME TO REWARD MY FAITHFULNESS.
I WOULD HAVE DISMISSED YOU ALL COMPLETELY IF YOU HAD NOT BEEN SENT BY LORD NORIYUKI.
WAIT HERE.
BUT WE WERE TOLD TO STAY WITH YOU.
NONSENSE. LORD NORIYUKI PUT YOU AT MY DISPOSAL. I WILL NOT HAVE THE SACRED TEMPLE GROUNDS DESECRATED WITH ARMED WARRIORS.
B-BUT...

DON'T ARGUE, OR I WILL REPORT YOUR INSUBORDINATION TO LORD NORIYUKI HIMSELF!
BESIDES, WHAT HARM COULD POSSIBLY BEFALL ME IN A PEACEFUL TEMPLE?
WELL... AS YOU WISH.
A TEMPLE IS NOT THE PLACE FOR SWORDS OR VIOLENT ACTIONS.
23.

PRIEST? PRIEST JEZO? WHERE ARE YOU?
I HAVE EVEN MORE TO BE THANKFUL FOR TODAY.
PLEASE ENTER.
AH, JEZO, WHAT AN ADVENTURE WE HAD!
OH! YOU'RE NOT JEZO!
UNFORTUNATELY, PRIEST JEZO MET WITH AN UNTIMELY ACCIDENT. I AM A VISITING PRIEST. COME, SIT, AND TELL ME YOUR GOOD NEWS.
BUT, FIRST, WOULD YOU PASS ME MY WALKING STAFF?
THE END

CONTRABAND

The first Europeans set foot in Japan in AD 1543. Six years later, Francis Xavier (1506–1552) arrived and started the Jesuit mission. This became very successful, and the Jesuits acquired almost complete control of the port city of Nagasaki. Soon, churches were founded even in Kyoto and Osaka, and seminaries were established for training Japanese preachers. The Jesuits recorded Japanese customs and the culture of the day, resulting in the famous Japanese-Portuguese dictionary called *Nippo jisho*. The book recorded the language not as written in Chinese characters, but exactly as it sounded to the Jesuits. By 1580, there were an estimated 200,000 Japanese Christians, including many more than a dozen *daimyo* (lords).

Oda Nobunaga (1534–1582), the first of the three great unifiers of Japan, was curious about the foreign religion and allowed the Jesuits to spread Catholicism. After being assassinated by Akechi Mitsuhide, one of his trusted generals, Nobunaga was succeeded by Toyotomi Hideyoshi (1536–1598). Hideyoshi established a ban on Catholicism, but it was nominal and the number of converts continued to increase. Catholic missions, closely tied to foreign trade, continued to flourish as late as 1613.

When Tokugawa Ieyasu came into power in 1603, he tightened his grip on the country, and foreign influences dwindled. Everything was done to stamp out Christianity, more for political reasons than for religious ones. It was suspected that Christians did not accept the government as a supreme authority, and it was feared that Christianity might serve to unify defiant *daimyo* against the shogunate. There were also fears of intrusion on Japan by European powers. These fears were exacerbated by disputes between Spain and Portugal, as well as between Jesuits and the more recently arrived Franciscans and Dominicans. As a result, each Japanese family had to officially register as members of a Buddhist temple. Villagers and temples filed annual reports stating that everyone in their district had been examined and that no Christians were found to be among them.

In 1637, a mostly Christian revolt led by sixteen-year-old Amakusa Shiro was put down near Nagasaki. Thirty-eight thousand peasants and *ronin* shut themselves up in Hara Castle on the Shimabara Peninsula and defied the Tokugawa government. The Dutch assisted the shogunate by bombarding the castle from the sea. After a four-month siege, Hara Castle was stormed and the starving Christians killed.

Only a few "secret Christians" (*kakure kirishitan*) survived, mostly practicing their religion on islands off the coast of Nagasaki. It was not until 1873 that the restrictions on Christianity were lifted.

Information for this story came from the following two sources:

- *Everyday Life in Traditional Japan*, by Charles J. Dunn (Rutland, VT/Tokyo: Charles E. Tuttle, 1969).
- *Cultural Atlas of Japan*, by Martin Collcutt, Marius Jansen, and Isao Kumakura (New York: Facts on File, 1998).

After the Rat

Nezumi Kozo (literally, "Rat Boy") was a thief who operated in 1820s Edo. He dressed in black and broke into only the residences of the rich, thereby delighting the general public. He would escape by nimbly traveling from one rooftop to another, giving the authorities the slip under the cover of night. The rumor spread that the money he stole from feudal lords and rich merchants was given to the poor. The truth was that he spent all that he stole on gambling and drinking saké. He was captured and executed in 1832. This "Robin Hood" later became the hero of Kabuki plays, novels, and dramas.

This information was taken from *Who's Who of Japan* (Japan: Japan Travel Bureau, 1990).

Nocturnal

The *hannya* (or *hanya*) was one of the most feared demons in Japan's pantheon of monsters. Though there were male *hannya*, they were usually depicted as females. According to legend, the *hannya* was once a beautiful woman who became insane and was possessed by a demon. She was a ghoul and a vampire, eating her victims and drinking their blood. Children and infants were a delicacy to her.

If a *hannya* had been an especially jealous woman in life, she would return to exact vengeance on an unfaithful lover or on men in general. Before fighting, a *hannya* screamed at her enemy, then attacked with her claws and horns.

Probably the most famous *hannya* story is that of the demon of Rashomon Gate. In AD 976, a demon named Ibaraki was said to have haunted the gate in Kyoto. Watanabe no Tsuna boasted that he would spend the night there. At about two in the morning, when he started to doze off, he felt something tug at his helmet.

Watanabe drew his sword and slashed wildly behind him. There was a shriek of pain, and he was surprised to find that he had cut off the *hannya*'s hand. He took it home and placed it in a box. A few days later an old woman appeared, asking to see the hand. He was reluctant to show it to her, but after she told him her son had been a victim of the terrible demon, he did as she asked. She revealed herself to be the *hannya*, grabbed the hand, and flew off.

The Treasure of the Mother of Mountains

I first heard of the Japanese gromwell in a television documentary about the mountains of Japan. The shrub grows in the presence of gold, and there are specks of gold in its berries as well as fine gold powder in its leaves. There are two other native Japanese plants that share the same properties—the spicebrush and the Japanese beech. The roots of these plants absorb gold from underground water and then distribute the metal throughout their systems to their leaves.

A January 25, 1993, article in *American Metal Market* reported that the Metal Mining Industry Association of Japan, an affiliate of the trade ministry, had been studying the gold content in plants that grew above twelve mines. This project began in 1987. Studying these plants would be much more cost effective than random drilling.

The Mother of Mountains was first conceived as a minor story arc, but as I worked with Noriko, she gradually came to life with a definite personality and a tragic backstory. The story changed from an events-driven story to one that is character driven. Subplots were thrown in with Motokazu, Lord Horikawa, and the suggestion of Tomoe's marriage.

The role of the woman in the samurai class was just as strict and regulated as that of the man. In earliest times, there are records of women leading men into battle: Empress Jingu led the invasion of Korea while pregnant. However, by Usagi's time, women of the military class did not go into battle but were submissive to their husbands or fathers and usually oversaw the samurai household. They were still expected to be proficient with weapons such as the *yari* (straight spear) and *naginata* (curved spear). One of these hung over the door in every samurai home. They carried a *kaiken* (short dagger), which would be used for defense or to commit *seppuku* (ritualized suicide).

Tomoe Ame was inspired by Tomoe Gozen, consort of Kiso Yoshinaka during the Genpei War. She helped lead the Minamoto forces, even killing several of the enemy in single combat. At the Battle of Awazu, she was almost captured by Uchida Ieyoshi. He had seized and ripped a part of her sleeve. Angered, she attacked him, cut off his head, and later presented it to her husband.

Fox Fire

Foxes (*kitsune*) are usually portrayed as tricksters in Japanese folktales. They are sometimes benevolent, but more often malicious. They can appear in human form, usually to play pranks on someone. They are able to create illusions, hypnotize and seduce men, and lure them to dangerous situations. They carry "fox fire" within their tails, which they use to lure travelers astray and which can set houses aflame.

At the age of one hundred, a fox's spirit can possess a man—causing insanity—and can assume human form. When the fox reaches five hundred years old, it turns from red to white, and it becomes capable of transforming itself into anything it chooses. At one thousand, it grows nine tails, turns golden, and gains great wisdom.

Shinto shrines may have a sanctuary where the deity of rice, Inari Daimyojin, is worshiped. The sanctuary guardians are two foxes made of stone, wood, or bronze, one carrying a jewel or scroll and the other with a key to a storehouse or treasure box. Foxes also act as Inari's messengers, and the deity sometimes assumes that form. In addition to the rice harvest, Inari is also the patron of swordsmiths and traders.

Tamamo no Mae was a nine-tailed fox who wreaked havoc in India and China before escaping to Japan in the twelfth century. She cast a spell on Emperor Toba (1108–1156), but was exposed by Abe no Seimei, the court astrologer, who held up a mirror reflecting her true form. The fox fled, pursued by the archer Miura Kuranosuke. As he was about to kill her on Nasu Plain, she transformed herself into a stone. Anyone who touched the stone died instantly. In the fifteenth century, a monk named Genno Osho destroyed the stone, but in so doing released poisonous smoke. According to modern analysis, there is a high arsenic content in the area.

My story was inspired by the story of Abe no Yasuna, a tenth-century nobleman. Abe was out walking when a fox, pursued by hunters who were after its liver for medicine, stopped in front of him. Abe hid the fox in his robes, and the hunting party rushed past him. Abe later met and married a young woman named Kuzunoha. They were happy for three years, during which she bore him a son. She died of a fever (or, in other versions of the story, she left him), but she came back to him three days later in a dream. Kuzunoha told Abe not to mourn her, because she was the fox he had saved. Their son grew up to become the court astrologer who cured Emperor Toba of a fox's enchantment.

Sources consulted for this story include:
• *Yoshitoshi's Thirty-Six Ghosts*, by John Stevenson (New York: Weatherhill, 1983).
• *Japanese Ghosts and Demons: Art of the Supernatural*, ed. Stephen Addis (New York: George Braziller, 1985).
• *Japanese Animal Art*, by Lea Baten (Tokyo: Shufunotomo, 1989).
• *Japanese Mythology*, by Juliet Piggott (New York: Hamlyn Publishing Group, 1969).

The Ghost in the Well

There are two versions of the story of Okiku. Aoyama Tessan, a major retainer of Ietsugu, the seventh Tokugawa shogun (1709–1716), was given a set of ten very valuable Dutch porcelain dishes. One was accidentally broken by his wife, who threw the pieces down the well and accused Okiku, her maid, of stealing it. Okiku was locked up and half starved but could not produce the missing dish. She escaped and, in desperation, drowned herself in the well. Each night, her ghost would appear and slowly count to nine, then break into a loud, plaintive wail. Mitsakuni Shonin, a friend of Aoyama, exorcised her by waiting near the well one night. Once Okiku had counted to nine, he yelled out "ten." This satisfied her spirit, and she never appeared again.

In the second version of the story, Okiku was a maid who had rejected Aoyama's advances. He entrusted her with the ten Dutch plates for safekeeping. He hid one of the dishes, and then told her to bring out the entire set. When she could not, he demanded she sleep with him or be punished for her carelessness. She still refused. In his anger at being rejected once again, he killed her and threw her body into the well. Her spirit haunted the well, counting to, but never reaching, "ten."

The Kabuki play *Bancho Sarayashiki*, or "the dish mansion of Bancho," was based on the second version of this famous story. Bancho is the district of Edo where the story takes place.

Reference for "The Ghost in the Well" came from *Yoshitoshi's Thirty-Six Ghosts*, by John Stevenson (New York: Weatherhill, 1983).

Chanoyu

Drinking tea, first for medicinal purposes, and then later for pleasure, was already widespread in China when it was introduced to Japan in the eighth century by a Buddhist monk. But it was the *chajin*, or Japanese tea masters, who made the preparing, serving, and drinking of tea into the ceremony that is still practiced every day.

Cha-no-yu literally means "hot water for tea." It is a communion whose ultimate goal is to establish a spiritual and harmonious relationship between the host and his guests. The tea ceremony finds its origins in Zen Buddhism. The first tea masters were priests who taught their followers that enlightenment can be obtained through the discipline of the ceremony.

By the eleventh century, the Japanese aristocracy was also partaking of *chanoyu*. Guests were invited to play *tocha*, where they were tested on their ability to distinguish teas of different varieties as well as from various tea regions and plantations.

The samurai class used smaller rooms or larger rooms partitioned by a screen called a *kakoi*. Later, small rooms were built especially for the tea ceremony, and they themselves became known as *kakoi*. One of the best-known designers of *kakoi* was the Zen priest Murata Shuko (1422–1502). He is regarded as the *kaisan*, or father, of the tea ceremony. He distinguished himself with his understanding of Zen at an early age and spent the later years of his life perfecting and teaching the art of tea.

During the age of wars in the late sixteenth century, the tea ceremony became a way to impress and court powerful allies. Oda Nobunaga extended invitations to the wealthy merchants who controlled trade with the West. His successor, Toyotomi Hideyoshi, held gatherings and used tea articles owned by Nobunaga to indicate that he had been chosen to carry on Nobunaga's work. The record of Yamanoue Soji states that Hideyoshi had eight tea masters working for him. The most renowned of these was Sen Rikyu. Rikyu was the first to fashion bowls specifically for serving tea. *Raku* bowls are simple earthenware, shaped by hand and fired at a low temperature. Previously, bowls had been imported from China and were not necessarily intended for tea. Rikyu was an innovator, constantly devising new ways to serve tea and new shapes for the utensils.

Though it is just the act of making a cup of tea, the ceremony requires years of training and practice. The host and guests meet in a small teahouse and share a sense of togetherness. They are not expected to communicate physically, but spiritually—though there are times when words are expected. Tea master Rikyu forbade any frivolous conversation within the tearoom. Every aspect of the ceremony, down to the simplest movement, was to be conducted according to a strict regimen. The goal of the ceremony is expressed in the kanji *wa* (harmony), *kei* (respect), *sei* (purity), and *jaku* (tranquility).

Religious scholars have likened the tea ceremony to the Catholic sacrament of Communion. Parallels certainly exist, including the wiping of the vessel, turning it in one's hand, and even partaking of a morsel. These scholars speculate that Master Rikyu may have been converted by European missionaries. Regardless of his religious beliefs, Rikyu's position under Hideyoshi grew, but so did his ego. A series of misfortunes, many brought about by jealous rivals, eventually incurred Hideyoshi's wrath. The final straw occurred when Rikyu had a statue of himself erected on one of the gates of Daitoku-ji Temple. Hideyoshi, angered to have to walk under Rikyu's statue, ordered the tea master to commit suicide. Rikyu was seventy years old. Hideyoshi also ordered the statue to be beheaded.

I had the good fortune to participate in three tea ceremonies, once as the second guest. My thanks go to the tea masters, particularly Masaye Nakagawa, who explained the entire event and patiently answered my questions.

The bound stone on page 18 of "*Chanoyu*" (page 512 in this volume) indicates a path that is forbidden to take. A comment on the relationship of Usagi and Tomoe? Perhaps.

Other sources consulted include:

• *Urasenke Chanoyu Handbook*, vols. 1 and 2, by Grand Master Soshitsu Sen XV (Kyoto: Urasenke Foundation, 1980).
• *The Tea Ceremony*, by Sen'o Tanaka and Sendo Tanaka (Tokyo: Kodansha International, 1973).
• *The Art of Chanoyu: The Urasenke Tradition of Tea* (Urasenke Foundation, 1986). Published to accompany an exhibition at the Doizaki Gallery in Los Angeles.

GALLERY

Stan Sakai's cover art for the issues collected in this volume.
Colors by Tom Luth, except on Sakai's painted covers.

SAKAI
LUTH
2004

SAKAI
2004
LUTH

稲妻
SAKAI
2004
LUTH

SAKAI
2004
LUTH

SAKAI
LUTH
2004

復讐
SAKAI
2004
LUTH

SAKAI
2004
LUTH

SAKAI
LUTH
2005

SAKAI
2005
LUTH

SAKAI
LUTH
2005

SAKAI
LUTH
2005

Usagi Yojimbo Volume Three #88

Usagi Yojimbo Volume Three #89

Usagi Yojimbo Color Special #1

SAKAI
©1991

Usagi Yojimbo Color Special #2

Usagi Yojimbo Color Special #3

Usagi Yojimbo Volume Three #90

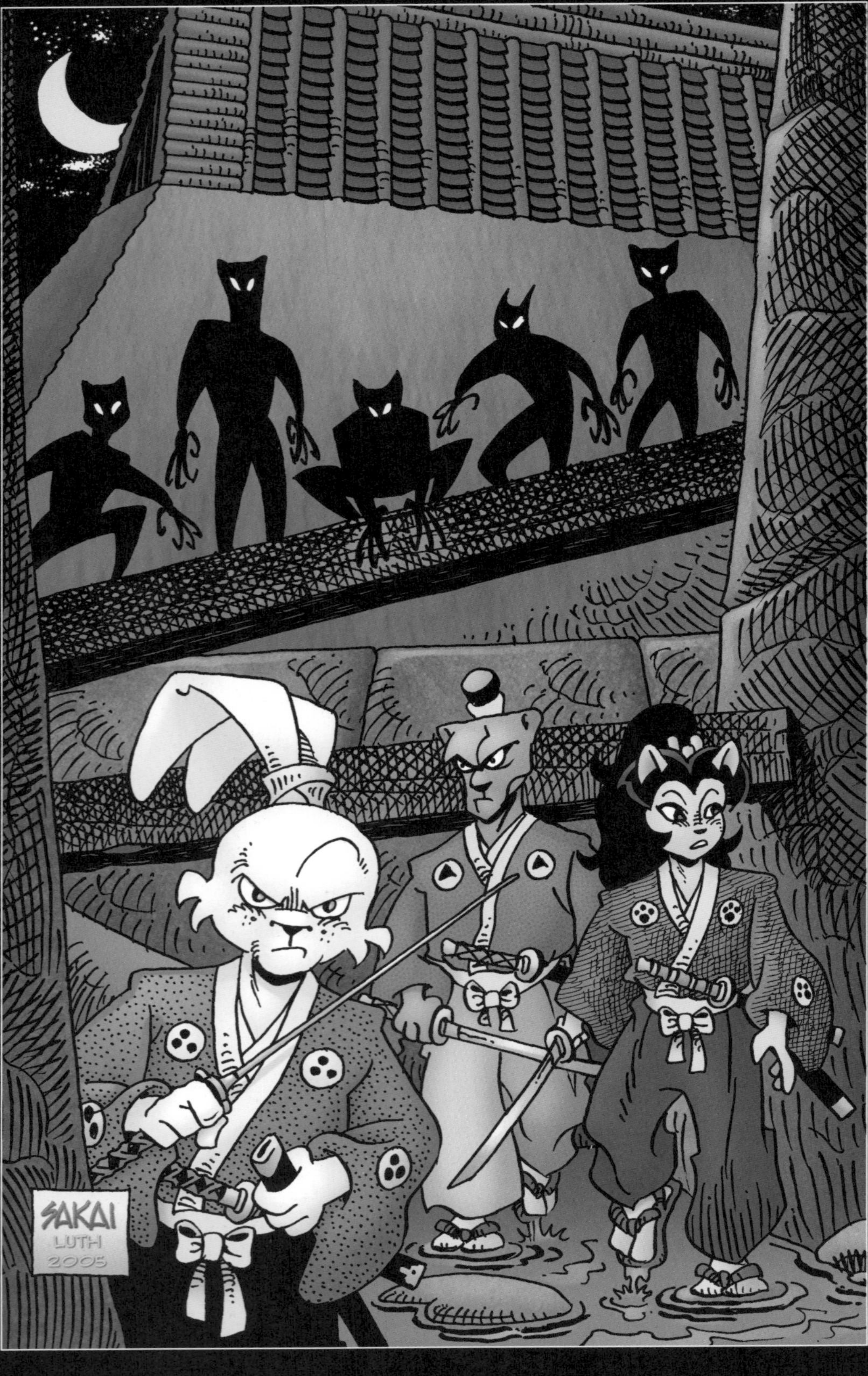

Usagi Yojimbo Volume Three #91

SAKAI
LUTH
2005

SAKAI
LUTH
2005

SAKAI
LUTH
2006

SAKAI

SAKAI

SAKAI

"TOMOE'S STORY," "THE DOORS," AND "FOX FIRE" were first published between 1989 and 1992 in Fantagraphics' *Usagi Yojimbo Color Special* #1–#3. Because Stan determined that the stories occurred later in *Usagi*'s chronology, they were not reprinted until Dark Horse's *Usagi Yojimbo* Book 22: *Tomoe's Story*, when Usagi's adventures caught up to the time of the stories' setting. The color materials for the three stories no longer existed, so "The Doors" and "Fox Fire" were printed from new scans of the original artwork. However, the art for "Tomoe's Story" had been lost, so Stan completely redrew the story, and it is this newer version that appears in *Tomoe's Story* and in this volume.

In order to preserve this unique piece of *Usagi*'s publishing history, select pages of the original version of "Tomoe's Story" were scanned from a copy of *Usagi Yojimbo Color Special* #1 for this edition. The art has been restored and the color has been removed for clarity.

The following pages present a comparison between the original story and Stan's later reinterpretation. While page layouts and dialogue remain nearly identical, the differences in panel composition, character designs, and line style show Stan's and the characters' evolutions between the time when "Tomoe's Story" was originally conceived and when it was re-created in 2008.

Page 1

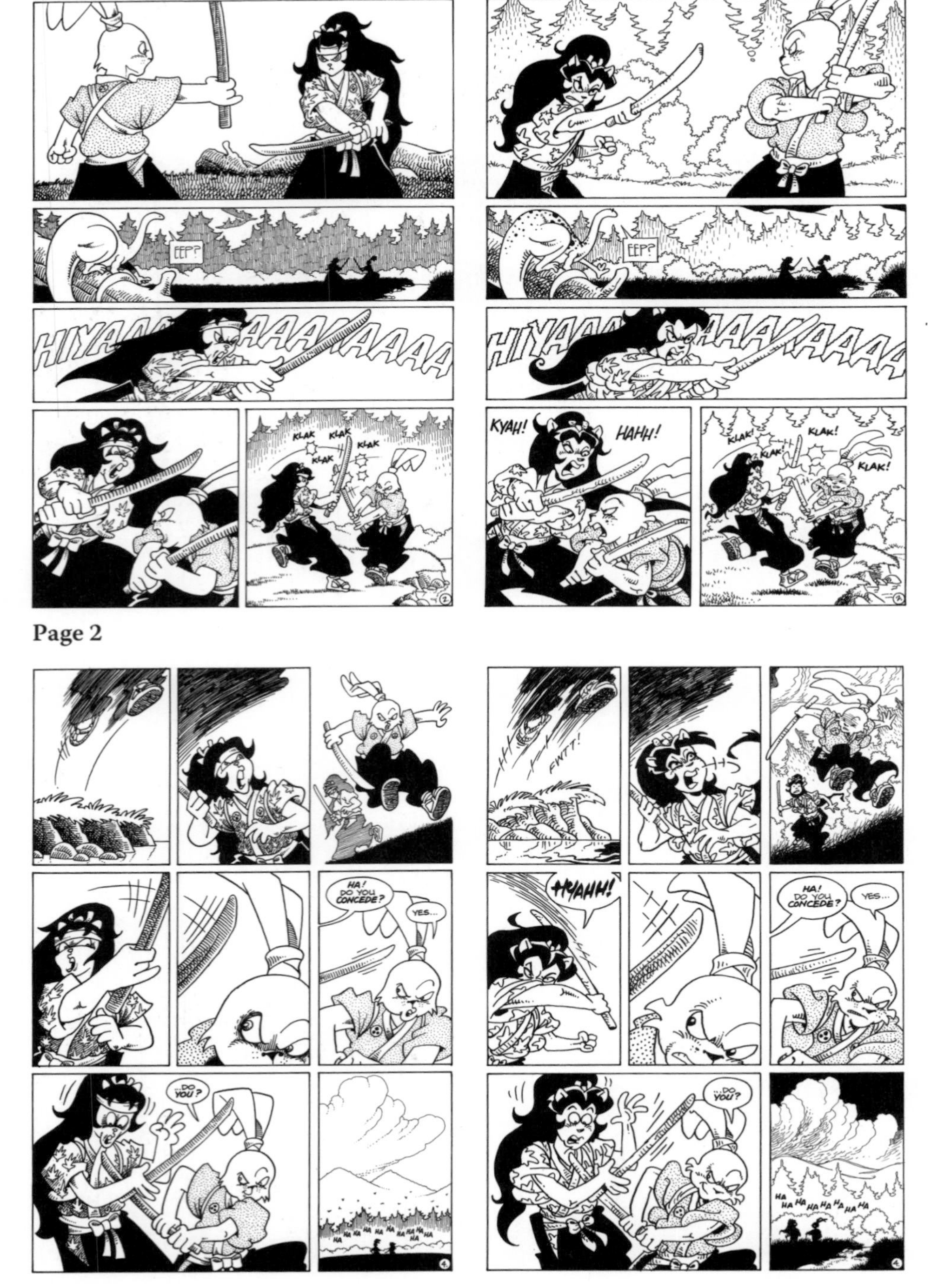
EEP?
HIYAAAAAAAAAAAA
KLAK
KLAK
KLAK
KLAK
2
EEP?
HIYAAAAAAAAAAAA
KYAH!
HAHH!
KLAK!
KLAK!
KLAK!
KLAK!
2

Page 2

HA! DO YOU CONCEDE?
YES...
...DO YOU?
HA HA HA HA HA HA HA HA HA
4
FWTT!
HYAHH!
HA! DO YOU CONCEDE?
YES...
...DO YOU?
HA HA HA HA HA HA HA HA
4

Page 4

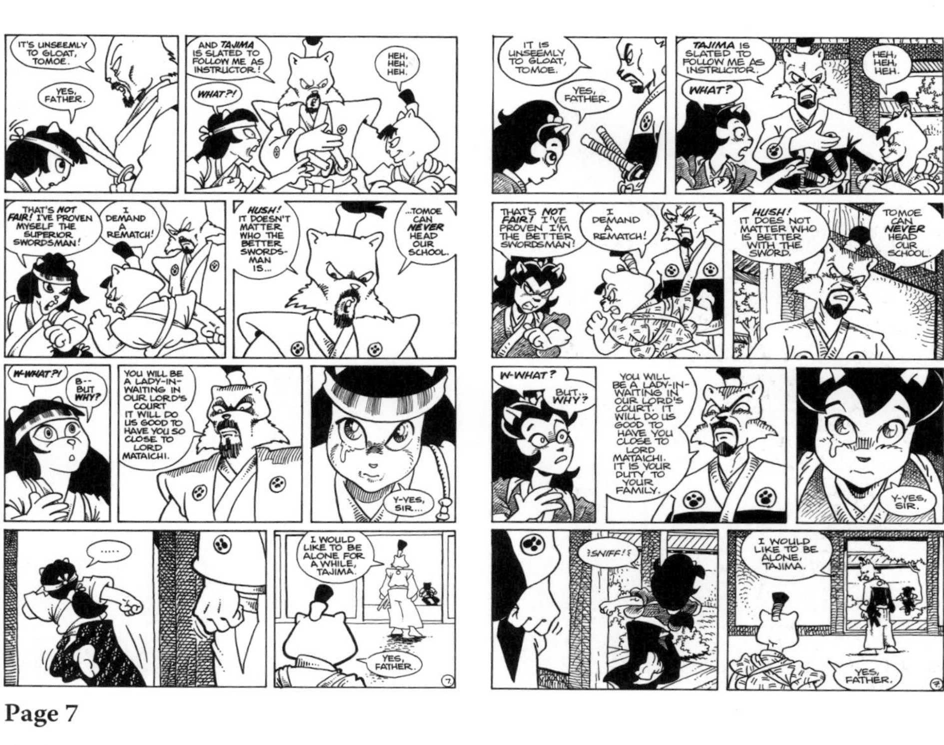
IT'S UNSEEMLY TO GLOAT, TOMOE.
YES, FATHER.
AND TAJIMA IS SLATED TO FOLLOW ME AS INSTRUCTOR!
WHAT?!
HEH, HEH, HEH.
THAT'S NOT FAIR! I'VE PROVEN MYSELF THE SUPERIOR SWORDSMAN!
I DEMAND A REMATCH!
HUSH! IT DOESN'T MATTER WHO THE BETTER SWORDS-MAN IS...
...TOMOE CAN NEVER HEAD OUR SCHOOL.
W-WHAT?!
B-- BUT WHY?
YOU WILL BE A LADY-IN-WAITING IN OUR LORD'S COURT. IT WILL DO US GOOD TO HAVE YOU SO CLOSE TO LORD MATAICHI.
Y-YES, SIR...
.....
I WOULD LIKE TO BE ALONE FOR A WHILE, TAJIMA.
YES, FATHER.
7
IT IS UNSEEMLY TO GLOAT, TOMOE.
YES, FATHER.
TAJIMA IS SLATED TO FOLLOW ME AS INSTRUCTOR.
WHAT?
HEH, HEH, HEH.
THAT'S NOT FAIR! I'VE PROVEN I'M THE BETTER SWORDSMAN!
I DEMAND A REMATCH!
HUSH! IT DOES NOT MATTER WHO IS BETTER WITH THE SWORD.
TOMOE CAN NEVER HEAD OUR SCHOOL.
W-WHAT?
BUT... WHY?
YOU WILL BE A LADY-IN-WAITING IN OUR LORD'S COURT. IT WILL DO US GOOD TO HAVE YOU CLOSE TO LORD MATAICHI. IT IS YOUR DUTY TO YOUR FAMILY.
Y-YES, SIR.
SNIFF!
I WOULD LIKE TO BE ALONE, TAJIMA.
YES, FATHER.
7

Page 7

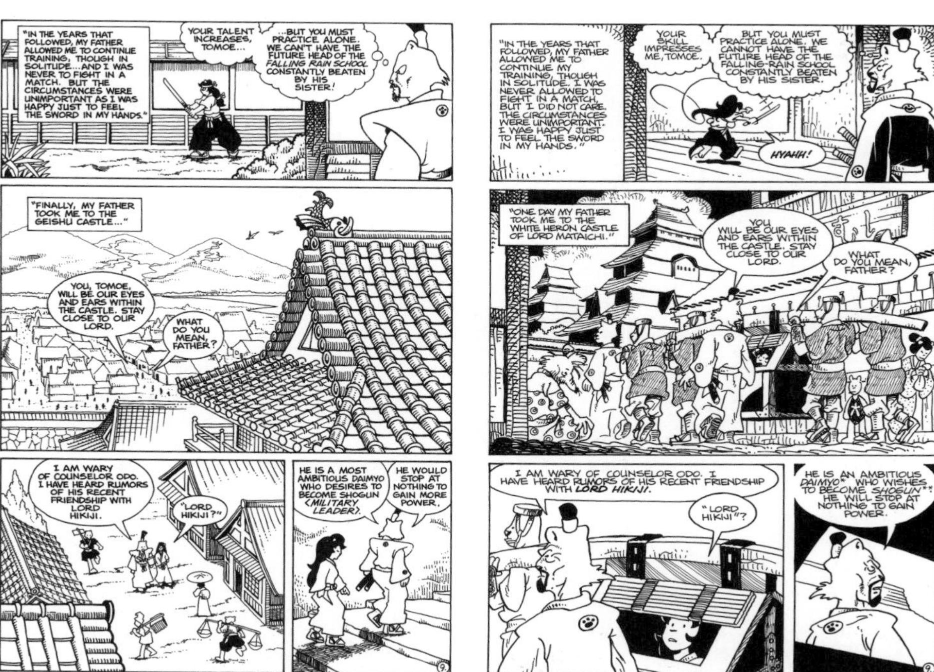
"IN THE YEARS THAT FOLLOWED, MY FATHER ALLOWED ME TO CONTINUE TRAINING, THOUGH IN SOLITUDE... AND I WAS NEVER TO FIGHT IN A MATCH. BUT THE CIRCUMSTANCES WERE UNIMPORTANT AS I WAS HAPPY JUST TO FEEL THE SWORD IN MY HANDS."
YOUR TALENT INCREASES, TOMOE...
...BUT YOU MUST PRACTICE ALONE. WE CAN'T HAVE THE FUTURE HEAD OF THE FALLING RAIN SCHOOL CONSTANTLY BEATEN BY HIS SISTER!
"FINALLY, MY FATHER TOOK ME TO THE GEISHU CASTLE..."
YOU, TOMOE, WILL BE OUR EYES AND EARS WITHIN THE CASTLE. STAY CLOSE TO OUR LORD.
WHAT DO YOU MEAN, FATHER?
I AM WARY OF COUNSELOR ODO. I HAVE HEARD RUMORS OF HIS RECENT FRIENDSHIP WITH LORD HIKIJI.
"LORD HIKIJI?"
HE IS A MOST AMBITIOUS DAIMYO WHO DESIRES TO BECOME SHOGUN (MILITARY LEADER).
HE WOULD STOP AT NOTHING TO GAIN MORE POWER.
9
"IN THE YEARS THAT FOLLOWED, MY FATHER ALLOWED ME TO CONTINUE MY TRAINING, THOUGH IN SOLITUDE. I WAS NEVER ALLOWED TO FIGHT IN A MATCH, BUT I DID NOT CARE. THE CIRCUMSTANCES WERE UNIMPORTANT. I WAS HAPPY JUST TO FEEL THE SWORD IN MY HANDS."
YOUR SKILL IMPRESSES ME, TOMOE.
BUT YOU MUST PRACTICE ALONE. WE CANNOT HAVE THE FUTURE HEAD OF THE FALLING-RAIN SCHOOL CONSTANTLY BEATEN BY HIS SISTER.
HYAHH!
"ONE DAY MY FATHER TOOK ME TO THE WHITE HERON CASTLE OF LORD MATAICHI."
YOU WILL BE OUR EYES AND EARS WITHIN THE CASTLE. STAY CLOSE TO OUR LORD.
WHAT DO YOU MEAN, FATHER?
I AM WARY OF COUNSELOR ODO. I HAVE HEARD RUMORS OF HIS RECENT FRIENDSHIP WITH LORD HIKIJI.
"LORD HIKIJI"?
HE IS AN AMBITIOUS DAIMYO* WHO WISHES TO BECOME SHOGUN**. HE WILL STOP AT NOTHING TO GAIN POWER.
9
*LORD **MILITARY DICTATOR

Page 9

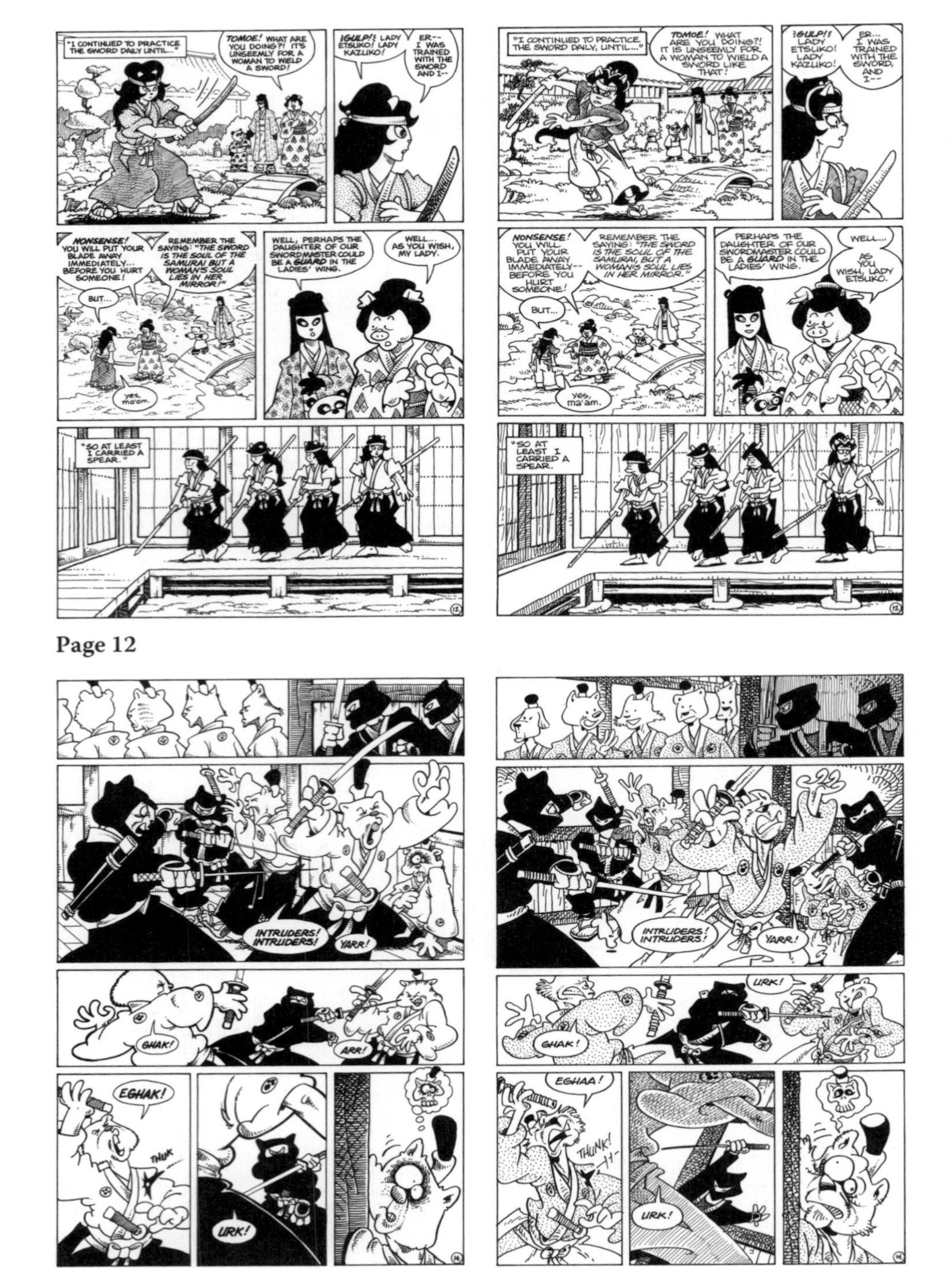

Page 12

Page 14

Page 19

Page 20

Stan's contribution to the 2004 San Diego Comic-Con catalog, which included a section dedicated to the rabbit *ronin*.

Mark Crilley

Nate Piekos

David Petersen

ABOUT THE AUTHOR

Stan in his studio. Photo by Julie Sakai.

STAN SAKAI was born in Kyoto, Japan, grew up in Hawaii, and now lives in California with his wife Julie. He has two children, Hannah and Matthew, and two stepchildren, Daniel and Emi. Stan received a fine arts degree from the University of Hawaii and furthered his studies at the Art Center College of Design in Pasadena, California.

Stan's creation *Usagi Yojimbo* first appeared in the comic book *Albedo Anthropomorphics* #2 in 1984. Since then, Usagi has been on television as a guest of the Teenage Mutant Ninja Turtles and has been made into toys and seen on clothing, and his stories have been collected in more than three dozen graphic novels and translated into sixteen languages.

Stan is the recipient of a Parents' Choice Award, an Inkpot Award, an American Library Association Award, two Harvey Awards, five Spanish Haxturs, ten Will Eisner Awards, two National Cartoonists Society Silver Reubens, and most recently four Ringo Awards, including one for Best Cartoonist in 2020. In 2011 Stan received the Cultural Ambassador Award from the Japanese American National Museum for spreading Japanese history and culture through his stories. Stan was awarded the inaugural Joe Kubert Distinguished Storyteller Award in 2018 and was inducted into the Will Eisner Hall of Fame in 2020. Stan, in partnership with Gaumont USA, is currently developing an Usagi animated series for Netflix.

USAGI YOJIMBO™

Created, Written, and Illustrated by Stan Sakai

Available from Dark Horse Comics

The Usagi Yojimbo Saga Book 1 Second Edition
Collects *Usagi Yojimbo* Books 8–10
$29.99 | ISBN 978-1-50672-490-4

The Usagi Yojimbo Saga Book 2 Second Edition
Collects *Usagi Yojimbo* Books 11–13
$29.99 | ISBN 978-1-50672-492-8

The Usagi Yojimbo Saga Book 3 Second Edition
Collects *Usagi Yojimbo* Books 14–16
$29.99 | ISBN 978-1-50672-493-5

The Usagi Yojimbo Saga Book 4 Second Edition
Collects *Usagi Yojimbo* Books 17–19
$29.99 | ISBN 978-1-50672-494-2

The Usagi Yojimbo Saga Book 5 Second Edition
Collects *Usagi Yojimbo* Books 20–22
$29.99 | ISBN 978-1-50672-495-9

The Usagi Yojimbo Saga Book 6
Collects *Usagi Yojimbo* Books 23–25
$24.99 | ISBN 978-1-61655-614-3

The Usagi Yojimbo Saga Book 7
Collects *Usagi Yojimbo* Books 26–28
$24.99 | ISBN 978-1-61655-615-0

The Usagi Yojimbo Saga Book 8
Collects *Usagi Yojimbo* Books 29–31
$24.99 | ISBN 978-1-50671-224-6

The Usagi Yojimbo Saga: Legends
Collects *Senso, Yokai, Space Usagi,* and more!
$24.99 | ISBN 978-1-50670-323-7

Book 29: Two Hundred Jizo
$17.99 | ISBN 978-1-61655-840-6

Book 30: Thieves and Spies
$17.99 | ISBN 978-1-50670-048-9

Book 31: The Hell Screen
$17.99 | ISBN 978-1-50670-187-5

Book 32: Mysteries
$17.99 | ISBN 978-1-50670-584-2

Book 33: The Hidden
$17.99 | TRADE PAPERBACK: ISBN 978-1-50670-852-2
$59.99 | LIMITED EDITION HARDCOVER: ISBN 978-1-50670-851-5

Usagi Yojimbo/Teenage Mutant Ninja Turtles: The Complete Collection
$17.99 | ISBN 978-1-50670-950-5

The Art of Usagi Yojimbo
$29.95 | ISBN 978-1-59307-493-7

The Sakai Project: Artists Celebrate Thirty Years of Usagi Yojimbo
$29.99 | ISBN 978-1-61655-556-6

Gallery Edition Volume 1: Samurai and Other Stories
$125.00 | ISBN 978-1-61655-923-6

Gallery Edition Volume 2: The Artist and Other Stories
$125.00 | ISBN 978-1-61655-924-3

47 Ronin
Written by Mike Richardson
$19.99 | ISBN 978-1-59582-954-2

The Adventures of Nilson Groundthumper and Hermy
$14.99 | ISBN 978-1-61655-341-8

Available from Fantagraphics Books
fantagraphics.com

Book 1: The Ronin
Book 2: Samurai
Book 3: The Wanderer's Road
Book 4: The Dragon Bellow Conspiracy
Book 5: Lone Goat and Kid
Book 6: Circles
Book 7: Gen's Story